I0724633

The Afghan Wedding

Gary Girod

Milton, Ontario

This is a work of fiction. All of the characters, events, and organizations portrayed in this novel are either products of the author's imagination or are used fictitiously.

Brain Lag Publishing
Milton, Ontario
http://www.brain-lag.com/

Copyright © 2022 Gary Girod. All rights reserved. This material may not be reproduced, displayed, modified or distributed without the express prior written permission of the copyright holder. For permission, contact publishing@brain-lag.com.

Cover design by Peter Dibble

ISBN: 978-1-928011-77-4

Library and Archives Canada Cataloguing in Publication

Title: The Afghan wedding / Gary Girod.
Names: Girod, Gary, 1990- author.
Identifiers: Canadiana (print) 20220219222 | Canadiana (ebook) 20220219230 | ISBN 9781928011774
  (softcover) | ISBN 9781928011781 (ebook)
Classification: LCC PS3607.I76 A69 2022 | DDC 813/.6—dc23

Content warnings: Gun violence, sexual suggestiveness

To Catherine who gave me my first chance and convinced me to take a second. To Daniel, Peter, and my loving parents.

Chapter One
Deserts of Sand and Ice

Unseen tears stream down puffy cheeks beneath the fifteen-year-old's white veil. She bites her lip as she strains to conceal her sobs. From outside her window she watches her Baba and uncles as they set up tents for the marriage festival. The wooden door to her small room opens as her mother, covered completely in an azure burqa, enters the room.

"Come Avizeh, let's take a walk together." The blue-veiled woman reaches out her hand. Avizeh does not even feel her own rise to accept it.

The brick and clay of the Fatah family's ancestral home breathes in the afternoon sun. Avizeh's kindly uncle Parviz once told her that her betrothed, Razaaq Hirat, owns a mansion near the border with Iran. Rumor has it the warlord occupies an old Soviet base built in the shade of an Alexandrian temple, a temple which had been converted into a mosque a thousand years ago, before it was shelled by the Americans during their first invasion. Two thousand years, a dozen empires and the only thing left is a pile of stones sinking into the sand as the ever-hungry Dasht-e Margo, the

'Desert of Death,' forever swallows history and people alike.

The young bride follows her mother past the sweeping tents set to hold her betrothed's one hundred most trusted men. Avizeh watches anxiously as her sisters, cousins and aunts lay out bowls of nuts and fruit across elaborate Persian carpets under the main tent while her father converses with the local mullah who will officiate the wedding. Her mother leads Avizeh to the house's other side, where the world opens towards the endless western expanses. The world feels still around her as if it is holding its breath. The mountains in the east and west hold back the wind, and any sparse rain that makes it past the Indian Himalayas is greedily swallowed up by Pakistan. Avizeh watches her mother's chest rise to reassure herself that time has not stopped completely.

"Do you have any questions before tonight?"

"No." Avizeh chokes out the word numbly, sounding like a ghost speaking with the shaking voice of a terrified child.

"Don't talk as if you walk to your own grave!" her mother berates her. "You must be happy tonight. A bride must be her husband's font of joy. When you leave with Razaaq Hirat you must always do as he says quickly and gaily. Learn what he likes and do what he wishes even before he asks you. When he goes back to war or when he takes a second bride then things will be easier, but if you shed a tear at one of his commands your life will be nothing but misery."

"Yes." Avizeh shudders, then quickly adds, "Yes, I understand Mother, and I will do as I am told. Mother, how can I sound happy when I'm not?"

"Remember how you were so thirsty when the sandstorm came to our village and no one dared go to the well? Remember how you imagined there was water in your mouth? How you played that game and when we finally did bring back water you hardly drank at all? Just imagine you are filled with happiness."

Avizeh bites her lip and clutches her mother's hand. For the first time she realizes she may never see her again. Razaaq is a man of war, fighting false believers, drug smugglers and American soldiers who still on occasion interfere across the fractured provinces of western Afghanistan. Above all regional squabbles, Afghanistan has always been the play toy of greater empires. Conflict is the spirit of her land, the young bride has no doubts. She closes her eyes and attempts to push away any thoughts that might bring tears to her eyes.

In the distant north, sand kicks up as a half-dozen Jeeps roll across the roadless desert. Mother and daughter watch as the war caravan approaches for a wedding. As the procession nears, the women can see individual men crammed on top of the vehicles. From beneath her veil Avizeh cannot tell the men apart; to her they are one man wearing a hundred black and gray robes, sporting a hundred chest-length beards, carrying a hundred assault rifles. As they near, the young bride looks for Razaaq among the men but as she does she feels an immense wave of dread and her knees shake violently.

"Come, you need to return to your room. Remember, the mullah will ask you three times if you'll accept the marriage. Say 'yes,' each time, walk out and when your husband lifts your veil to kiss you, you must be smiling."

"Yes, Mother." Avizeh tries to sound happy even as the ground begins to spin. She glances up just in time to see the sky before the roof of the house appears above. Her mother ushers Avizeh into her room, commands her to sit on the bed, keeping her clean white burqa off of the dirt floor, then walks out, closing the door behind her. The trembling young bride listens as the Jeeps close in around the house. A chorus of a hundred pairs of stomping boots on hard ground mingle with jubilant greetings as she sits silently alone. The walls muffle the noise from outside until the dozens of conversations become one alien sound, expressing happiness she does not share. She thinks she hears her Baba among the voices talking to Razaaq as they hash out the Nikah. Avizeh knows it is a mere formality; Razaaq is a powerful warlord, her father will agree to whatever terms he dictates to him. She smells warm bread and lamb meat from the nearby kitchen and listens to her empty stomach growl. After an hour of listening to Razaaq's men conversing with her extended family she hears light footsteps from outside her door. The door opens and the mullah stares down at her. With his flowing black robes, wrinkly bald head and sharp-eyed stare he looks like a vulture examining a fresh carcass. The young woman bows to her elder respectfully.

Without closing the door, he asks, "Avizeh Fatah, do you accept Razaaq Hirat as your husband in marriage?"

"Yes," Avizeh says, forcing out a smile, which is hidden behind her veil.

"Avizeh Fatah, do you accept Razaaq Hirat as your husband in marriage?"

"Yes," she hears herself say.

"Avizeh Fatah, do you accept Razaaq Hirat as your husband in marriage?"

"Yes." No word has ever sounded so ugly to her ears.

"You are now Razaaq Hirat's wife. Follow me, Avizeh," the mullah commands as he turns his back to her room.

Avizeh cannot feel her feet yet somehow she is pulled like a spirit from her home into the wedding tent. Her uncle plays the sitar as her eldest cousin sings *Asta Boro*. Her extended family and some members of the village stand on her right while Razaaq's men stand on her left. The soldiers have removed their face coverings and laid their assault rifles on the edges of the tent, though they remain in easy reach. At the end of the hall a tall man with a long black beard, broad chest and piercing dark eyes holds her gaze.

Smile. Smile. One foot, the next. Breathe. Happy, be happy.

A mere step from her husband, Avizeh realizes that it is only important that he thinks she is happy. The thought cracks through her and she hears herself gasp for air within the silent tent. She stands next to Razaaq and looks up to meet his gaze. He smiles broadly and lifts her veil. He leans down to kiss her and she feels his large lips cover her own, feels his beard on her chin. He pulls back and looks down affectionately at his new bride. Congratulatory cheers resound through the tent. Avizeh cannot hold her smile any longer as two tears stream down her cheeks and she gives a small sob. As her vision blurs she sees her husband's face contort into a hateful glare.

Gunfire explodes from behind the wedding tent. A man howls in pain behind her. Instantly, Razaaq's men grab their weapons and run outside. The sudden stampede brings the tent crashing down and Avizeh's family cries out as they run for cover. A strong arm circles Avizeh's waist and she is carried like a disobedient child on her husband's hip as he sprints towards the cover of a Jeep. Fiery-golden gunfire bursts through the dark night, a cacophony of overpowering light and sound that leaves Avizeh senseless.

Razaaq presses Avizeh against the wheel of one of the Jeeps. "Stay here and stay low, do you understand?" he roars at his young bride.

His new wife cries and puts her hands on her face.

Razaaq smacks his new bride hard across the face and she tastes blood. "Don't make a sound, idiot girl! I won't have you die before tonight." He grabs her head and forces her to the ground before running off into the darkness to join the chaos.

Avizeh lies on the ground and tries to stifle her cries when a nearby explosion blinds her. The sound of gunfire is suddenly replaced by a metallic ringing and she blinks madly to clear her vision. The newlywed starts as she sees something move in front of her. A dark form walks toward her, cautiously. The shadow crouches on one knee and lifts a long black rifle. A sound like a high-pitched whistle breaks through the night and a tiny spark illuminates a man wearing camouflage garb. The gun whistles again and a body hits the ground behind her.

Avizeh rises, legs shaking uncontrollably, and stares at who she assumes must be an American soldier. The world in front of her is a wall of imperceptible darkness broken only by flashes of gunfire. The way the man stops in front of her makes the young woman think he is studying her, gauging a potential threat. Suddenly she runs towards him. Through eyes clouded with tears she sees the gun point towards her chest but keeps running. As she nears he turns the barrel away from her.

"Please don't let him hurt me! Don't let those men hurt my family, please! Please, please don't kill us! Don't let them kill us, please!"

The man stares at Avizeh, his demeanor unreadable behind his night vision goggles and mask. A shot rings clear through the chaos and a fountain of blood explodes from the man's chest, covering her wedding gown. Avizeh screams and falls to the earth, feeling warm blood trickle down her clothes. The young woman stares through bleary eyes at the man before her even as he convulses. She tries to wipe tears away but that only makes her vision worse. She blinks furiously and looks down at her hands and sees that they are covered in a dark mixture of blood, sweat and dirt.

"Avizeh!" a rage-filled voice roars close behind her.

Avizeh stiffens as she recognizes her husband's murderous tone. She turns and sees his face covered in blood as he glares hatefully. "I told you to wait by the car, you faithless whore!" Avizeh gasps and turns back to the American's corpse, eyeing his gun. Avizeh runs to the body and tries to lift the rifle. She tugs on the heavy gun but it slips and falls to the ground. Between flashes of gunfire the terrified bride realizes that the now-motionless body lies on the rifle's sling. She drops the gun and searches the body, praying for a pistol. She pulls on his bloodstained shirt and sees a blinking blue light. Avizeh reaches for the light and pulls back a silver disc-shaped object roughly eight inches across and half as wide. Blue-crystal digital numbers run across its glowing screen.

"Whore!" Razaaq thunders as he aims his Kalashnikov at her.

Avizeh shakes and grips the disc as tightly as she can. She closes her eyes and prays for mercy.

The sound of gunfire disappears instantly. A chilling breeze, colder than she has ever felt before, cuts through her wedding dress and she shivers furiously. Through chattering teeth, she thinks she hears the sound of water splashing all around her. She opens her eyes. All around her are titanic blocks of ice, their snow-covered tops floating over frigid blue water. Avizeh looks down and realizes she is kneeling on pure white snow beneath her.

Did I die? Is this heaven? Or hell? How can this be either when both are supposed to be warm? She looks down at her burqa and jumps, seeing the wet crimson stains across her dress for the first time. Her hand shakes uncontrollably from fear and sudden cold. She touches the sticky dark crimson across her belly. *Did my husband kill me?* She pulls back her trembling hand and watches the scarlet liquid solidify on her fingertips.

A deep, inhuman wail explodes from just behind Avizeh, causing her to scream and fall to the ground. She looks over and sees the marine's corpse, at first thinking he might be alive. Then her eyes fixate on a massive creature that looks like a fat dog with flippers instead of feet. She stares, wide-eyed, numb hands clawing at the snow beneath her, pushing herself away. The creature bares its huge yellowing teeth towards her and Avizeh cries out again. The young woman's heart pounds even as she shivers violently from the cold. Her mind races as she looks for some escape, even as she begins to feel light-headed. She knows the gun is useless as its sling is trapped underneath the corpse between herself and the creature. She looks around frantically for somewhere to run. To her horror, she realizes she is on a tiny ice floe only a dozen meters long and about as wide. She looks up to the sky as her tears freeze on her cheeks.

Are you still there, God? Or did I leave you in the desert?

The dog-creature turns from Avizeh and barks at the water loud enough for her to feel its panicked cries reverberate through her chest. The terrified young woman watches it open its maw, exposing long yellow teeth as it yelps. Out of the corner of her eyes she sees movement and follows the creature's gaze downward.

Against the still, dark blue abyss a massive black fin rises in the water and races towards the ice floe. Avizeh watches as the fin gains speed, moving faster than she could run. Once it reaches the ice floe the fin dives downward and a colossal black lower body and tail descend into the water. A small wave splashes onto the ice floe in its wake. Avizeh pushes herself backward to avoid the chilly water as the ice teeters beneath her. The dog-creature backs up to the middle of the small frozen island, so close Avizeh can smell its putrid breath. It yelps and looks nervously back out at sea.

Avizeh watches horrified as four more fins race towards them, moving even faster than the first. A huge wave rises above the fins and the creatures dive just before hitting the ice floe. A wave of freezing water rolls over the surface and Avizeh is paralyzed as she tumbles backward in the freezing swell. When the wave passes, it leaves her body stiff in the deathly cold. She only barely registers that she is on the very edge of the block of ice, her feet dangling above the water. The body of the American slips down, sinking into the blackness.

Avizeh is completely numb. She is barely conscious of the dog-creature awkwardly pushing itself back to the middle of the small island as the four fins take up positions again. She knows she must join it to live but her will is weaker than the cold. The only feeling in her is the disc in her left hand. With what little strength she has she clutches onto it, hoping for another miracle.

A humming from far away turns into a deafening whipping sound just above her. A pair of boots drop down in front of her, kicking snow into her face. An arm reaches around her waist as a strong man lifts her, though she barely feels either. Suddenly she flies through the air just as another wave rolls over the ice floe and the dog-creature tumbles into the depths. The man holding her barks something in a language she cannot understand and someone seizes her from behind and places her in the back seat of a helicopter. Avizeh jerks violently and holds her arms across her chest as she shivers. The man who rappelled her to safety closes the sliding door. Beside her, another man pulls out a hot water bottle and presses it against her chest, which she grabs. She holds it tightly against her and thinks its life-saving warmth is the best feeling she has ever had, like the feeling of happiness filling her and spreading outward to every part of her being. The men wrap her tightly in a thermal blanket as she shakes.

Feeling returns to Avizeh's numbed fingers and she realizes that the disc is still in her left hand, underneath the hot water bottle. She eyes the men around her. Her rescuer says something to her in a language she cannot understand. She thinks he means to sound friendly but his voice is gravelly and comes out as a bark. He waits for her response;

when it doesn't come he turns to the other man who says something that sounds like Arabic, which Avizeh can recognize but not speak. When she doesn't respond to him the man shrugs his shoulders and looks out the window.

Avizeh looks back and forth at these strange men. They sport long black rifles at their sides and look like the soldier that died in front of her. While their eyes are turned she cautiously slips the disc down inside her clothes.

This device and God's grace are the only things I have in this world.

The unusual group sits in silence, with only the semi-muffled whirring of the helicopter blades above them breaking the peaceful journey above a snow-white landscape that stretches as far as the eye can see. Avizeh peers out the window and thinks she sees strange black birds that waddle instead of fly. After a long flight over endless white expanses the helicopter slows as it approaches a large hexagonal building, surrounded by smaller buildings that look like half-cylinders on their sides, with a concrete wall surrounding all of them. A large American flag waves gently from a nearby pole.

The helicopter descends onto a platform amidst the buildings, blowing snow in all directions. The door to her right opens. A strong hand on Avizeh's back pushes her forward, through the biting cold, towards a non-descript building with the words 'Medical Center' painted above the door. As they enter, a seated man in green scrubs looks up from a computer screen, his face rapidly displaying shock, worry, confusion, then sympathy. Unintelligible words pass between the medic and the soldier behind her and the former leads her to a bed. He steps away and returns with a set of clothes which look too large for her small frame. He pulls the curtains around the bed, points at the clothes and says something before ducking out. Avizeh takes the hint and shakily removes her drenched wedding gown. As she does the teleporter falls to the bed. She catches her breath and her gaze shoots up to the closed curtain. She removes her soaked layers and dons the baggy clothes. She then grabs the teleporter and stuffs it inside her shirt. She opens the curtain and nearly jumps to see the medic standing just outside. He motions for her to lie back, covers her with a heated blanket while holding a thermometer to her forehead.

Warmth courses through Avizeh and she suddenly feels incredibly tired. Just as she thinks she is about to nod off, she notices a figure walk towards her. She looks up into the heart-shaped face of a tall, dark-haired woman who stares back with apparent compassion.

"Hello," she says in Farsi.

"Hello," is all Avizeh can think to reply.

"How are you feeling?"

Avizeh stammers.

"That's understandable. What's your name?"

"Avizeh."

"Avizeh, that's a pretty name. My name's Clara."

"Clara," Avizeh sounds out the foreign-sounding name.

"Is your head spinning? Do you feel nauseous? Are—"

"Am I dreaming?" Avizeh interrupts her checklist of medical questions.

"What?" Clara asks, taken aback. "No, you're not dreaming, though you've had quite a day."

"Where am I?"

"Antarctica."

Avizeh's eyes go wide.

"This is the US military base Fort Powell. You must have touched a teleporter, that's how you were transported here."

Avizeh closes her eyes and wonders again if she is dreaming. "What about my family?"

"Are you hungry, Avizeh?"

Avizeh suddenly realizes how famished she is and nods. She thinks back to her wedding, remembering the smell of warm bread and cooked lamb. After the marriage she would have feasted with her new husband and family. Tears well up in her eyes and she sobs.

"It's okay to cry, Avizeh." Clara puts a hand on her shoulder. "Take your time, cry it out."

Avizeh thinks of her family, left behind in the firefight. She lowers her head to her chest and weeps, feeling the teleporter pressing against her with every heaving breath.

*   *   *

Somehow Avizeh manages to sleep, though for how long she can only guess. When she wakes up, Clara is still sitting beside her. She offers Avizeh a cup of water and escorts her to the bathroom, which Avizeh tells her is unnecessary. A few minutes later Clara steps out, returns with a tray full of food and assures Avizeh that the chicken soup is halal.

"How did I get here?" Avizeh asks as she lies back and picks at a piece of bread.

"You must have taken a Q-Leap."

Avizeh tilts her head to the side.

"You must have accidentally touched the emergency jump button on that fallen soldier's teleporter. I can't tell you much; only what is publicly known. The man who you were set to marry, do you know who he was?"

"Razaaq Hirat?"

"Yes... do you know what he did?"

"He's a warlord. He took over the Hirat tribe and moved into Farah territory."

"He made bigger enemies than that, otherwise you wouldn't be here, Avizeh." Clara watches with a slight smile as the youth shoves food into her mouth. "They're going to ask you what happened to the teleporter."

Avizeh looks up at her innocently.

"Do you know what I'm talking about? It's a disc-shaped object, has a lot of lights..."

Avizeh shakes her head. "I don't know what you mean. Whatever it is, it must have fallen into the ocean with the dead American. What's going to happen to me?"

Clara's face doesn't move and Avizeh feels a pit open in her stomach. "That's not for me to decide. I'll get you clothes tomorrow. If you're hungry or need anything, just ask me. Not many other people here speak Farsi."

Avizeh hears boots stamp across the tiled floor and looks up. A tall man with gray hair and wolf-like eyes approaches them. He walks as if his upper half is completely stiff and unaware of how quickly the lower half is moving. He stops beside Clara and says something to her in English but in an accent that is impossible for Avizeh to understand. She stands, salutes, responds and waits for his reply. The man finishes speaking and both his and Clara's eyes turn to Avizeh.

"Do you feel well enough to walk around, Avizeh? This man is my commanding officer and he wants to speak in his office."

The young bride looks nervously at the pair.

"Avizeh, I want to help you but you have to trust me."

Avizeh meets her gaze, which is neither soft nor warm, but possesses an inner strength which calms her. The Afghan bride stands up slowly. Clara assists Avizeh with her coat and gloves and the trio walk in silence towards the exit. As Clara opens the door, Avizeh covers her eyes and squints against the light reflecting off the snow. After a moment of confusion she realizes that the sun moved to a different position in the sky though the world is just as bright as it was hours ago, and she wonders again if she is alive and conscious. Clara's gloved hand presses on her back, feeling as real as anything Avizeh has ever felt, guiding her to a large rectangular building.

The sudden move from the negative sixty-degree outside to the balmy interior gives Avizeh a sudden vertigo, and she grabs onto Clara, who leads her down a series of hallways to the gray-haired man's office. Inside is a desk and several gadgets and trinkets whose purpose Avizeh cannot guess as they occasionally flicker and emit a little beep or hum. The gray-haired man and Clara take off their coats and hang them on hooks on the wall. Underneath his thick coat the man wears a finely-pressed green suit with medals pinned to his left breast. Clara starts to help Avizeh remove her snow gear when she shrugs her off, pulling her coat around tighter; Avizeh is used to wearing a full burqa in temperatures twice as hot as the room. The stiff man takes a seat on the other side of the desk and the two women sit in chairs opposite him. He says something to Clara while still looking at Avizeh.

Clara explains, "Avizeh, this man is Colonel Gregory Mueller. He wants to ask you a couple of questions." Avizeh nods and she continues. "Can you tell us your full name?"

"I already told you."

"Say it again."

Colonel Mueller presses a button and a faint buzz comes from a small microphone between them.

"Avizeh Fatah."

"Where do you come from?"

"Afghanistan."

"Where in Afghanistan?"

"Near Anar Dara, in Farah, a little village southeast of there."

"Who did you live with there?"

"My family. I have two brothers, Aamir..." *Small hairs beginning to grow on his chin, standing by a bowl of nuts, his hand on the table waiting for the feast.* "Daoud, Fahima's son..." *Beside his uncle, fidgeting, sucking on his thumb, wondering why his sister is wearing white instead of her usual black.*

"My sister..." *Laily, the pretty one with sparkling eyes, a gentle face and soft hands. She is promised to Razaaq's second-in-command on her thirteenth birthday.* "My three sisters from my father's second wife Fahima..." *All younger than me. Elina, Omira, Ilaaha hiding behind Fahima, shielding the little ones from the eyes of the soldiers.*

"My mother..." *Still as a statue. When I walked between my family and the soldiers, did she even look at me? Was she worried about what would happen to me? That after he took me back to his mansion maybe I'd be killed during a fight with Razaaq's rivals or the Americans? Was she sad? Was she ashamed of me? Did she think I couldn't be a good bride? She always loved Laily more...*

The young woman feels a sudden overwhelming weight press her down into her chair, feeling for the first time as if today's events are a break with her entire previous life. Her family, her friends, her village, her entire existence transformed from an *is* to a *was*, and all that *is* is a young Afghan woman sequestered in an American military base on a frozen continent, alone with only Clara who understands and sympathizes with her, and even the last part she doubts. Avizeh looks down at her hands, studying the black snow gloves, remembering when her delicate fingers were covered in white.

"Was that all?" Clara asks.

Avizeh closes her eyes, too tired to cry anew.

Colonel Mueller says something to Clara.

"Was that all, Avizeh?"

"I don't want to think about it."

Clara conveys her message to Colonel Mueller. He offers a stern reply.

"You have to answer," Clara adopts her superior's tone.

Avizeh sighs deeply. She wonders why it matters. What do they want? Will they help her? Avizeh looks up at Clara and decides she must trust her. She thinks back to that night. She remembers perfectly what she saw when she was halfway up the aisle. "Baba." *My father never smiled much when I was around but as he watched Razaaq lift my veil he was smiling, showing his teeth, finally proud of me.*

"My uncle Parviz." *Singing Asta Boro with gusto, looking to impress the soldiers, who he admired so much.*

"And my aunts Hadi and Yalda."

Colonel Mueller's gaze does not leave Avizeh as he asks the next question.

Clara translates, "Can you tell us what happened just before you teleported here?"

Avizeh slumps in her seat and looks aside. "Do I have to?"

Clara nods.

"I... I was getting married."

"Who were you getting married to?"

"Razaaq Hirat."

Something flickers in the Colonel's eyes.

"Did he come with anyone?"

"One hundred of his men. His soldiers."

"Did you recognize any of them?"

"No." Avizeh shakes her head. "I only know him."

"Can you tell us what happened?"

Avizeh recounts the events up to her rescue from the ice floe.

"What happened to the teleporter?"

"It fell into the water."

Colonel Mueller's eyes narrow. Avizeh clutches her sides and wishes she had her veil to shield her from the man's look. After a moment's pause to process this new information, he says something to Clara, who then turns to

Avizeh. "He wants to know if you know anything about Razaaq's men. His plans, his territory, his weapons."

"There was a hundred men there, I think. He controls most of the territory north of Farah. His men had lots of guns."

Clara says four words to Mueller and he rolls his eyes.

Before he can pose another question, Avizeh asks, "Is my family okay?"

Clara pauses before translating to Mueller.

"We can't say," she responds.

"Are you sending me back?" Avizeh replies nervously, looking up into Clara's face.

"You would be in danger," Clara says without changing her expression. "Do you want to go back?"

Avizeh pauses. "You killed Razaaq, yes? It's safe for me to see my family?"

Clara looks at Mueller. Without translating to him she turns to Avizeh and says, "We can't reveal any of our operations."

"What about my family?"

Clara speaks to Colonel Mueller. After a tense back and forth she turns back to Avizeh. "I'm sorry, we can't tell you what happened."

Avizeh looks down, defeated. "What will happen to me?"

Clara asks Mueller, who gives a curt reply and responds with a wave. Clara stands up and motions for Avizeh to do the same. "You'll be staying in the women's dormitories under my supervision until we can get you off base. Now, it's time to go."

Avizeh rises to her feet and dares a look at Mueller. He stares back placidly at the women as they step out the door. Clara puts her hand on Avizeh's back and leads her past the reception hall, into the cold.

"Avizeh, listen to me. The army is probably going to arrange to have you adopted by a family somewhere where you will be safe. Probably somewhere remote, like in Iceland, or rural Canada. It's too dangerous to send you back to Afghanistan. And one rule you must abide by, Avizeh: never, ever say what happened that night. We work in secret up here and the man who you were going to marry belongs to a very dangerous group. If you ever tell anyone what happened that night it could endanger you and your family."

Avizeh looks up at Clara and starts breathing quickly, feeling the biting cold fill her lungs. She wants to protest but realizes she can't afford to anger Clara as she is the only person who understands her. She drops her eyes, squinting against the light reflected off the snow.

Someone yells something in English so suddenly Avizeh jumps, her eyes shooting to her right to a raised concrete platform. A machine suspended on a crane projects a holographic image of seven soldiers in different positions. There are two in the back on their bellies holding sniper rifles, four men in front of them holding machine guns and one man in the center holding a grenade. On the ground below each are seven 'Xs.'

A group of seven real men walk past Avizeh, towards the holograms. They take up the same positions as the projections, guns leveled ominously towards her and Clara. A final man steps forward and holds a grenade in his hand. A loudspeaker begins a countdown. The two men in back put their hands near their hearts and Avizeh sees the familiar shape of teleporters. The two snipers disappear. Avizeh blinks as she tries to comprehend what she knows just happened. The loudspeaker issues a command and the four infantrymen disappear. A final countdown begins and the man in front pulls the pin on his grenade. He cocks his arm back, ready to throw. Avizeh puts her arms in front of her and closes her eyes. When nothing happens, she looks up and sees he is gone.

Chapter Two
The Orengh Incident

Avizeh stands in a palace of white marble, with a domed ceiling stretching to infinity as stars flicker in its endless expanse. A hundred villagers stand on her right, dressed in every color that exists, smiling and crying in joy. Ten thousand masked men hold rifles pointed towards her, following her as she walks forward. Avizeh steps to the front of the huge chamber and looks up into a hideous face that shares attributes with Razaaq Hirat and Colonel Mueller that refuse to blend with each other, as if each man's personality is too strong to give in to the other. Two sets of overlapping eyes, one dark brown, the other steely gray, lock on the young bride. Three lips open as her monstrous husband moves to kiss her. Its lips touch hers and a wave of icy water rolls into the palace.

Avizeh wakes up sweating. Heavy boots thud across linoleum floor and a dozen women scattered throughout the women's dormitory converse or watch television together. The young bride from Dasht-e Margo contemplates her dream and recollects the previous day's events. She rolls over and peers down at the bunk below her, searching for Clara only to find the bed empty. Avizeh's breathing quickens and she scans the dormitory for the only person on the base she knows will understand her. She climbs down the cold metal ladder, places a foot on the floor and slips, falling on her stomach. She looks over her shoulder and sees oversized pant legs trailing well below her feet. She hears laughter from two women in front of her, blushes a deep red and rises to a sitting position. She rolls up her pant legs and sleeves, then stands up and continues her search, nearly running away from the women who had laughed at her.

"Clara," Avizeh squeaks as she walks down the line of bunks. She reaches the end with no sign of Clara and pauses at the bathroom door. She steps inside, thankful not to find any strange women changing or showering. Avizeh looks at the bathroom stalls and suddenly gets an idea. She reaches into her shirt to pull out the teleporter when the disc slips out and hits the floor with a loud *clang*. Avizeh's eyes shoot to the door. The muffled chatter of the women behind it is all she hears. She picks up the disc and rushes to the bathroom stalls. She walks up to the toilet on the far right, opens the lid and puts the disc inside. She realizes the device must be waterproof as it still lights up as before, even after it was drenched on the ice floe. Avizeh turns it so the lights face down and hides it at the bottom of the tank. With the contraband device securely hidden she leaves the bathroom and continues her search for Clara.

Avizeh walks along the length of the dormitory until she approaches a pair of women, one with blonde hair and the other with a buzz cut, who stare at a screen playing a music video of a woman in a field of lilacs strumming a guitar. Avizeh stands next to them and watches mesmerized. The two women look over curiously at the Afghan girl in oversized clothes. "Clara?" she asks. The blonde looks at the other and shrugs. The two give Avizeh a bewildered look, then turn back to the screen.

Avizeh turns toward the dormitory's exit, wondering if she is allowed to walk around alone outside when suddenly the door opens and Clara walks in. The woman removes her hood and gives Avizeh a reassuring smile as she walks up to her.

"Good morning," Clara greets her in her native tongue. "How are you feeling?"

Avizeh shrugs.

"Understandable," Clara replies. "I'm going to a little town not too far from here to get you some clothes. Until then you can have breakfast with a friend of mine who's learning Farsi."

"Can I come with you to get clothes?" Avizeh pleads.

"No. It's odd enough that I'm going to buy clothes for someone your size, can you imagine what the world would think if they knew there was a non-American minor at our Antarctic base?"

Avizeh gives Clara a look that shows her that she doesn't know. Without stopping to explain, Clara helps her put on her coat and they trudge through wind and snow towards the mess hall. The cafeteria is nearly full and Avizeh tries not to look at any of the large men flanking her as they wait for their helping of eggs and toast. After filling up her tray, Clara leads Avizeh to a table where a lanky man with brown hair tied in a ponytail, green eyes and tan skin smiles and waves at her.

"Avizeh, this is James Dinapoli."

"Hello, Avizeh," he says in terribly accented Farsi.

"Hello," she responds timidly, grateful to finally have someone else to speak with.

Clara turns to James and says something to him in English as Avizeh sits down. She leans in and gives him a kiss, turns to Avizeh and says, "I'll be back before you know it," and leaves the two to their breakfast.

Avizeh flips over her scrambled eggs with her fork, ignoring the man in front of her, even as she feels his eyes on her. She takes a few bites of the bland but warm food, then looks up at James.

"Hello," she says again.

"Hello."

"So, you are learning Farsi? Why do you want to learn?"

"Go maybe to Farsi speak place," James replies.

Avizeh tilts her head.

After a moment James asks, "Feel how?"

Avizeh squints.

"Feel how?" he repeats.

Avizeh looks down at her plate, feeling horribly alone yet again.

James does not try to talk to her for the rest of breakfast, leaving the two to eat in silence. After she empties her tray, he escorts her back to the women's dormitory. Once inside, Avizeh walks slowly, trying not to trip in her baggy clothes as she stumbles over to her and Clara's bunks. She decides to collapse onto the lower bunk and wait. With the lights on and the constant activity of women conversing, she knows she can't get any peaceful shut-eye. She stands up and quietly approaches two women huddled around a desk. The two watch a screen showing a fine-suited handsome man and a beautiful long-haired woman in a forest during a storm. The woman's dress is drenched and clinging to her every curve. The man leans in, says something in a husky voice and kisses her. He reaches for the back of her neck with one hand and begins to fondle her breast with the other. Avizeh puts a hand on her mouth. The man reaches for the strap on her left shoulder and pulls it down. Avizeh blushes and walks away.

Avizeh notices a woman with flowing, curly red hair siting

at another desk. The Afghan approaches her, smiling at the long curly locks draped over the woman's chair, marveling at the brilliant orange hair. The woman remains oblivious to her and reads from a tablet held in her right hand while holding a finger on her left temple with the other. Avizeh looks up at the shelf above the fiery-haired woman and sees a knitting kit with a dozen spools of yarn and instantly perks up. *Even if I can't speak their language, I can knit and maybe make a connection that way.*

Without looking up from her tablet, the woman reaches across the desk with her left hand. She gropes around the desk for something and after a few seconds of not finding it, glances up. She sees Avizeh standing in front of her and gives her an annoyed and suspicious look. She stands up, puts her tablet down on the desk and continues her search. After failing in her attempts to find the mystery item, she turns to the Afghan refugee, anger clear on her face. She walks up to Avizeh and says something very stern which she can only respond to with a frightened look, when a cheery voice calls out from her left. From the next bunk over a Chinese woman smiles with a half-eaten orange in her hand. The redhead turns to the woman and yells at her. As she approaches, the Chinese woman shoves the rest of the orange into her mouth and drops the skin on the side of the bunk. The redhead yells and chases after the woman, who jumps from bunk to bunk, while the rest of the women in the dormitory howl with laughter.

The noise is too much for Avizeh, who runs into the bathroom, sees two women showering and averts her eyes, blushing furiously. She nearly stumbles again as she runs to the bathroom stall. She slams the door, locks it and sits on the seat with her head in her hands, eyes watering. She thinks of her room, how last night she waited in the dark while the muffled sounds of merrymaking outside attested to her own isolation. There, as here, she waits as a man she has never met decides her fate, and she remains helpless against forces greater than herself. She turns around and looks at the tank. She knows removing the lid and taking the teleporter out would cause a commotion; she would only have a few precious moments with it before the showering women wondered what was happening.

Avizeh stares at the tank through tear-filled eyes. *If I press the button where will it take me? Will it teleport me to the ice floe, or just above the freezing water? Will it take me back to my village? What if I can't go back? What if Razaaq is there? Or American troops? What if they find me with the teleporter and kill me for lying to them?*

Avizeh turns, drops her head in her hands and cries.

*   *   *

The distraught teenager from the Desert of Death sits inside the stall until the tears stop flowing. She wipes her nose, takes a calming breath and exits, careful to avert her eyes from the shower section as she reenters the living quarters. She walks to Clara's empty bunk, lies down, closes her eyes and wraps herself in a blanket. Between the coat, the oversized clothes and the blankets, she begins to sweat but remains bundled, enjoying the warmth which feels like a hug from a loved one. It is a snug, all-embracing feeling, like cuddling beside her mother when she was little.

*   *   *

A desert appears. She walks endlessly alone. The ground slopes down and her sandals sink into the burning sand. Her feet begin to tingle but there is no cool place to put them. She walks forward, panting. Below her is a small stream bordered by lush green grass and trees. She runs forward; each step is like walking on coals.

She reaches the stream, carefully puts her water jug down, falls to her knees, lifts the lower part of her veil and drinks. A shadow rises over the water in front of her and she looks up. Seven men stand on the other side of the gently flowing water, hiding amidst the trees. Avizeh thinks of running but she knows she would be caught.

A man emerges from the brush and steps into the water. He wades across the stream and approaches Avizeh. His face is wet, as if he had been washing himself in the river, but there is a stink on him, as if it had been the first time in a long time. A rifle is slung across his back and as he approaches its muzzle comes too close to her face for comfort. He grabs her jug, dips it in the water for her and hands it back.

"Do you live near here?" he asks, while the girl nods quietly. "We will escort you home."

*   *   *

Avizeh is lying in one of the bunk beds when she feels a tapping on her shoulder and turns to see James is standing over her. He raises a hand to his mouth in an eating motion. She sighs, throws off the covers and stands up to join him. The two walk outside and back to the mess hall. They load up their trays with pasta and meat sauce, a fruit cup and water, then take their seats at an empty table. Avizeh takes a few lazy bites of her pasta before looking over at James. He has a little smile on his face but isn't looking at her, giving all his attention squarely to his food. She sighs again.

Avizeh leans over and touches his cup of water. "Ab," she says. James looks up at her. She repeats, pointing down into the cup. "Ab."

"Bale, ab," he replies.

Avizeh smiles. She points to the slice of orange in his fruit cup. She waits a moment. When he doesn't respond, she says, "Portaghal."

"Portagle," he tries.

"Port-agh-hal." She leans in so he can see her lips.

"Port-agh-hal."

"Bale! Bale bekheir!" She smiles. She leans in and touches his slice of apple.

"Sib!"

Avizeh smiles wide, showing her teeth. The two cycle through the whole plate. She points to each item slowly and after a few minutes James is able to name them all, looking very proud as he does. After passing the test he looks over at her, as if wondering what's next. Avizeh barks at him, causing the people at the next table to stare. She barks again, loudly and lets her tongue drop out of her mouth, panting.

"Mush!"

"Nist." Avizeh shakes her head. She wags her tongue again. She waits for him to answer, but when it becomes apparent he doesn't know the answer, she says, "Sag."

James rolls his eyes as if he should have known. Avizeh tilts her head back, pulls up her nose back with her thumb and oinks. The next table over bursts into laughs. James laughs and Avizeh smiles and snorts again.

"Umm... khuk?"

"Bale!" Avizeh exclaims, clapping.

The two spend the next hour conversing the only way they know how: with wild gestures and exclamations. Suddenly their language barrier no longer impedes their mutual understanding but facilitates it as they engage in the universal language of play. Avizeh acts out every animal she knows, then pivots to clothes, then weather, which she accomplishes by blowing for wind, fanning herself for hot, and covering her head with her tray for rainy. She ends by putting a hand on her chest and saying, "Esm e man Avizeh ast," accentuating her own name. She repeats the phrase, then waves at him.

"Esm e man James..."

"Ast."

"Esm e man James ast."

Avizeh smiles and claps. Deciding that was enough Farsi, she leans in and says, "English." In response, he touches his glass.

"Water."

"What-er."

He reaches over and holds up her slice of apple, as he had finished off most of his food. "Apple."

She repeats, before he moves on to the next item.

"Orange."

"Orengh."

"Orange."

"Orengh."

James leans in. "Or."

"Or."

"Ange," he makes a show of opening his mouth wide.

"Ange."

"Orange."

"Orengh."

James smiles and waves it aside.

"Orengh!" Avizeh insists.

"Orange," he replies.

"Bale, orengh!"

"Yes!" he says.

Avizeh tilts her head.

"Bale... yes."

Avizeh nods, understanding. "Yes."

"Yes!" James throws his hands to the side, smiling.

"Yes, orengh!" She smiles back.

James laughs and puts his hand on his chest. "Yes, orange." After a moment, he composes himself and looks back at her. They work through the rest of the food on her plate. He skips the animals and weather and finishes with, "My name is James."

"Meh nam ees Avizeh."

He tries it two more times before ending their session. They both realize they still have a huge grammar barrier to overcome to truly speak to each other but they made progress. He waves at her tray and Avizeh finishes eating, saving the orange, which she puts in her pocket. When she finishes, they bus their trays and he escorts her back to the women's dormitory.

Avizeh enters and walks slowly toward the redhead's bunk to find her still reading. Her look hasn't softened since before and her hair is even frizzier. The Afghan woman stands beside her and the redhead looks up from her tablet at her. Avizeh reaches into her pocket and holds out the orange towards her.

"Orengh."

The woman looks down at it curiously. She takes it and says something incomprehensible with an awkward smile on her face.

"Meh nam ees Avizeh."

"Oh... Jaina," she replies.

Avizeh smiles and does a little bow. She starts to head back when Jaina calls, "Avizeh." She turns around and Jaina points to her knitting kit. Her eyes light up and Jaina hands Avizeh her knitting needles. Avizeh takes off her coat and puts it on the bunk next to her. She sits down, takes the needles and nods. Jaina points to the yarn and waves, indicating that it doesn't matter which color she picks. The Afghan grabs the spool of red yarn and looks at Jaina, who smiles and nods.

Avizeh smiles in return, sits down and begins to knit. Quietly, she says, "Orengh."

"Red."

Avizeh looks up. Jaina points at the yarn. "Red."

"Rad."

Jaina points up at another spool of yarn. "Orange," she says.

Avizeh gives Jaina a confused look. She points at the orange on the desk. "Orengh."

Jaina nods. "Yes, orange," then she points at the spool of yarn. "Orange." She points back to the slice of orange. "Orange. Orange."

"Orengh," Avizeh says. She breathes and gives a helpless look.

"Orengh."

*   *   *

The far door opens and Clara walks down the length of the bunks holding a large plastic bag. She reaches her own bunk and notices that Avizeh isn't there. She drops the bag and looks down the length of the hall, a sudden panic swelling inside her chest. She walks towards the bathroom when a cheery voice calls, "Clara!"

Clara turns and sees Avizeh sitting on Jaina's bed, knitting needles in hand.

"Hey," Clara says in Farsi. "Are you doing all right?"

"Yes," Avizeh replies in English with a smile.

"Oh, has James been helping you with English?"

"Yes," then in Farsi, "and I have been teaching him Farsi."

"Wonderful. Here, would you like to see the new clothes I bought you?"

Avizeh nods and stands up. Clara whispers in the young woman's ear, and she turns and says, "Thank you, Jaina," and puts the knitting needles and thread down on her desk.

"Tell her she can continue working on whatever it is she's making when I'm around."

Clara nods, places a hand on Avizeh's shoulder and leads her back to her bunk. She opens one of the bags and holds out a pair of light blue cotton pajama pants and a white-sleeved shirt. "This should be about your size," she says while handing her a pair of undergarments. She retrieves a winter coat and pants and says, "Yeah, this looks like it will fit, and will keep you warm, even in the most extreme cold." Finally, she pulls out a pair of shoes with pink laces and a pair of teal socks.

"You can try these on in the bathroom."

Avizeh nods, takes the lot and walks to the end of the hall. Clara pushes the bags aside, sits down at her desk and turns on her computer. She opens a web browser and types in 'Razaaq Hirat.' There is a *BBC* profile and a few stories dated months ago to his involvement in attacks as far west as the Iranian border but nothing recent. Clara wonders if her new guest's husband still lives. It irks her that she has to look on civilian news sources to find out what her own organization is doing. Ever since she was taken off combat duty, her knowledge of the outside world has been limited.

Avizeh steps out of the bathroom in her new clothes, which thankfully seem to fit her. As she walks down the hall she gets a catcall from one of the women near her. Avizeh cringes for a moment, but then smiles and says, "Thank you!" which draws a smattering of laughs.

"Ready for dinner?" Clara asks.

"Yes," Avizeh replies in English.

"Do you know what 'no' is in English?"

"No," she says with a smile.

Clara smiles. "That's all right. I'll be sure to teach you a few words at dinner."

Clara leads her outside into the biting cold. As they walk the familiar path to the mess hall, Avizeh looks over at the concrete platform. Just then a man appears out of thin air, gun leveled at the ground, and Avizeh jumps. Another man appears, then another. Six more men emerge from nothingness. After a moment a final man appears, covered in blood, his shirt visibly drenched in it; warm stink spewing from him. He takes a casual step forward and Avizeh realizes that none of the blood is his own. He saunters right past Avizeh, leaving a trail of scarlet footprints in the snow. As he passes he looks down at her. A few tiny flecks of crimson fall in a mist that freezes in the frigid air between them. His squad members follow him, the heavy pounding of their boots disturbing the winter calm.

Avizeh shudders. Clara reaches down and puts a finger under her chin, pushing it up. The young woman takes two long steps, hoping that she stepped over the frozen bloody prints.

Chapter Three
From Ramadan to Rabi

"Good morning." Avizeh peeks down from the top bunk just as Clara rubs sleep from her eyes. The young Afghan adjusted to barracks time remarkably fast despite December's permanent sunlight. In place of natural light, the inhabitants of the Antarctic base's lives are decided by clocks, meal times and the automatic dimming of artificial lights for bed.

Clara slides her legs to the ground. "You're not busy again today, are you?" Avizeh asks in Farsi with imploring eyes.

Clara shakes her head. "They don't need me anymore."

"Good!" Avizeh says enthusiastically in English. Switching back to her native language, she adds, "I can only watch so much TV, though it's helped. And James and Mehmet have been busy, so I've had no one to talk to."

Clara rubs her eyes and thinks. "When's your birthday, Avizeh?"

"The twenty-fifth of Dhul Qa'idah."

Clara furrows her brow. "So, June third?" she says aloud. *From early May to the end of July the base will be in total darkness. It would be a pretty dour time for a birthday...*

"Let's go for a walk outside," Clara changes the subject.

"Really?" Avizeh beams. "Will anything try to eat us?"

"Probably not," Clara replies with a wink. She stands up and before Avizeh can ask another question, grabs some clothes and walks down to the showers. She returns to find Avizeh sitting on her bed in full snow gear. She has even zipped up the top of her jacket so her face is barely visible. As tired as she is, Clara cannot help but smile. She walks over to the desk and pulls out a small camera which she hands to Avizeh.

"Do you know how to work a camera?"

"Yes, I've used one before," Avizeh remarks as she toys with it. She is about to take a photo when Clara grabs the lens.

"One rule: no pictures of the base. You can take pictures of animals and icebergs and anything you think is pretty but nothing of the base."

"Can I take a picture of you? Or us?"

Clara thinks about that for a moment. She sighs and says, "Outside. Nothing of the base itself."

"Okay!" Avizeh cheers using her favorite new English phrase.

"One more thing." Clara opens another drawer and pulls out a pair of snow goggles for herself and a smaller pair for Avizeh. The young Afghan puts them on and Clara laughs. "Very stylish."

The two set off outside the barracks. A pair of guards at the main gate scan an ID chip in Clara's hand and take a retinal scan. She answers a few questions about the purpose of the trip before the gate opens.

Avizeh's mouth drops open in wonder as she looks across the empty fields of snow that stretch for all directions. A visible gust of wind throws tiny white flakes into the air.

Clara looks down at Avizeh. "Well, care to lead?" Avizeh

looks back up at her questioningly. "We can go anywhere you like."

For a long while, Avizeh considers which way to go. She lifts her camera and takes a photo. The young woman puts the camera back in her pocket and heads straight forward. Avizeh takes a step and her eyes go wide as she sinks waist-deep in snow.

Avizeh struggles walking down the lip of the dune. She can hardly see with her veil in front of her, forcing her to look up towards the nearby town, then down again to her feet. She looks up again as she lowers her right foot. Her toes only tickle the sand and she stumbles and falls to her knees. Strong arms grab her under her ribs and lift her up.

"Always keep your eyes on your feet, Avizeh," her mother breathes into her ear.

"But then I might head the wrong way."

"You will make this trip many times in your life and one day you won't need to look to know it's there. Your destination will always be the same but the sand will forever shift beneath you."

Strong hands enclosed in puffy gloves grab Avizeh's overcoat and struggle to pull her out. "Are you all right?" Clara asks, worry clear in her voice. Avizeh turns to Clara with a smile which is enough of an answer for her. "Let's take this more slowly, shall we? We have all day and there's food and water in my pack so we won't have to head back anytime soon."

Avizeh nods and leads her forward. They march until the base rests on the far horizon. The amazed Afghan looks out and sees a dark-blue sliver which must be the ocean at the edge of her vision and marches towards it. After a few minutes of walking, Avizeh hears a squawking noise and jumps. Recovering, she marches towards the noise more quickly, with Clara racing after her. After a long time, they near an inlet flanked by glaciers and Avizeh stares in amazement at an encampment of hundreds of emperor penguins. She pulls out her camera and starts taking photos.

"How about we get closer?"

Avizeh looks up at her curiously. She nods vigorously and the two head down towards the icy beach. As they near, Clara points to a group of penguins jumping into the water. "They're hunting for food. Look, you can see some coming back with fish in their mouths."

Avizeh watches an especially large bird waddle towards a stationary penguin. The penguin opens her mouth and slimy fish fall out and into the mouths of the chicks.

"See that? The males stay with the eggs and sit on them, keeping them and the babies warm while the female goes to hunt."

Avizeh's eyes widen. "Is there anything that eats them?"

"Seals," Clara replies.

Avizeh thinks back. She remembers the terrified seal howling like a mad dog on the ice floe beside her. "Do orcas eat penguins?"

"No, orcas eat the seals."

Avizeh decides that she doesn't like orcas. "Can we get any closer?"

"Sure, just not anywhere near the nests."

Clara leads her to the edge of a beach. A handful of the penguins look at them curiously but otherwise ignore them. Avizeh pulls out her camera and starts taking photos. She stoops to one knee and leans in for more.

"Look!" she says excitedly. "I caught a penguin as it was jumping into the water!"

"Very nice!"

Avizeh puts her camera away. The two climb up a nearby ridge and look out at the horizon. "What's out there?" She points out towards the sea.

"Well," Clara thinks. "Straight that way is Brazil and the

Amazon rainforest. It rains for months and there's pumas and toucans and all sorts of colorful birds. And people too. The best football players in the world come from there, I'm sure you know."

Avizeh nods. Even her little village in the Desert of Death has football fans with Brazil jerseys.

"And that way?" Avizeh points to the right.

"That's Africa, where there are jungles filled with monkeys and crocodiles. And farther up savannas and lions."

"That way?" Avizeh points farther to the right.

"Far out, across thousands of kilometers of ocean, is India. And a little to the left," Clara guides her hand, "is Pakistan. And just past that is—"

"Afghanistan."

Avizeh holds her hand out and looks toward the horizon. Across dozens of kilometers of icy desert beyond their inlet, far past the sea is a desert of sand, and a place where the stars shine in blazing silver glory over the tumultuous land below. Avizeh gazes out towards her home for a long time.

"And not too far that way," Clara pulls her hand and turns her nearly fully around, "is Australia. It's got koalas and kangaroos and spiders..."

"I hate spiders," Avizeh remarks. "More than I hate orcas."

"Well, then don't go there. The spiders there are bigger than your face." Clara puts her hand in front of Avizeh, clenching her fingers. The 'spider' jumps at Avizeh and she falls back against Clara and giggles.

Still leaning against Clara, Avizeh looks up and says, "I'm thirsty."

Clara unbuckles her pack and swings it forward. She hands Avizeh a thermos filled with water and a sandwich before retrieving her own.

"Shall we head back?"

Avizeh nods. She takes a step forward, leading Clara on an

arc towards the base. When they are halfway there, Avizeh cries out and grabs her leg.

"Are you okay?"

"Yes, I just banged my foot on something." Avizeh takes a small step backward. Grimacing, she leans over and brushes snow off a small hump, uncovering a large steel tube. Avizeh looks down, following the hidden but still visible upraised snow, and realizes it leads back to the base. She steps on top of the tube and looks down its length. Opposite the base is an enormous solar farm, stretching as far as she can see.

"What's that?"

"Those collect energy and heat from the sun. That's taken via this steel pipe to the base. That's how we get our power."

"So you can power the teleportation machines."

Clara nods. "This is the perfect place for it. The land is open and the sun shines for six months."

"Six months?"

"From Ramadan to Rabi... well, close to that. Then it begins to get darker. From the end of Jumada to Sha'ban the sun will be completely gone."

Avizeh tenses as she tries to imagine that.

"It's not so bad; in fact, it can be quite beautiful. With no cities nearby you can go outside every night and look up and see the Milky Way and more stars than you can count. It's one of the most breathtaking sights you can imagine. Sometimes when I'm feeling sad during those months I just remember that I'll get a sky full of stars soon. Here, I think there's a photo on your camera."

Clara leans over, puts a hand on the camera and flips through photos. She flips quickly but Avizeh sees a few pictures of Clara in front of a small, two-story home with a girl that looks a lot like her and two older people who must have been her parents.

"Here we go."

A picture of a blazing silver night sky appears in the small screen. In the middle of the photo is a brilliantly shining streak of white lights, appearing like a gash in the universe where all the stars spilled out. Avizeh studies the photo and remembers how she had walked out a few paces from the meager lights of her little village and saw a sky bursting with starlight just like in Clara's picture. She looks at the image, then up at the cloudless blue sky. As she does she sees a palm tree to her left, her home behind her and the Desert of Death in front of her. *This whole time I was looking at my future and I didn't even know it.*

Chapter Four
Anywhere in the World

"**V**ery good!" Jaina exclaims as Avizeh holds up a blue snow cap she just finished knitting.

"Thank you," Avizeh replies, stressing the 'th' as she mimics an American accent. "I hope it fits."

"It looks amazing." Jaina smiles while turning the computer screen. She presses the camera button and Avizeh appears on the screen, grinning shyly with a deep blue snow cap over her long, dark hair.

"Here, let me grab mine." Jaina reaches over for the red snow cap Avizeh made for her, which is one shade darker than her own fiery hair. She leans over and puts her arm around the young Afghan. "Look at you, kid. Smiling, making the best of life." She presses her cheek against Avizeh's. "Up here people can get crazy, especially around now, in the perma-night, but you seem to be holding on to your sanity better than most."

Avizeh doesn't fully understand the last part but gets the gist of what Jaina was saying. "I like looking at the stars."

"You're nuts. I don't know how you stand being in negative sixty-degree weather. Especially when you come from a place that's so hot. You are a tough little bird."

Avizeh understands each word but has no idea what she means and offers a shrug with an endearing smile.

"Well you've handled the change pretty well. I'm proud of you. You're a keeper." Jaina reaches out and squeezes Avizeh's cheek.

"Thank you, you are good friend," she replies, feeling sudden warmth. At first she thought she would only be speaking to Clara and James, but ever since the orengh incident, a word she still cannot properly pronounce, Jaina lets her use the computer to watch TV, read English stories and listen to music. All of this has to be done with someone watching her, ensuring that she won't send out any e-mails, video or so much as comment on a webpage, as Avizeh is not allowed access to the outside world. In those six months, she managed to pick up a fair amount of English and even meet two new people who she helps learn western Afghanistan's Farsi dialect.

Life in the barracks isn't always exciting; by all accounts her world in Fort Powell is as confined as in Anar Dara. She is not allowed anywhere but the women's dormitory, mess hall and the common outside area, and is forbidden any contact with the rest of the planet for reasons of 'national security,' which are never explained to her. In Afghanistan, she was only allowed outside a few meters of her home and was forbidden from contacting anyone outside her village due to moral reasons, which were detailed even less. It is a different box to live in, but she is familiar with the boundaries.

"Ready to go to dinner?"

Avizeh nods, then dons her snow pants and overcoat. Even though the walk to the mess hall is only twenty meters, the average temperature hangs around negative sixty to seventy degrees Celsius, regardless of the time, as daylight won't return in full for six months and not at all for another three. Bundled up with warm underclothes, a second layer of pants and sweater, scarves, snow caps and a final layer of bulky snow pants and coat meant specifically to combat extreme subzero temperatures, the two women waddle outside like mother and daughter penguins. Once outside, Avizeh begins to feel the chill on the scant exposed parts of her face. She has been told that stepping outside is akin to jumping into a pool of frozen water and could blast the air out of the lungs. So garbed, the two walk outside until they reach the mess door, which Avizeh clumsily opens with her thickly gloved hands.

"Surprise!"

Avizeh's eyes widen. At least a quarter of Fort Powell's occupants smile at her with Clara in their center. Clara steps forward, pulls back Avizeh's hood and whispers in Farsi, "We've prepared a little party for you to celebrate your sixteenth birthday!"

The young Afghan gives a shy, shocked smile. "Thank you!" she says timidly. Clara leads her forward toward a large cake with a penguin family drawn in icing on it. As one, the small cohort of fifty sings 'Happy Birthday.' Avizeh blushes and feels a warmth that she hasn't felt since long before her arrival.

"...happy birthday, dear Avizeh, happy birthday to you!"

The group applauds and Avizeh grins from ear to ear. Clara picks up a large cutting knife and asks, "Which part of the cake would you like?"

Avizeh points to the baby penguin. Clara cuts it out and hands it to her, then proceeds to cut up the rest of the cake.

Jaina leans in next to Clara. "How'd you get the cake? You didn't carry it from the Chilean camp, did you?"

"Oh god no, can you imagine? I got the ingredients and cooked it myself."

Jaina gives her a sidelong glance.

"I can cook!"

"Apparently. Working intel has done wonders for your domestic abilities." After an uneasy pause, Jaina says, "Hey, I love working with you. Field work's a bitch anyway. It all worked out for the best, you being here with the kid."

"Tavallodet mobārak, Avizeh," James exclaims.

"Thank you!" Avizeh smiles. James' accent has vastly improved since she arrived.

"You like it? It's been a long time since we've thrown a party. I didn't have cake on my birthday. You're pretty special, Avizeh."

The sixteen-year-old Afghan blushes and takes another bite.

"Avizeh." Clara walks up beside her. "We got you something."

A broad-shouldered man named Tom with a spiral Maori tattoo on his left arm holds out a small box with blue and white stripes and an ice-blue bow.

"What is it?" Avizeh asks, putting her plate down.

"Well, open it and find out!"

Avizeh reaches for it and tears off the wrapping. Inside is a stuffed penguin doll holding a camera. "Now you don't have to use my camera. You can take your own pictures and save them on my computer to look at."

A warm tear falls down Avizeh's left cheek. She sniffs and puts a hand up to her face. Jaina places a hand on her back. "Thank you!" Avizeh calls. "Thank you everyone!"

"You're welcome," James replies.

Jaina looks at him while huffing.

"I was accepting her thanks on behalf of everyone. Also, I was the one who had to travel to Las Estrellas, in the dark, alone."

"Khafe sho!" Jaina tells him to shut up, one of the only

phrases she has bothered to learn.

Avizeh fiddles with the camera and accidentally takes a shot of the chair.

"Hey, we should get a picture of us all!" Jaina calls out. One of the men gives her a look and she says, "We can save it on an external hard drive that's not connected to the server. No one is going to see your big dumb face, and honestly you think someone will come looking for you up here?"

The whole barracks squeezes together near the lunch counter as Clara helps Avizeh set the timer on the nearest table. The two run together and Avizeh jumps on her lap and smiles just before the camera flashes. "Wow, cool," she says as she looks at the result and her Americanism makes the room burst out laughing. As the party ends, Jaina and Clara walk Avizeh out towards the women's dormitory when Avizeh stops halfway between the two buildings. "Can we step outside, away from the lights? I want to take a picture of the stars."

Jaina eyes Clara. "You take her if you want, I'm freezing my ass off."

Clara gives Jaina a look that says she doesn't appreciate the language, but Jaina has already scampered off. Clara escorts Avizeh past the gate, where the two walk out into the snow. With each step the white powder, illumined by the lights of the base, turns a shade darker. They march over a snowbank that obscures the spotlights. The world around them is a majestic dark purple, with a gentle but all-encompassing cold felt with every breath and exertion. As they stop, Avizeh looks upward at the Milky Way. As she stares up at the wondrous glittering she thinks how still the sky is; unlike the sand and snow that forms the foundation of her life, the sky appears solid and unmoving. A gentle breeze whispers across the plains and she feels a peace unlike any she has ever felt. Avizeh lifts the camera and snaps a photo.

"You can hold it the other way too," Clara says from beside her. Avizeh prefers her way but obliges, turns the camera sideways, then takes a shot of the dark Antarctic landscape gently illuminated by blazing lights above.

"Do you still know where the Amazon is? And Africa? And... my home?"

"I think so," Clara replies. She points to the left. "That should be the Chilean base, and farther on the Amazon. That way is Africa. And that way should be India, Pakistan and Afghanistan."

Avizeh snaps pictures of each direction. "Now I will know where they are. I can follow the stars."

"Good thinking." Clara smiles. "I have a GPS inside the bunk. Some night when I'm not working, we can check which stars lead home. Come on, let's go inside."

Avizeh turns and follows her back to the golden lights of the base. As they do, Avizeh remembers the last celebration for her. She pictures her wedding night, hears the crack of gunfire, feels Razaaq's strong arm pushing her down. She stops mid-step, suddenly feeling faint.

"What's wrong?" Clara turns on her.

"Cold," Avizeh forces out, her voice trembling.

"Come on, stay close to me." Clara puts a hand around her.

"Thank you," Avizeh says as they recommence their march back to Fort Powell.

*   *   *

Morning dawns with the raising of the lights. The recruits rise to begin anew their fight against terrorism from their vantage on the bottom of the world. Avizeh sits at Clara's desk while knitting a second pair of mittens and watching a cartoon about a girl who can talk to obnoxious discolored rainbows in order to convince them to shine with their proper hues when Clara steps over, turns off the TV and announces, "Colonel Mueller wants to see you in his office."

Avizeh vaguely remembers his office from six months ago, though time hasn't lessened her sense of nervousness and dread. She dons her snow gear, takes a calming breath and follows Clara to the central command building and the Colonel's office where Mueller greets them with his usual cold-faced look and motions for them to sit.

"Avizeh," he stresses every syllable until the word is unrecognizable. The young Afghan woman's friends have learned to pronounce it as one uninterrupted sound, but Colonel Mueller, who hasn't spoken to her since her arrival, knew her name as nothing more than an underlined phrase in a file. "I hear you are working on your English."

"Yes, I am learning."

Mueller's eyebrows arch and Avizeh thinks that at least that part of him isn't carved from marble. "Impressive. Perhaps we don't need Clara for this." Changing tones on a dime, he continues, "We've found a potential family for you, in a rural town of sixty people in northwestern Ireland where they primarily speak Gaelic. You would be cared for; you would never have to worry about getting married off to a warlord or living in a war zone again, but you would be sworn to utter secrecy. If anyone asks, you will have to tell them that you are a refugee from Pakistan, adopt a new name, and never once mention this base or anything you saw here."

Clara takes the initiative of translating. Avizeh clutches at her snow pants, looks up at Clara, then back to Colonel Mueller.

"Do I have to go now?"

"No, not immediately," Colonel Mueller replies, his tone unreadable. "You have made yourself sufficiently useful here by teaching our men operating in the field Farsi and its regional dialect. Keeping you here would make it easier to ensure you weren't blabbing any military secrets to civilians." He says that more to himself than the other two. His lips turn up slightly in what Avizeh imagines is supposed to be a smile. "And I hear you're pretty well-liked."

Clara puts a hand over Avizeh's and translates again.

"You can stay for now. If you change your mind, I'll have to look for another family. Just know that secrecy is an absolute, and as well-liked as you are here, we do expect you to work. It doesn't matter how young you are, this is an active military installation. You need to be teaching Farsi, washing dishes or scrubbing toilets to earn your stay here. Do you understand?"

Avizeh nods.

"That's all, you're both dismissed."

Chapter Five
One Day Later

Six months of day as blinding golden light from the sun blares back even more intensely from the white plains of ice and snow. One month of civil twilight, as the sun begins to fall at the edge of the world and the sky turns orange against white clouds while a few of the brightest stars gleam in defiance of the sun's waning rays. One month of nautical twilight as the sun itself disappears except for a sliver of golden red line on the horizon. One month of astronomical twilight as the stars take firm hold of the heavens and the last of the daylight disappears. Three months of night follow and the naked cosmos illumines the world in crystalline silver. Rarely, a stray cloud formation from a warmer climate wanders over the frozen bottom of the world, leaving it in cave-like darkness, save the cold steel fortress with its artificial pinpricks of light. On windy nights when flying snow blots the stars from the sky, it is as if all of creation is a void and Fort Powell is the last holdout of humanity in an endless abyss of invisibly spinning chaos.

A single day that lasts an entire year passes at the bottom of the world. This thought reverberates without end as

Avizeh contemplates the strangeness of her life. A single day on Mercury lasts fifty-eight Earth days as the planet spins so slowly. On Venus it's even longer, as a Venusian day lasts one hundred and sixteen days. The gas giant Jupiter spins so fast a day lasts less than ten hours. Only Mars shares the Earth's cosmic rhythm as a Martian day lasts just thirty-seven minutes longer than on its sister planet. Beyond the two siblings, every celestial body in the solar system moves to astronomical patterns wholly alien to the pale blue dot. Yet, no world is so distant from Earth as its own southern extremity. Dancing gales with millions of ice crystals in their gowns bite across endless plains before leaping up glacial mountains as the Antarctic day is more than three times longer than any known planet's.

After six million years of hominid evolution, Captain John Davis became the first sentient being to set foot upon this world in 1821. In over two hundred years, human beings still have not adapted. Calendars, clocks, work schedules, timetables and automated lights cannot turn the creep of time into anything resembling that of Earth. Constant work becomes the only way to hold on to rational time. Nearly every second the Afghan-Antarctican is awake she sits at a computer, watching videos, listening to music and reading as she rapidly learns English. When Jaina needs her computer back Avizeh watches, asks her what she is doing, how she does it. So she perfects her third language: computer programming. Like English, she knew a fair amount before her arrival at the South Pole. As in Antarctica, so in Afghanistan, she was primarily confined to her house, though the reasons for her sequestration varied. The family's antiquated computer taught her the basics of English writing and grammar, alongside programming. Despite her father's groans that computing would not bring a husband, Avizeh took to her solitary instruction with passion. Now, stranded in a timeless steel enclosure, she receives a crash course in both subjects. After a few months, Jaina even shows Avizeh how to do some menial tasks assigned to her. The work frees the Afghan from boredom for a few hours while Jaina pretends to supervise between watching movies on her phone.

Avizeh sits at Jaina's computer examining a website that broadcasts messages from northern Nigeria proclaiming global jihad. On another screen she writes a long line of code which she enters into another program that traces the origin of the website's latest uploading computer. She pulls up a digital sticky note and writes 'Lat: 11° 40' 19.4664, Long: 9° 21' 17.4888.'

The door opens with a howl of wind and a bundle of clothes that Avizeh recognizes as Clara.

"Hey," Clara greets her in English as she approaches her desk. "How have you been?"

"Bored," Avizeh replies. "Oh, I found Sheik Yusuf for you, or at least where he's been updating his Twitter feed."

Clara studies the location. "Let me take over." She sits down and looks through Avizeh's process, then offers her a little grin. "Since when did you get so good at infiltration?"

"I have a great teacher. Jaina's been working with me every night, usually while watching one of her romance movies," Avizeh mentions slightly uncomfortably.

Clara's grin subsides. "Yeah? Well, you've gotten really good."

"I hope so. I mean, I'm going to need a real job when I leave here. I can't be wiping floors and scrubbing toilets when I get out of here."

"But you're the best at it," Clara smiles and squeezes Avizeh's arms. Seeing Avizeh's annoyed look, she adds, "So, now that I am finally back, did you want to go for a walk?"

Avizeh nods, suddenly appeased. Outside, the sun is

halfway up the horizon, high enough to grant visibility but not so bright that they are wholly dependent on protective eye-wear.

"I was thinking about how I arrived here. Do you know why I ended up on an ice floe? Why didn't I appear in the teleport bay?"

"Because of the scrambler written into the teleporters. If any of our soldiers were killed in the field and we kept our location saved, terrorists could just teleport back and shoot up the base. Teleporting back requires a manual code, but in emergency situations the teleporters can still be used, though they spit you out in a random location in a hundred-mile radius of the base. That way if you're friendly, we can pick you up; if you're not, you freeze to death."

"Has that ever happened before?" Clara gives her a 'you-know-you're-not-supposed-to-ask-those-questions' look and Avizeh preempts her. "So, to make it work you have to enter the private's personal code on the teleporter, then the coordinates, and that's it?"

Clara eyes her suspiciously. "Why do you ask?"

Avizeh shrugs, a difficult thing to do in her heavy layers. "I have to be curious about something. I've been stuck up here for a whole year. I can only watch so much TV, scrub so many floors, wash so many dishes, and teach the word 'bicycle' in Farsi so many times." All the while she thinks back to the teleporter still hidden in the women's bathroom, grateful that she'd been given the task of cleaning since it kept others from finding it.

As they walk, Clara replies, "Have you thought about being adopted by a family?"

Avizeh sighs. "Every day. But from what Mueller describes, it would just be another exile. I would have to stay in a rural area and almost never leave. I wouldn't know anyone. I'd never see or even hear from you, Jaina or James again. I'd just be thrown into another world without knowing anyone. I don't understand, didn't you guys kill Razaaq and his entire organization? Why do I have to live in a cage?"

"It's not about them anymore." Clara sighs. "It's what you know about this place. The higher ups are worried that if you told anyone anything—"

"I don't know anything!"

"Avizeh... you aren't waiting for things to calm down in Afghanistan so you can return to your family, are you?"

The Afghan meets her gaze. "I don't know," she says, pain clear in her voice. "I don't want to go back to that world, but if the military made Afghanistan peaceful, then I could return and see my family again."

"I don't think Afghanistan is going to be peaceful for a long time."

"Isn't it your guys' job to make it so? Why send so many soldiers there if you're not going to change it?"

"It's a dangerous world, Avizeh. There are a lot of unstable regimes, a lot of terror organizations."

Avizeh has heard that before many times, always following a question her superiors refuse to answer. "I want to go to Villa Las Estrellas." Avizeh meets Clara's eyes and sees her friend look down at her with a mixture of empathy and sorrow. She has seen that look from Clara a hundred times; it is a look that says, 'you know I *want* to give you what you want, but my job is to keep it from you.'

"Come on, I won't even be leaving the continent and no one will know that I'm not supposed to be here. I'll be covered head to toe in snow gear, no one will read anything unusual in it. Let me have some human contact."

"It's not up to me," Clara snaps back. Avizeh regards her with a look of tired resignation that tells her that a year trapped in Fort Powell has finally become too much for her. "I'll take it up with Colonel Mueller, I promise."

*   *   *

Avizeh scrubs the floors of the claustrophobic intel room while Clara types busily beside her at the single computer, which is hooked up to a series of towering servers with flashing blue lights. After a year of spotless floors in the mess hall and women's dormitory she had her clearance upped, allowing her to clean the offices when there is someone present to keep her from stealing state secrets, the clinic when trained staff are present to keep her from carrying off drugs, and the intel room and the battery facility, where the actual teleporters are charged. She had been allowed access to everywhere in her frozen prison except the interior energy storage unit, the guard towers, the men's dormitories and the command center, where the actual mission objectives, targets and operations are laid out.

Despite its name, the intel room is little more than a safe for lines of code. Radio frequencies are issued regularly with ever-changing passwords, satellite links are monitored and re-coded, and the internet connection is observed, maintained, and every two days the connection is routed through a randomly chosen military proxy server to ensure all codes are scrambled. All this is done out of the paranoid fear that the Russian science outpost three hundred kilometers away that primarily monitors weather patterns is secretly trying to snipe data from the base using sensitive receivers that have not yet been invented. Or maybe the Australians are in league with Arabian splinter groups that are trying to steal information from Antarctica and use it to dislodge the American military bases near Mecca. Or perhaps the penguins have teamed up with the mole people and are trying to take over the world. Avizeh cannot be sure and in lieu of any real information she is left to speculate. The reasoning behind government secrecy is supposedly so self-evident that it makes utterly no sense. But the result is that Clara, Jaina, Eugene, José, John and Albert take shifts reassembling lines of letters, numbers and punctuation marks in an endless fight against world terror.

Avizeh looks up from a spot she has been scrubbing for the past five minutes and watches Clara, who is busy keeping America safe by acting randomly.

"Did you talk to Colonel Mueller?"

Clara's fingers don't miss a beat. After a minute she presses the 'enter' key. "Yes," is all she says then returns to typing. Avizeh knows better than to interrupt so she puts her head down and keeps scrubbing.

"He said I could take you."

"Really!" Avizeh jumps, not believing someone as stiff as Mueller could compromise on anything. "Thank you, thank you, thank you!" she cries as she leaps on Clara and hugs her.

"Hey, watch some spy movies before we go there. Act totally cool. Mueller wasn't going to let you go but I told him we couldn't keep you up here forever and that this would be your first test to see that you can blend in and act inconspicuous. Think you can manage?"

Avizeh nods over and over. "Yes, I can be cool. I am totally cool. When can we go?"

"Whenever I finish my work." Clara smiles and rubs at the back of her neck. "You missed a spot," she points.

"You can't be too busy if you're looking at the floor instead of the computer."

"I know how to keep America safe, can't you tell?" Clara waves at the lines of gibberish.

"I think so, a little," Avizeh replies. "I've noticed that all the weird code like that is something you get out of an algorithm, right? Some sort of generator specific to here that enters a random line of code, like a password that no one could guess. But whenever you are done inputting it you can start to tell when it makes sense."

"When did you learn all this?"

"Jaina told me. One day she was bored and asked if I wanted to trade places. She explained a little."

Clara purses her lips. "That's unprofessional of her."

"You don't think I'm going to give away government secrets to terrorists, do you?"

"No, but we're not supposed to be sharing details like that."

"It's okay; Jaina said she doesn't know either. She says she just copies José's stuff and adds zeroes and q's."

Clara shakes her head. Avizeh can tell she is annoyed but Clara is more loyal to her compatriots than her supervisors, especially as it concerns Jaina.

"Don't repeat that to anyone."

"Of course. I'm cool." Avizeh grins and pretends to clean the floors. After twenty minutes she sits down in a corner, unable to pretend any longer.

"Why are you sticking around if you're done?" Clara asks, eyes still on the screen.

"I've hardly seen you," Avizeh replies. "I even heard that you were looking for a transfer. Someone said you were trying to get back into the field."

Avizeh and Clara eye each other through the screen's reflection. "You don't have to worry about that; not many people who've been out of combat for two years get another shot at it."

"Are you getting bored here too?"

"Let's head back." Clara pushes back from the terminal while logging off.

As they leave, Avizeh dumps what little water she has left on the side of the building where no one will slip on it. The soapy residue freezes almost as soon as it hits the snow.

A scream cuts through the glacial peace. Six figures standing on the teleportation bay huddle around a seventh man lying on the ground clutching at a bloody stump where his left leg should be. The entire left side of his uniform is in shreds and soaked with the blood of a hundred weeping cuts. Two of the six men lift their comrade as he jerks and throttles against them, screaming until his cries become a half-wheeze. The soldiers march him towards the clinic, leaving a heavy trail of thick, dark blood in the snow.

*   *   *

The clinicians miss a few spots when cleaning up Private Andrew Donovan, leaving Avizeh to mop up flecks of dried blood left over the next two days. After she finally finishes wiping down the gruesome scene, she trudges back to the women's dorms, head down. Avizeh's hand is on the door when out of the corner of her eye she sees Clara entering the intel room. The young woman throws her equipment to the floor and follows her.

"Clara, where have you been?" Avizeh almost shouts.

Clara walks over to the computer and logs in. "Avizeh, now is not the time," she states evenly while still eyeing the screen. Just then Avizeh notices the teleporter in her hand and her eyes widen.

"You aren't leaving me, are you?"

"We just lost a man on an important mission in—" Clara catches herself before she reveals any details, "an area I specialize in. They need me."

"What about Las Estrellas? You promised me!"

"Avizeh!" Clara shouts back while finally turning to face her. "I'm not your babysitter; this is a military base. We are the first responders for the most immediate covert operations. Nothing compares to that."

Clara pulls back a plastic flap on the back of the teleporter, grabs a long black cable hanging from the computer terminal and connects the two. A program opens up with the text, "Please enter master code to reprogram." Clara pulls out a piece of paper with a two-hundred character code and begins to type.

"Talk to Mueller, maybe he'll let Jaina take you."

A notification pops up with the text 'Finished' and with a prompt to put in a new master password. She pulls out another piece of paper and types. When she finishes, another prompt asks for a six digit 'New Lock Password' for quick access in the field. Clara enters carefully, then re-enters. When she finishes, she clicks the 'disconnect' button. She takes a deep breath and turns to Avizeh, who has been watching the process intently.

"We might be on the edge of the world but we're always on the front line, always ready to jump into the most dangerous circumstances. That's what I was trained to do, that's what I did for six years, until one day shit happened and they benched me. I'm a soldier, Avizeh. I know five languages so I can perform interrogations, learn secrets and scope out targets. I know how the constellations should look in every continent for when we go dark and have to raid hideouts with electric equipment detectors that would give any other troop away before they got into sight range of the target. I care about you deeply, Avizeh. But..."

The last word hangs between them. Avizeh's deep brown eyes begin to water. Clara meets her gaze stoically, refusing to show any emotion. "I'm leaving and you're not authorized to be here alone."

Avizeh turns her back on Clara and storms out the door. She runs as fast as her heavy clothes allow back to the women's dormitory, wiping away frozen tears. She throws off the extra layers onto her bed and runs for the bathroom where Jaina stands in her way. "Hey, hey, look at me," Jaina instructs as she puts her soft hands on Avizeh's shoulders.

She looks up and sees only a blur of red through her tears.

"You knew that Clara was going into the field."

Jaina nods. "She'd been trying since the day she got placed in intel. She never liked sitting behind a desk. I figured she'd be out kicking ass one day or another." Jaina wipes a tear from Avizeh's cheek.

"I don't want to be here anymore," Avizeh sobs.

Jaina sighs. "I know it hurts, kid. Clara told me to take you to Las Estrellas. Who knows, maybe we could even go to a Chilean jungle. Let me work my magic, okay?"

Avizeh sniffs and tries to meet her friend's eyes. Nothing Jaina says makes her feel any better but she appreciates the attempt.

"Tell me you're going to be okay."

"Yeah, I'm going to be okay."

"Good. Sleep it off, watch some bad TV. Take a break from coding. It's about time I did my own work anyway." Jaina manages a laugh.

"I just need to be alone right now."

"Okay. But don't mope, or I will have to smack you. And don't be late for dinner." Jaina runs her thumb across Avizeh's chin.

Avizeh nods slowly, trying not to cry and not look like the defenseless loner she was nearly a year ago. Jaina lets go and Avizeh walks past her into the bathroom. Avizeh scans the room, sees it is empty and takes the familiar stall. As quietly as she can, she opens up the tank and sees the quantum teleporter. As the janitor of the women's base she is the only one to clean the toilets but she still fears that one day she will look for her hidden treasure and find it missing. She presses a button and the screen flashes 'Enter Coordinates.' She presses another button and it asks for a six-digit password. Avizeh knows it would be pointless to guess; she has no idea what the previous soldier would pick as his code. The battery symbol flashes. Avizeh closes her eyes and turns it off.

*   *   *

Three twenty-four hour cycles pass since her fight with Clara and Avizeh's sadness turns to frustration and anger. By day four she is weary. Without knowing what else she can do, she takes Jaina's advice and sneaks food out of the cafeteria so she can eat while watching action movies. By the seventh day she is back to cleaning in the intel room while Jaina types away. After ten minutes of arguing with Jaina over who the best James Bond is, a notification pops up and the redheaded intelligence agent steps out. When Jaina returns she is holding a teleporter and a piece of paper with a two-hundred character long code.

"Is someone else going to the front too?" Avizeh asks.

"This is a very long sequence; don't distract me," Jaina replies.

Avizeh leans in and sees Jaina deep in concentration. Slyly, Avizeh lowers her camera's lens out of her pocket and takes a picture. She pushes it back in, hoping the sequence was in focus. Avizeh continues cleaning until Jaina finishes typing in the code. She enters a new password before putting the page in her pocket, ready to shred. Avizeh notices that the coding process is the same as last time and smiles discreetly.

"Jaina, where do the teleporter codes come from? What process do they use?"

"I don't know, some randomized code. Why do you ask?"

"Well, what are the odds that someone else learns how to use our tech?"

"Not really a possibility. Even if they can figure out the password, the teleporters are only good for two jumps and this base is the only one with the correct plug-ins capable of charging them. On the off-chance someone gets their hands on one, I'm guessing they would try to test it out, teleport to some nearby desert, then it'd be out of energy."

"Do you know who's getting that teleporter? Anyone I know?"

"Daniel Haussman. You two aren't friends, are you?"

"No, but I know him. I helped him learn Farsi... is he going to where Clara is?"

Jaina looks back at Avizeh. "Don't talk to him. I'm sorry, but if they keep sending out the B-teamers it means that we're running low on people and the last thing he needs is a distraction... I'm sure Clara's thinking about you and you two will be reunited before too long."

"Okay, I won't talk to him." Avizeh ignores the last part.

Jaina chooses not to confront Avizeh about her now-habitual brooding. "Are you done cleaning? I want to head out."

Avizeh nods. As they leave she briefly wonders if Clara and Jaina realize that such a small room that's regularly used by one person at a time doesn't need an hour's worth of cleaning a day. As they step out into the cold, she realizes that they must have and that they must be just as stir crazy as her.

Except every nine months they're allowed to go home.

*   *   *

Avizeh waits until the women's dormitory is completely empty. When the last soldier leaves, she uses every illicit programming technique she's learned from years of sitting in front of computer screens and compiles a profile on Daniel Haussman. She collects his full name, birthday, family relations, social security number, credit card numbers, nationality, hometown, military ID, every piece of information she can find. After she finishes she enters all his information through a number of algorithms. After trying hundreds, she finds a handful that can produce the sequence of letters and numbers that formed the code she caught Jaina inputting. Avizeh feels her heart beat fast, and for the first time in a long time she flushes with warmth. *Perhaps the code for the teleporters isn't fully randomized,* she postulates, knowing that is her only hope for reprogramming the teleporter. Still, one code isn't enough to determine the correct code generator.

Avizeh enters the intel room the following night and sets her cleaning supplies near Jaina, who eyes her and laughs. "Are you trying to send me a message? Do I smell?"

Avizeh dons her most innocent face. "Do you mind if I hang around with you? I've already watched all the Bond movies three times now."

Jaina softens. "Sure, kid. Come on, pull up a seat."

Avizeh pulls a black swivel chair over to the console and sits by Jaina. "Is it okay that I see this?"

"Even I barely know the important information; that's the level of secrecy. Here, I'm tracking known individuals associated with anti-American soldiers in southern Tajikistan. That gets sent to the command room along with any notable chatter or observable upticks in internet-based activity or large electronic patterns. I send all that info to the old guys in the command center and they decide where to move the troops. It's mostly objective numbers and details; the actual plays get made in the field."

"Can you see Clara on here?"

"No, only the guys in the command center know where our people are. I just send them data on potential threats and try to screw with their systems when I can. I'm Q to her Bond."

Avizeh watches as Jaina sends off logistics information and monitors dark net chatter, though she can tell there is hardly any activity in the area regarding violent incidents even before Jaina explains just that. Most of what they observe is code-speak for the opium trade and human trafficking, both of which disturb Avizeh but she remains far more concerned about terrorist cells that might endanger Clara.

"If you could go anywhere in the world for a day, where would you go?"

"Oh god, don't make me dream," Jaina moans. "I won't get leave for another three months and I'll probably have to go to my sister's wedding in Nebraska. But if I could go anywhere... Paris. Visit the Louvre, climb Montmartre, go to Saint-Denis, see where kings were buried. That's where I'd go."

"Yeah? Have you been?"

"Oh yeah. You'd love it. It's beautiful. And it has the best art in the world. And the kebab shops... I know everyone says French food is great but when I go I head straight for the Turkish places. Cheapest food you can ask for and it tastes amazing. Paris would be great for you, it's like European class with Middle Eastern food."

Avizeh rests her chin on her hand as she imagines it, realizing it has been over a year since she ate anything other than American-style barracks food. "Does Las Estrellas have kebabs?"

"No, sorry. And it looks like it might take a little longer for me to get time off. We're sending someone else to the front, so that'll take more work..."

"Who?"

"James."

Avizeh freezes. "Him too? How bad is it? Is Clara okay?"

"You know I don't know," Jaina replies. "Just have faith."

Avizeh bites her tongue before she can ask if Jaina means to have faith in Clara or something else; something she hasn't considered for a while now.

Jaina steers their conversation back to spy movies, and Jaina argues that *Leon: The Professional* is too good a film to be made today. By the time they discuss the plausibility of the Bourne films, Jaina announces that she has to step out. When she returns she is holding another page of code. Avizeh waits until Jaina is deep in concentration, then subtly takes a photo. After she does, Avizeh stands up. "I'm going to go say goodbye to James. I didn't get the chance with Clara."

"Okay, I'll probably be here all night so don't wait up for me. Glad I could teach you the finer points of being a spy."

Avizeh smiles, sure that the campy, gadget-based spies Jaina admires would be immediately killed in a realistic scenario. She packs on her layered clothing, picks up her cleaning supplies, and deposits the latter before making a beeline for the mess hall where she spots James in line and steps up beside him.

"Oh hey, I'm glad you showed up." He beams at her in his overly-enthusiastic manner. "I haven't seen you around for a while. I was wondering if we could practice Farsi together one last time."

"I'd love to." Avizeh smiles back, feeling suddenly happier. After they grab their food and sit down at an empty table she asks in her native tongue, "How are you?"

"Good, feeling good," he replies naturally and with an accent that almost matches hers. "When I first got here I would take my leaves in Arizona, New Mexico," he lists the states with the same accent she would expect from someone from western Afghanistan, "because I was tired of the cold. Now every time I go somewhere warm it makes it that much harder to come back. Hopefully when I ship out things won't be too hot."

"Have you been to Anar Dara?"

"Maybe," he says coyly.

"Is Arizona anything like it?"

"Yes, except it has water, and big cities... Mexican food. And you can hike in the hills without getting shot at by jihadists. So, no, nothing like Anar Dara. Oh, god, it's wonderful. My family has a house in the middle of nowhere in the northwest, near the border with Nevada and Utah. There's hardly a cloud in the sky most days but every so often dark thunderclouds will roll in and cover everything, and thunder will crash down all night. It's amazing. You wouldn't believe it, but I can fall asleep to that. When I was little, growing up in South Dakota, I lived next to a train station, and every couple of nights the horn would blare. Something about loud powerful noises helps me sleep, it's like the tangible proof that there's something larger out there, something powerful yet non-harmful. How's my Farsi, by the way?"

"It's amazing," Avizeh laughs, "I remember when you could hardly say a word. How'd you pick it up so well?"

"Mostly you. And lots of movies. I've watched a lot of Iranian films. They really help with the vocabulary and grammar but for the actual accent I just copy you... and exaggerate."

"Exaggerate? How so?"

"When I was in high school my class went to France. I knew a little French and one of my friends told me to sound French I should just copy Pepé Le Pew. I thought that was going too far but all the French people I met thought my accent was amazing."

"Do I really sound that foreign to you?"

"Only when you speak Farsi. In English you have a great American accent. It's part of being young. I wish I had learned languages when I was your age. Now it's like teaching a cat quantum physics."

Avizeh gives him a quizzical look. "What was that last thing you said?"

"Quantum physics," he replies in English.

"Oh. Wow, you know a word I didn't," she responds in

Farsi.

"There's an Iranian cartoon about a child scientist who saves the world from monsters, called 'Gholam's Laboratory.' There's lots of obscure vocabulary there, and I can copy his accent. Great show."

"I'll check it out. I have a lot of time on my hands."

"It won't last forever," James replies, suddenly serious. "I hear you're getting sick of being up here. Just think of all the good times you've had; it'll make it pass quicker."

"Colonel Mueller told me that when I decide to leave I'll be put somewhere isolated. Somewhere where there's probably even less people than here; it'll just be another box."

"I'm sure you can sneak away," James smirks. "You don't believe me? Ah, I get it. You must think that the military and the government are some all-powerful entities because your whole life you've either lived under warlord rule or barracks rule but just outside the walls of this base, nearly everything is open and free. I swear to you as soon as you leave here you'll end up in a place where you can drive off into the mountains at two in the morning. You can fly from one coast to another. You can get drunk and go to a rock concert and scream at the stage. There's so much out there and no one's going to be able to do anything, I promise you. They tell you what you can or can't do but they can't enforce it."

"Really?" Avizeh's eyes widen. "This whole time, I was afraid that I'd be moved from one isolated place to another. You mean if I break the rules they won't put me in Guantanamo or something?"

James falls backward laughing, his face turning red as tears stream down. "You're not going there or to any black ops prison, I promise you. I've gotten in enough trouble as a kid, as long as you don't hurt anyone then no one is going to punish you too harshly. Have you really been afraid of angering the higher-ups? You've really been scared that they might hurt you?"

Avizeh shrugs, suddenly feeling dumb for admitting it.

"Well, I understand. All you've known is authoritarian oppression, but most of the world isn't like that. All you have to do is cross over to that other side. You'll be fine."

Avizeh smiles back at him, thankful she caught him before his departure. "If I do leave soon, will I ever see you and Clara again?"

"I wouldn't count on it."

"That hurts me," Avizeh admits. "Especially the thought that Clara might not come back from this mission."

"Hey, don't say that, I'm set to join her. Oh shit, I shouldn't have said that. You know most of our conversations have been pretty light, but I can't help but wonder; how have you handled not seeing your family?"

Avizeh looks aside. "I miss them, a lot. I try not to think too much about them, since I may never—" She stops and takes a breath. "If you could go anywhere in the world, where would you go?"

Avizeh wishes that he didn't make her so happy. For the next two hours they sit together as he talks about all the places he has visited and the indiscretions he has committed when he was young and looking for exotic love. He tells her about all of the things his father told him that he forgot only until later, after making his dad's same mistakes. They talk about literature and he tells her that Lord Byron's decision to fight for Greece during its war of independence inspired him to join the military. Before, he was a struggling writer who could only put food on the table with his parents' help. The idea struck him that as wonderful as words were, he could be out somewhere making the ideal become real. One day he deleted his novels and poems and signed up to join the Navy SEALs, having come to the philosophical conclusion that moving a single stone was worth more than a thousand different stories imagining it.

Thirty minutes after everyone else has left James announces, "I need to do a couple things before tomorrow." The two stand up and he holds his arms out. Avizeh walks into his embrace, feeling an incredible weight in her stomach from the knowledge that this might not only be their last moment together, but he may never return to Fort Powell alive. They bus their trays and walk outside where she utters, "Goodbye," so faintly she is sure James only sees her mouth the word. He smiles, waves and turns towards the men's dormitory, leaving Avizeh to watch him walk away before she returns to the comfort of the women's quarters. Only when she reaches the door does she remember the wistful look on his face and the way he recounted every bad decision with an acceptance and humor that he was talking to her as if convinced that he wouldn't come back. Avizeh's breath catches in her chest as she realizes that one of her only connections to the outside world suddenly disappeared.

Chapter Six
The Way Out

Avizeh sits uncomfortably opposite Colonel Mueller inside his office for the third time. He has bags under his eyes but he still carries himself with the stiff, disciplined manner that she has come to expect.

"Thank you for seeing me." Avizeh fidgets nervously. "I know the base has been busy so I'll be quick; I was hoping to leave Fort Powell."

Mueller pauses and Avizeh forces herself to meet his gaze. "Have you thought this through?"

"Yes. I think it's time."

Mueller furrows his brow. "It's been months since you even considered it, but perhaps the time has come. It'll take a while to find you an adequate place and alibi but I can start a new search."

"Thank you. How long do you expect it to take?"

"I don't know!" Mueller spits back with a sudden vitriol. "Getting you off my base isn't my highest priority. In fact, I am somewhat disinclined to see you leave."

Avizeh stiffens. "What do you mean?"

"I mean you've been such a great help and the situation in

the destabilized areas of Afghanistan and southern Tajikistan has taken a turn. Your language and cultural instructions have been invaluable for the part of our garrison assigned to the 'Stan countries. Our expert in the area was Clara but ever since the Sudanian War we've been so strapped that we had to send her and even her replacement James. We're getting another expert but I'm told he won't arrive for another week, and one is too low."

"Then ask for more people."

"I have. They'll come, eventually. All I'm saying is you've done a lot of good work. I'm not supposed to tell you this, but we're going to have to send a lot more people into the field soon. Any help you can give us would go a long way towards victory. And keeping Clara alive."

Avizeh holds his steely gaze for a long moment. "Why is this on me to keep her safe? Isn't that your job?"

Mueller gives off an angry snort that reminds Avizeh of a bull about to charge. "How about three months? Three months and you're out, no matter what. We'll get a Farsi expert up here to start training people in a week, then I'm getting a team of Navy SEALs to bolster our ranks, and if I pull some strings I'm sure I'll even be able to get more people on board. How about it? Three months and I'll find you a home?"

Mueller reaches out towards Avizeh.

"If I'm not gone in three months, don't expect me to help anymore."

Mueller's expression sours but his hand remains outstretched. Avizeh lifts hers and shakes it.

*   *   *

Avizeh is assigned to help two men she hardly knows learn Farsi as her janitorial work is reassigned to a recruit who smuggled alcohol into the base. After nearly eight hours of stunted conversations she manages to sneak away to the intel room. As she enters she notices Jaina entering another line of code. Avizeh grabs a chair behind her. As she does she pulls out her camera and snaps a photo before rolling a chair over beside Jaina.

"Hey kid, what's new?"

"I'm leaving in three months; James convinced me."

Jaina turns to her with a shocked expression but quickly recovers. "Good for you. Do you know where you're going?"

"No."

"Anywhere you're hoping for?"

Avizeh shrugs. "If the place I end up in is boring I can always sneak away to somewhere interesting."

Jaina smiles. "I bet you will. You have a habit of ending up in strange places."

"I'm going to miss you."

Jaina's lips purse and she looks back at the screen. "You'll be fine, kid. I'm sure you'll make some friends your age."

Avizeh looks at Jaina through the screen's reflection, watching as Jaina evades her gaze. She wonders if Jaina will miss her. "Will you be here a while?"

"This is my new home, kid. I might as well bring a pillow."

"That's too bad. I won't be cleaning much anymore. I'm going to be a full-time Farsi instructor. I don't suppose you need me to teach you?"

Jaina smirks. "The curse words are all I needed to know."

"Once I leave I'll never see you again."

Jaina's eyes briefly meet Avizeh's in the screen's reflection.

"I'll have to wonder what happened to you."

Jaina stops typing. She takes a breath and lets her head fall back. "Hey, you're going to be starting a new life soon. A real one, where you can make real friends, travel. Just pretend like this is all some crazy dream."

"And my family?"

Jaina turns to eye Avizeh. "Been thinkin' about them recently?"

"I've been thinking I don't want to forget everyone I've ever known again."

Jaina shrugs. "That's life sometimes. I had best friends in high school and college that I thought I'd be close with forever. I haven't spoken to most of them in over a decade. Ah, I'm getting old!" Jaina laughs in an attempt to ease the tension.

"Except you chose to leave them." Silence passes between the two, interrupted only by the eternal hum of the terminal fan and their own gentle breathing. Avizeh suddenly realizes that it takes a special kind of person to live in frigid isolation for as long as Jaina has. She thinks about apologizing but she has already returned to her work.

"I'm tired," Avizeh lies, "I'm off to bed."

"Catch you later, kid," Jaina mutters without looking up.

*   *   *

One of the advantages of widespread chaos across the world is the privacy afforded by the base's low occupancy. The women's dormitory is completely empty and Avizeh is able to enter her newly-acquired code into Clara's computer without so much as looking over her shoulder. The number of algorithms capable of creating the code narrows to four. That isn't too bad of odds but a mental image of orca fins racing to an ice floe reminds her that she shouldn't take any unnecessary risks. The next day she sneaks a picture of another code and the possible algorithms are narrowed to one. Avizeh inputs all the info she has of the fallen soldier whose teleporter transported her to the ice floe. She takes a picture of the new two-hundred-character code, instinctively looks over her shoulder and turns off the computer, panting in panicked excitement.

The young Afghan practically runs to the bathroom and retrieves the teleporter. The weighty metallic object suddenly feels alive with a hidden potential and Avizeh's eyes widen at the sudden knowledge that the innocuous device, barely larger than her palm, could transport her anywhere in the world. She stuffs the smooth silver object beneath her shirt, replaces the lid on the toilet tank and walks out of the bathroom as inconspicuously as possible, only to find the sleeping quarters still empty. Avizeh layers up and steps outside, dodging the odd passing soldier as she does. She grabs her cleaning supplies and makes for the teleporter charging facility. Since Antarctica is experiencing permanent noontime she figures that another teleporter won't cause any discernible dip in the base's energy. Avizeh pretends to clean the same spot for an hour, eyes fixed on her teleporter, heart drumming incessantly in her. The second the teleporter is charged she bolts up, disconnects it and stuffs it into her clothes.

That night she sleeps with the teleporter over her fast-beating heart. Hours pass until the dormitory is filled to the now-normal half-capacity. The lights dim as the artificial night envelops Fort Powell. The excited and terrified teenager reminds herself that the hardest part is yet to come, but still cannot find sleep as she imagines herself suddenly appearing in every place she has ever seen on her computer screen. She thinks of home and wonders if her family still lives in lonely, little Farah, or if they live at all. Her hand finds the device. As her fingers run across its length she imagines it thrumming with power. She forces her eyes shut and hopes the darkness will bring her sleep.

*   *   *

Avizeh's gentle breathing is her only measure of time. She cannot tell if she ever truly sleeps, just that she opens her eyes and the dormitory is empty. A strange serenity grips her and she rolls her feet over the bed's edge. She calmly begins her daily routine, brushing her teeth and her hair. In spy movies the hero always acts calm even when the world is seconds from implosion, and they are always attractive just before saving the day. She figures there must be a connection, that the time Pierce Brosnan and Sean Connery spend in front of a mirror offers a moment of unintentional meditation. Once she finishes brushing her hair for the third time the young Afghan steps into an empty stall to vomit.

After brushing her teeth a fourth time, Avizeh forces herself to march into the intel room, having decided to skip breakfast. Once inside, Avizeh eyes her lone friend left on base and notices her long curly red hair is even more unkempt than usual, and she is struggling to stay awake. She tries not to think of Clara, and how the disorderly nature of the base must reflect the deterioration of the war. Avizeh calls, "Morning," and then immediately tells her about her most recent findings. She explains that she discovered a dangerous insurgent's location by tracking his still-in-use playlist on a music streaming site, which he was logged into while in the mountains of Uzbekistan.

"Wow, smart thinking. I'll check that out and pass it on to command. You know, I'm not worried about you at all, Avizeh. You've got big things ahead of you. Me? I'll probably settle down in a house in the Carolinas somewhere and hope that the VA will keep sending me checks. But knowing as much as you do at your age..."

Jaina closes her eyes for a moment before shaking herself awake.

"I'll be right back. Got another thing, to, you know."

"You should really grab some coffee on your way back.

You look like you're going to fall over."

"Yeah, coffee, boy you think of everything." Jaina laughs and tussles Avizeh's hair, undoing nearly an hour of nervous procrastination.

As soon as Jaina leaves, Avizeh jumps into her seat, pulls out her own teleporter and hooks into the computer. She retrieves her camera and pulls up the photo with the code. She enters it slowly, tense, knowing a single mistake would result in a security warning. Her eyes fly to the door, and she hopes that Jaina took her advice and grabbed a hot cup before returning. Fingers shaking, she types in the last of the code and hits 'Enter.' A tab pops up asking for a new password and the young Afghan hears her heartbeat so loudly in her ears she thinks it might explode. Avizeh enters '823598.'

Password confirmed.

Unbelieving, Avizeh has to read the message three times before disconnecting the teleporter, finally convinced her scheme worked. She hides the device under her clothes and exits the program. As she does the door opens with a loud creak and a sudden blast of cold air as Jaina walks in with a piece of paper and a teleporter in one hand and a steaming cup of coffee in the other.

"Sitting down in my spot? You better not be getting me in trouble."

"Just watching the chatter." Avizeh stands up and takes the spare chair.

"Looking for Clara?" the tired redhead asks while depositing her things on the computer desk.

Avizeh pauses, then nods overly-enthusiastically.

"She's cautious," Jaina says as she removes her layers. "Eager for a fight, but she won't actually get into one unless she knows she can win."

"Are you telling me to have faith that she'll come back?"

Avizeh asks skeptically, tired of being talked to like a child.

"I'm saying if anyone comes back, it'll be her."

Jaina puts her coffee down and sits beside Avizeh.

"I don't have an assignment today so I'm going back to the dorms," Avizeh announces while standing up. "I'm not feeling so well."

"Hey, give me a hug," Jaina says and waves her over. "Don't tell me you're leaving and then just get cold on me."

Avizeh wraps her arms around Jaina. "Sorry."

"That's okay. Feel better, kid."

Avizeh puts on her snow clothes feeling light-headed and uncoordinated. She glances over her shoulder at Jaina, feeling a mixture of excitement and guilt. Jaina looks just as tired but now more focused than before. The Afghan teenager wants to say something, to tell Jaina that she doesn't want to lose her as a friend after she leaves the base. *No. I can't distract her from her work.* Clara is out there, and James too.

Avizeh leaves her friend behind and returns to the perpetually-empty women's dormitory. She lies down in her bunk, sleeping with the teleporter inside her jacket pocket. She looks over at the clock impatiently before closing her eyes.

Chapter Seven
The Return

Avizeh awakens at midnight to find the lights out and the few remaining women soundly asleep. Cautiously she sneaks down from her bunk, walks into the bathroom, picks her familiar stall, closes the door and sits down. With shaking hands she turns on the teleporter and enters her password. The screen then prompts her to enter coordinates. She meticulously types in the latitudinal and longitudinal coordinates and presses 'OK.'

The entire world instantly changes. The cramped bathroom becomes an open series of small, rolling hills topped with mud-brick houses. A sudden breeze carries the smell of sand and parched grass. The sky is a deep hazy purple with thunderclouds in the distance. The sudden change so overwhelms her senses that Avizeh falls to her knees and clutches her mouth to keep from throwing up. For a full minute she feels the cool earth as the vertigo passes. Once the world stops spinning, she lifts her head and looks at the paltry, squat building before her.

Home.

Avizeh rises to her feet. She takes an energetic step

towards the door. Then she slows; her foot drops to the ground as if testing for a trap. Her third step is so slow that she nearly stumbles over mid-step. She imagines her beating heart expanding in her chest until her lungs press against her ribs, and struggles to understand why every breath is agony. She stows the teleporter underneath her jacket. She raises a shaking fist despite an invisible weight pulling it down. She meekly knocks at the door.

Time becomes meaningless, sensation is everything. The prodigal daughter returns as a stranger, awaiting permission to enter a house that is no longer hers. The door retracts. A figure just a few inches shorter than Avizeh, covered in a black burqa, looks up at her. A hand reaches up and pulls back the fabric on her head. Laily's beautiful night-dark hair flows down her shoulders. Her younger sister's gleaming almond eyes stare into hers with wonder. The two collapse into each other, crying, both grasping each other as if to keep a phantom from slipping into the ether. The parched dirt drinks their tears.

Avizeh lifts a finger and brushes back her little sister's hair. "You've grown so much since I last saw you."

"I thought you were dead," Laily gasps.

"I feared the same for you."

Laily wipes her face with her sleeve. "Where have you been?" she asks, looking down at her clothes, which are so out of place in Anar Dara.

Avizeh's hand cups the side of Laily's face. "I..." She trails off, her silence explaining more than she cares to say.

At that moment, a lanky boy with unkempt curly black hair and the beginnings of a goatee walks into the entryway. He looks at Avizeh with shock before turning and yelling, "Mom! Come here now!" Avizeh looks up in time to see her mother rush into the room. She wears a hijab but no veil and the homesick Afghan girl watches a torrent of emotions play across her mother's face like ripples in a pond. Her mother runs to her and wraps her arms around her. Like her sister, she holds her as if afraid she might vanish. Her sobbing mother lifts her face and kisses Avizeh.

"My beloved girl, oh how I've mourned you! I thought you were dead."

Avizeh can only weep in her mother's embrace. As she does, her brother Aamir falls to his knees beside the two. After waiting a long time, her mother finally lets go long enough for him to hug his big sister.

"Where is Father?" Avizeh asks, looking inside the house. As she does, her brow furrows. Their family had always been poor, but they had some few decorations in the room the last time she was there. Now, the entryway is completely bare, aside from one box pressed against the far wall.

A silence pervades the once joyous reunion until Aamir hastily adds, "He's alive, and well... er... he's healthy. He wasn't hurt on your wedding night."

"What about Fahima," Avizeh asks of her father's second wife, "and her children?" She watches her mother and Laily's faces, knowing something is wrong. "Please tell me they're okay!"

"They live," her mother replies, "don't you worry about that. They're just not here with us now."

Avizeh looks back and forth between each face. "There is something you're not telling me. What's wrong?"

"That night," Aamir replies, seeing it as his duty to tell his sister the uncomfortable truth and spare his mother and Laily the pain of recounting, "was a horrible night. Most of our family were unhurt, except our second cousin Faisal, who lost his leg. Nearly all of the men killed were Razaaq Hirat's men, and Razaaq himself. I'm sorry, your husband is dead." Aamir states the last part with genuine grief, not realizing Avizeh's relief that her murderous spouse is deceased.

After a pause, Aamir continues. "The whole village looked everywhere for you. I still did, even after everyone else gave up. But after three months we believed you were dead. Since you disappeared, we were no longer protected. Every month, what's left of Razaaq's gang comes into town demanding money to fund their jihad."

At that moment Avizeh realizes how skinny her mother and sister have become. Her brother has always been built like a stork but now his skin seems stretched across his prominent cheekbones.

"Fahima's family came for her and her children. Father refused to give her up, he said it was a sin to take a man's wife from him. But they were armed and said they wouldn't let their kin starve to death... this has all been very hard on Father."

Avizeh's gaze trails back towards the bare room. "You're leaving?"

"We have to," her mother replies. "The bandits keep demanding more each month."

"Don't they see you can't give any more?"

"They persecute us," Aamir says. "They blame you for leaving Razaaq."

Avizeh's mouth drops. "They starve you because of me?"

Her mother gives a sidelong glance at Aamir, clearly indicating he should not have said that.

"I didn't have a choice! Razaaq threatened to kill me!" Even as she says the words she realizes it does not matter. A long, uncomfortable pause ensues as the long-lost girl looks back to each set of eyes watching her. "Where are you going?"

"We're going to try to cross the border, into Iran," her mother replies.

"What will you do there?"

"Survive. That's all that matters. But now that you're here, we can go together as a family."

Avizeh stiffens. *Is this my new life? Begging for scraps in a foreign land while my father and brother...* She almost laughs upon realizing the South Pole is more hospitable than her ancestral homeland. *What of my friends? Jaina and James? And Clara...* She grimaces as she thinks of the woman who cared for her when she first arrived in the crimson-stained tatters of her bridal wear.

Avizeh locks eyes with her mother. *How can I abandon you again? You need me, I can see it. It's not just hunger in your eyes. Something broke in you when I left. Now, maybe you can heal.*

She clasps her mother's hand.

*　　　　*　　　　*

The familiar sway of twin car headlights beam through the window to light the kitchen. A sputtering motor coughs and falls silent. Avizeh's heart thunders inside her as she awaits her father. It takes far longer than usual for the car door to screech open before it is slammed hard back into place. The entryway door's rusted hinges hum a note, announcing his return. Avizeh bolts out of her chair just as he enters.

An old man stands before her. His black mustache speckled with gray hairs is now a gray mustache with a few dark patches. His head is shaved and sunburnt. His large cheeks have thinned. His once-prominent gut is gone and his belt is cinched as tightly as possible around his pants.

"Baba!" Avizeh leaps on him even as he registers her presence.

He places a trembling hand on her back.

"Avizeh!" he breathes the name. "Oh, Avizeh, I thought you were lost forever."

After a long embrace he holds her at arm's length and looks down at her clothes. "What are you wearing?"

"It's a long story," she replies.

"Well, I want to hear all about it. Praise Allah you have returned!" He hugs her tight and spins her around as if she were a child again. "Allah has blessed us! I have prayed that our family would be whole again and soon it will be now that you've returned!"

Avizeh looks at the three mirthless faces behind her. She turns back to her father, confused. "We are whole. We're all together."

Her father looks down at her with a smile. "That night you left was so hard for me. I didn't just lose you, I lost Fahima too. And my children, Daoud, Elina, Omira, Ilaaha. But now that you are back she can return!" He cheers triumphantly.

"I don't understand," Avizeh asks with a tinge of worry.

"Fahima's family took her, against the teachings of the Book, from me, because of how the Glorious Soldiers of Allah's Wrath have treated us since you left. Curse them, they claim that my girl ran away!" he says with incredulity. "But you did not abandon us in him. As is right, you must marry Razaaq's brother Behzad. Then we will receive protection and gifts. When Fahima's kin realizes we are favored again they will have to return her and my children."

Avizeh's breath catches in her throat. "I don't want to marry."

Her father looks down at her, confused and angry. "You must! It is only natural. And you will save our family."

"Razaaq said he would kill me!" Avizeh replies, begging him to understand. "And now you want me to marry a stranger?"

"Why else would you come back other than to do your duty and save our family?"

"Because I love you!" she shouts. The words reverberate through the small room. Avizeh turns and sees the wan faces looking back at her. Teardrops hang on her lashes. "I love my family and I came back to see that you were alive."

Her father pauses. His eyes show understanding but not compassion. "You are my daughter and the rightful bride of Behzad Hirat. Will you disobey Allah and bring death on us all?"

Avizeh hears a chair scrape across the ground as her mother rises but her father raises his hand to silence her.

"I don't want to marry him," Avizeh says timidly. "I came back for you, not him."

"Girl, you must do what is right for your family. You abandoned us once. Allah help you if you do so again."

Avizeh gasps and lets out a sob. She takes a step back, hunched over, tears falling freely. "I won't," she breathes. "I won't."

"You will, now!" her father says and grabs her arm. "We go now before you can run away again!"

Voices cry out from behind her. Laily appears beside them, begging her father to show compassion. Aamir tries to be the voice of reason in a world with none. Her mother grabs her and tries to pull her back. Her father yells at them all, raising his fist, shaking it at his eldest daughter, his wife and his own cruel fate.

"Please," Avizeh adds a small note to the discordant chorus of her family's screams. Her pitiful plea goes unheeded and her tears fall unnoticed to the floor. Her father lowers his other hand, grabs her by the shoulder and pulls her towards the front door. Three voices cry out from behind as she is pushed outside towards the car. An iron grip digs into the thin flesh of her shoulder while his other hand releases and reaches for the passenger-side door handle. Avizeh sees his angry reflection in the dirty window, alongside her own terrified visage.

Suddenly she spins around and claws at his eyes. Her father cries out in pain and falls back, releasing her. Avizeh looks down at her father, who rises to his knees, blinking. He catches her in a glance as furious as the one Razaaq had given her when last their eyes met. He rises to stand to his full height and marches towards her, pounding his feet on the ground with every step as a father does to assert his power over a frightened child. Avizeh takes a small half-step backward. Her father sputters curses about her disloyalty, impiety and faithlessness. Her mother steps between the two and begs him to stop. He shoves her aside as Laily and Aamir cry out.

Avizeh bolts towards the dark hills. She hears her father shout at her to return through pants as he runs after her. The crying girl flees without direction. As she does she feels the teleporter pound against her chest. She takes it out and tries to meticulously enter the dozens of numbers that will teleport her exactly back to that bathroom stall. A heavy arm pounds against her back and she falls to the ground while the metallic disc flies into the darkness. Her father falls to his knees and reaches for her. She struggles and presses a hand towards his face and he instinctively falls back. She crawls away, searching desperately for her only escape. She notices a small flashing light and makes for it. She grabs the teleporter, bolts to her feet and turns, seeing her father appear over her. She enters the last numbers and hits 'enter.'

Avizeh stands staring at the bathroom stall door, panting. She falls backwards and sits on the toilet. She lets a torrent of emotions flood through her: relief that her family is still alive, betrayal by her father, self-loathing that she abandoned them, anger at all the pain life has given her. She sobs.

"Hey, you okay in there?" a soft voice of a new recruit calls.

"Just crying it out," Avizeh replies as best she can.

"All right, just checking," the woman replies before leaving.

Avizeh lowers her head to her hands and tries to weep silently.

Chapter Eight
Distractions

Avizeh's whole body feels weighed down with dull exhaustion, though she thankfully has no tears left to shed. She quietly returns the teleporter to its usual hiding spot before cleaning herself up and stepping into the common area. The lights are on and she realizes it's morning, or what passes for it here. Having spent the past hour crying, she can't bear to be alone with her thoughts. She numbly dons her winter clothes and heads to the mess hall. She fills her tray with pancakes and sausage, not caring if it isn't halal. She sits down and forces food down her throat. As she does, a familiar face framed in flaming red sits opposite her.

"Whoa, you look…" Jaina starts. "Well, we all look like shit, since the mailmen refuse to deliver beauty products here, but you usually pull off the natural look." Jaina waits for a response and when none comes, she says, "Okay, I am too funny for you not to at least give a little smile. Something's bothering you."

Avizeh breathes, meets her gaze and makes to say something. Instead, she sighs and spears another piece of pancake.

"That bad, huh?"

Avizeh grimaces. "I just... I can't explain it."

"You feel you're going crazy down here? And somehow even though it doesn't make sense, you feel like your thoughts are echoing back at you from the tight walls and the sound has gotten so loud that your head's about to split?"

Avizeh frowns.

"No? That's usually what I feel. Which is actually why I came up to you. I figured you were near your wit's end so I would offer a distraction. If you need it that is; either you need sympathy or a distraction. Sympathy's more Clara's thing; she's kind of the motherly type, which I have had more than enough of, giving and receiving." Her eyes flare open and she looks aside to emphasize her point. "But I am great with distractions so if that's what you need..."

Avizeh considers and thinks that an excuse to escape her own mind, if even for a little while, is exactly what she needs. "What are you thinking? Movie night?"

"Nothing so lame. I'm taking you to Las Estrellas."

Avizeh gives her a shocked look. "Really? When?"

"Whenever you finish stuffing your cute, youthful, naturally-tanned face."

"How did you get permission?"

"For me or you?" Jaina laughs. "Honestly, I don't know which of us is a bigger security risk sometimes. Henry is taking over for me on intel for a few days; Mueller says I've been working too many late nights. While I was there I asked him if I could take you. I think he doesn't want you to leave so soon and figures if you let off some steam you wouldn't be such a sour puss."

Avizeh slowly shakes her head. She takes a few more bites and stands up. The two reenact the familiar ritual of donning their layers before stepping outside. They set out to the garage which is little more than a small tin box that houses a couple of snowmobiles. Jaina sits down in the driver's seat with Avizeh behind her. Jaina cruises to the gate where a guard opens the slow-moving metal wall and waves them off. As the pair take off across the plains, the titanic black-metal stronghold shrinks until it is a speck on the horizon. The path takes them down a hill and Fort Powell disappears completely.

Jaina brings the snowmobile to a stop. "Want to drive?"

"Really?"

"Sure. It's not hard. Just put your hands here. Hold on tight. Try not to go too fast until you can get the hang of it. Just like that. Now work on easy turns, this is government property and Mueller will be pissed if we break it."

Avizeh's heart pounds as she urges the snowmobile forward. Jaina squeezes her and she slows for a second, then brings it back up to a fast clip.

"Wooo!" Avizeh cheers and Jaina joins her.

They finally near Las Estrellas after what feels like hours, though Avizeh cannot be sure given how the sun remains stationary. The little town is an assortment of flat, one-story red, blue and white metal rectangles that look like shipping containers with doors and windows cut into them. The small assembly of oddly-shaped buildings rests on a black sand beach, with only a few patches of snow defying the summer sun dotting the landscape.

Avizeh slows the snowmobile before stopping beside a grocery store with the letters 'Comida' painted on its side and right underneath it 'Food.' Avizeh looks back at Jaina who pats her once on the head with her oversized snow glove before taking out the key. A high-pitched cry breaks the calm as a mob of children as young as seven and as old as fifteen run out of a large blue building with the word 'Escuela' painted on its side. Upon seeing Avizeh and Jaina, the whole of the school rushes towards them.

"How's your Spanish?" Jaina quips.

Avizeh looks down as a chubby-cheeked girl with pale brown skin and curly dark hair asks her rapid-fire questions.

"Um, hello?" Avizeh stammers.

As one the children burst out laughing. "Hello," one mimics.

"Hello," another tries his best Avizeh impression.

"Hello."

"Hell-o."

"Ah..." With an august look, one scrawny teenager turns to a girl on his left. "Hello."

"They speak English too, they're just being wiseasses," Jaina explains.

"You two US military?" the chubby-cheeked girl asks.

"Um." Avizeh looks at Jaina. "Yes."

"Wow!" chants a small circle to Avizeh's right.

"Do you teleport around the world? Kill terrorists?" the lanky teenager asks.

"If we did, we couldn't tell you. It's all top secret, hush-hush, don't ask or..." Jaina draws her finger across her throat. "My friend Eva," Jaina says, putting a hand on Avizeh's shoulder, "has never been here before. Your siesta usually lasts two hours, right? Care to spend it showing her around town?" The little kids in front perk up and grab Avizeh's arms and lead her to the beach, while rapidly telling her their names.

"You will love this place, American Eva. I show you around, I best guide. My name is Franco Manuel," pipes up a twelve-year-old who poses as the leader of his class of three.

"You don't know anything Franco, you can't even skip a stone three times," a little girl with blonde hair shouts, then turning to Avizeh, adds, "I skipped a stone five times."

"Camila lies."

"Shut up Franco!"

"I saw her do it!" a boy Avizeh thinks is named Alonso barks. "But I can throw farther."

The scrawny teenager, Javier, picks up a rock and shoves it into Avizeh's hand.

"Now, show us, American, your military skill."

Avizeh looks down at the rock, then at the cold black water as the children egg her on. She has seen in movies what they were talking about but has never skipped stones before. She cocks her hand back and all the children fall silent. Avizeh throws the stone, which promptly sinks into the water, causing the entire crowd of children to roar with laughter.

"No, no, no, like this," Alonso says as he throws a stone, skipping it twice.

"No, this better." Franco throws a stone, which skips twice.

"No, like this!"

Soon all the kids are picking up their own rocks and throwing them out to the ocean.

"Mine went farthest!"

"That was mine Philip!"

"No, you lie Camila!"

Avizeh picks up a rock and throws. Again, it sinks into the water to laughs.

"Like this." Javier motions. "With hand."

"Wrist," Camila corrects.

"Wrist, fast." The lanky teen turns his shoulders and in a fluid motion throws his stone, skipping it four times. The younger kids marvel at his skill and promptly imitate his style. Avizeh picks up a smooth stone and throws it as instructed. To her amazement, it skips twice and she jumps up in triumph. Most of the other kids are too engrossed in their own play to notice her achievement, but Camila cheers and gives her a high-five. For the next half hour the whole school population of Las Estrellas throws rocks as each tries to match Javier's four skips.

What if I had been born somewhere where I wouldn't have been given away to a warlord? Where it was more than just a token of exchange? A place where I could have friends and have fun? The children here live on plains of ice but they seem to be even freer than I've ever been.

A few of the children's arms tire so they congregate around Avizeh and ask her questions.

"What is America like, Eva?"

"Warm," the young woman with a false name replies. "With lots of tall buildings. And everyone has a car," Avizeh says, reciting what she's seen in movies. She thinks they probably grew up with American movies too and have perhaps seen many of the same that she has. From their wide-eyed looks she confirms that what they have seen onscreen was true: mansions, beaches, skyscrapers everywhere and hamburgers the size of their heads.

"So, what else is there to do around here, aside from skip stones?"

"We have theater," Javier says.

"Oh? For movies?"

"No." Camila shakes her head. "We put on plays. Some of the adults are in them too."

"Oh that's wonderful."

"They're in Spanish," Franco says.

"Well, I'll have to practice my Spanish."

"Can you count in Spanish?" Philip asks.

"Um..."

"No, uno!"

"Uno, dos, tres."

"Uno, dos, tres..." Avizeh repeats awkwardly.

"Cuatro, cinco, seis, siete, ocho, nueve, diez," the children sing together.

"It rhymes like a poem." Camila explains. "Uno, dos, tres.

Cuatro, cinco, seis."

"Uno, dos, tres. Cuatro, cinco, seis."

"Siete, ocho, nueve, diez," the other children join in.

"Siete, ocho, nueve, diez."

"Wow," Franco remarks. The other children laugh and mimic him with bad American accents.

"Wow."

"Wow."

"Wo-ow!"

"Now try," Camila prompts.

"Wow?"

The children holler and Avizeh realizes what she meant. "Uno, dos, tres. Cuatro, cinco, seis. Siete, ocho, nueve, diez."

The children applaud and Camila pulls on her arm excitedly.

"Wow," Javier says to more giggles.

"What else do you do for fun?" Avizeh asks.

"Play video games," Javier replies.

"Sometimes we take a boat," Alonso chips in.

"Last year our class went to Argentina," a teenage girl adds.

"Really?"

"Yes, it's right there," she says, pointing out to sea. "It's right next to Chile."

"What's there?"

"Alouatta!" a little kid shouts while jumping.

Before Avizeh can ask, the kids start making howling noises.

"It's a... monkey," Camila explains. "Little monkey. Screams a lot."

"What else?"

"Serpientes!" The same child hisses.

The children start naming and impersonating the animals they saw. Avizeh can only guess a few, as Camila is incapable of translating fast enough, when a loud whistle screeches over the sounds of the feral children. The noisy group turns and watches a woman step outside the school, waving at them.

"Vienen!" she shouts.

Camila looks over at Avizeh. "We have to go back to school."

The little children gather around Avizeh, grab her hands and walk back with her. As they near the village, Jaina approaches them.

"Did you have a good time?"

"Yes, we are friends now, yes Eva?" one of the older girls asks.

"Yes, good friends," Avizeh replies.

The whistle echoes again.

"We have to go. Goodbye!"

The little children cry, "Goodbye Eva! Goodbye Marnie!" and scamper off.

Avizeh laughs until she feels her eyes water. "Marnie?"

"That was Clara's doing. You can't give out a real name, so she's got a list of dumb old-timey names to give to newbies. Still, they're easier to remember than regular names. Say, I noticed you were in the same spot I left you in. Did they not show you around town at all?"

"No, they wanted to skip stones."

"Lazy little... Well, there's not much to see anyway. I just like getting out to meet some normies. That's where I was for the past hour; talking to an old friend. Here, let's hit the store and head back."

Jaina leads the bewildered teenager who wonders if she is Avizeh again towards the large building marked 'Comida.' Inside is only slightly warmer, and the half-filled shelves make Avizeh think they are in a giant refrigerator.

"Most of the food you get here we already have, and it's

crazy expensive. But there are some good novelty items…" Jaina spots the candy bars and picks out a large bar wrapped in sheer plastic. "When was the last time you had chocolate?"

"I'm not sure I ever have."

Jaina's mouth drops open. "Well, this might ruin you for chocolate for a while. This stuff is imported straight from the cacao fields up north, so you know it's the good stuff. And they mix it with this hot pepper, that's the red dust on top. You'd think spices and chocolate wouldn't mix but you would be wrong."

Jaina grabs a second one before they step out.

"I'll drive, you try that out."

Avizeh takes a seat and bites into the chocolate. "This is amazing!" she exclaims before scarfing it down. Her cheeks suddenly flush and her throat begins to constrict.

"It's so hot."

"Yeah? When's the last time you felt that?"

"I need water."

"No, that'll make it worse. Just ride it out, swallow your saliva."

Avizeh does as she is told, though it doesn't help, as the heat stays with her until they are nearly back to the base. The same guard from before ushers them in and Jaina parks the snowmobile in the garage.

"The children said they had a play in Las Estrellas. Can we go to it?"

"Yeah." Jaina nods. "If I'm not busy, sure. It's a pretty great place; you can definitely get attached to people there. But never give them any details about your life or who you are."

"What about you and your friend?"

"She has no idea who I am. She knows Marnie is a fake name. Every now and then I'll tell her a story and some of it will be true, but I'll say New York when I mean Boston, or a lake when I mean the coast, or something else made up. I know, silly stuff; rules are rules though. Everything we do here is a secret, even our identities. You have to keep your friends at arm's length, okay, Eva?"

Avizeh sighs but forces herself to mutter, "Okay."

"Good. How about we grab lunch before we part ways?"

As they approach the mess, two large male soldiers sprint up to them. Their eyes affix on Avizeh and the man on the right announces, "Colonel Mueller wants to speak with you immediately."

Avizeh's eyes go wide. She looks at Jaina, who looks on with confusion both at the summons and the horrified look on her face. Without a word to Jaina, she follows the men to the officers' building. The soldiers usher her to the colonel's office, where she steps inside alone. Her eyes lock with Colonel Mueller before falling to the space between them. Resting in the center of his desk is a teleporter.

Mueller's wolf-like gaze locks on the heavily-layered young woman before him. "Take off your coat and hang it up."

He speaks calmly but Avizeh still shakes. Moving at a quarter speed, she does as commanded.

"Sit down."

She obeys.

Mueller looks at her as if he wants to start a conversation but doesn't know which of the pre-meditated things he wants to say first.

"Do you know how teleporters work?"

Avizeh shakes her head.

"The satellites bounce back the atoms."

Avizeh waits for him to say more.

"I graduated from West Point with a diploma in logistics; science was never my field. Suffice it to say, these teleporters aren't magic items; in order for them to work they have to link up with our network. The second you used them, that information appeared on our system. The shocking thing was that the signal came from a teleporter belonging to a dead man.

"You told me Private Harold Manning was dead."

Avizeh doesn't want to look at him but cannot tear her eyes from the menace in front of her. She remembers her childhood in Farah. Shielded by a veil, she could close her eyes when powerful, angry men talked to her; she has no defense now. "I didn't know what else to do."

"This is a crime of the highest magnitude. These are some of the most valuable items on Earth and you withheld one from the United States government. Moreover, the fact that you were holding onto this makes me question your involvement in Manning's death. Perhaps you aren't as innocent as you seem."

"I was fifteen!" Avizeh cries incredulously.

"I've killed child soldiers younger than you; girls too. How do I know you didn't kill Manning and then used his teleporter to escape?"

Avizeh sits in paralyzed silence, feeling a bead of sweat trail down her face.

"How did you do it?"

"I didn't kill him," Avizeh whispers pitifully, her eyes watering.

"I mean, how did you get his password? You had to get his password somehow, since you used more than just the emergency leap. You entered specific coordinates that require user access. How did you do it?"

Avizeh sits in uncomfortable silence for a long time, but Mueller is unfazed.

"I've been stuck here with nothing but time and a computer in a barracks full of computer geniuses who specialize in hacking. Some of them showed me how to monitor dark net chatter, make algorithms and programs to get passwords. When I was cleaning, I saw how the passwords were given; I made a guess that the people who give them use a randomized code consisting of data on the person. I managed to take three pictures of other people's codes—"

"With this camera?" Mueller reaches into his drawer and holds the incriminating evidence up.

Avizeh sniffs and nods, tears clouding her vision. "I tried putting all their data into a few hundred algorithms we use to uncover passwords of terrorists and other targets. One worked. I entered Manning's information. I tried using the code I got to gain access to the teleporter and got a new password."

Mueller leans back in his chair. "Impressive. And here we all thought you were an innocent little girl, but I always knew better. I suppose seeing people die around you at a young age might have traumatized you, loosened your morals."

Mueller looks aside, freeing her from his gaze for a brief second. Avizeh looks down at her feet. *You were so close. You had three months and they would have shipped you off this frozen rock. Why...* But she knows she could never have abandoned her family. She had to see that they were still alive.

"How advanced are your skills?"

Avizeh shrugs. "Some of the techies taught me, and I have been helping monitor dark net activity." Suddenly, she thinks she might be able to save herself. "I've cleaned in the intel room and learned about advanced stuff too."

"When the women you've worked with talk about hacking and coding and all that stuff, is there anything they say that you don't understand?"

Avizeh shakes her head.

"You understand all of it?"

Avizeh nods.

Mueller holds her gaze. "This is a grave offense you've committed. You withheld information, secreted important military equipment and possibly even killed a US Marine. All this done in military space, meaning that you won't be tried as a civilian; you will be tried by a military tribunal. Do you know what that means?"

Avizeh shakes her head.

"That means the death penalty is still on the table."

The young Afghan is hit with a wave of paralyzing nausea. Her gaze falls to the floor and her vision clouds. She barely resists passing out, but her head feels so heavy she doesn't dare lift it.

"Please don't," she begs. "I didn't mean to hurt anyone. I just had to make sure my family was okay. That they were alive."

"That's no excuse, and your ultimate fate is out of my hands. Someone on the other side of the world is going to make that decision and I will comply with whatever order I am given. Stand up and put your coat on."

Avizeh looks up, shaking, eyes watering, head pounding. A shifting form walks over, grabs her by the arm and forces her to her feet. He throws her winter coat over her and practically shoves her into it.

"Let's go."

Mueller pushes Avizeh out of the office and marches her across the base to its far northeastern corner to a small, unmarked, square-shaped building slightly larger than the garage. Mueller puts his hand on a small door panel which lights up. The door opens and he practically throws her inside a stark room, completely bare save a clear counter dividing the right half of the room. In front of her are two large steel doors; just past the counter is another door marked 'Interrogation.' Mueller puts his hand on her back and pushes her towards one of the two unmarked doors. He puts his hand up to a panel on the wall. There is a clicking sound and the door opens, revealing a small prison cell with a mattress, toilet and a single small light.

"Please, I didn't mean any harm. I'll do whatever you want."

Mueller grabs her arm and throws her to the ground before slamming the door shut behind her.

Chapter Nine
Homeward Bound

Trapped and shivering, the young Afghan lies on a hard, old mattress. Every inhalation chills her insides and she never knows when the exhaustion overwhelms her, only that she suddenly jerks awake. Ten meager meals passing through the slot at the door's base inform her that she has been imprisoned for four days. She wonders what Jaina will do when she learns about her predicament, or any of the other women, but she knows not to hold on to hope. They are all like Clara: friendship is second to duty. Avizeh thinks back to Las Estrellas and how Jaina told her she had given her 'friends' a fake identity. *Is she the same with me? Was I just someone to pass the time with in this frozen hellhole, one she'll never trust, never be honest with? Have I been living under the illusion that these people were my friends?* Avizeh is tired of crying. She's cold, defeated and huddled up tight to conserve as much warmth as possible, but still she shivers, and has a terrible headache from suddenly waking up with her teeth chattering.

A clicking sound emanates from the door and Avizeh prepares to ignore whatever meager food is offered when three pairs of black boots stomp just in front of her face. Avizeh jumps, rushes to stand and finds herself meeting Colonel Mueller's hawkish gaze.

"Colonel Mueller," she utters cautiously. She sneaks a glance at the two rough-looking soldiers behind him who stare impatiently at her, standing as stiff as posed mannequins. The two men appear to be Arabs, with the toned physiques required of Navy SEALs. The one closest to her glares with an unnerving intensity at her with piercing dark brown eyes, while the other leans against the near wall in a relaxed pose that reminds her of a coiled snake.

"Avizeh, I relayed your crimes to my superiors. They decided that since you were a minor at the time you are less responsible for your actions. The decided punishment will be life imprisonment. You will be transferred to a maximum-security prison to a three-point-five by two-meter cell, just smaller than this," Colonel Mueller motions with his eyes, "that you will only leave once a day for one hour to a slightly larger box, neither of which will let you see the sky. You have no hope of parole and will live in that box until you die."

"How?" Avizeh shouts, her weariness replaced by blind anger. "You people came to my village, opened fire while my family stood in the crosshairs, and when I try to defend myself you call me a criminal? Or a terrorist? What gives you the right?"

"You are a persona non grata. You have no rights and ever since you arrived on my base I could have done with you whatever I pleased with the full authority of the United States government behind me; which is why I am granting you a way out."

Avizeh glares at him with pure hatred, but she holds her tongue.

"I've spent the past three days reviewing your work on dark net activity, I've interviewed those privates who have inadvertently been your mentors and your work on discovering the teleporter password itself was ingenious, if illegal and unethical. We have quite a few people with programming acumen but we need someone who has specific language skills in Farsi, particularly the Afghan dialect." He pauses, letting that sink in.

"I have a mission for you. It'll be dangerous, possibly lethal, but it's this or you live in a box for another seventy years."

Avizeh shakes from the cold and her own fury.

"I'm not giving you a long time to consider this. We need someone on the ground and I'm not going to ask nicely for you to decide to make things right."

Avizeh bites her lips with chattering teeth.

"Yes."

"Yes, you will comply, do exactly as you're told and serve the United States military in whatever capacity we ask of you?"

"Yes, dammit."

"Good," Colonel Mueller approves nonchalantly. "Follow me."

Mueller leads the two men and Avizeh to the counter, closing the door to her prison cell behind him. He pulls out a projection cube no bigger than his palm and presses a button. A holographic image appears alongside a projected keyboard. He presses a few buttons and rotates an image to better face them.

"Does this look familiar, Avizeh?"

"No."

"This is Kabul, capital of Afghanistan. Ever been there?"

Avizeh shakes her head.

"Kabul's different districts have been trading warlords since the first war; that's something you'd know just from watching the news. We have evidence to believe that the slums of Char Qala have been taken over by a warlord named Latif Ghilzai Khan. He's managed to take over the opium trade in the city, meaning he must be connected to terrorist cells operating in the mountains. Wahlim and Yasin," Mueller motions to the two at his side, "will take you into the city where you will meet up with our soldiers already there. Step two of the plan is to covertly approach the slum house where he has been traced to." He points to a stunted two-story building flanked on all sides by larger, decrepit buildings with bullet holes and broken facades from shells so old they could have been fired during the Bush administration. "Khan's men not only use encryption codes to mask their communications, but their chatter sounds like something out of a bad translation machine. Obviously, he's using expressions and maxims which go far beyond a classroom knowledge of just Iranian Farsi, which is what most of our ops speak. That's why we need you to solve the puzzle."

Avizeh looks at him while trying not to convey worry. She wonders if she would avoid prison just for trying, but the look in his eyes says failure is unacceptable.

"Are you still in?"

"Yes," Avizeh replies flatly.

Colonel Mueller bends down and pulls out a box which he places on the counter in front of Avizeh. "This should be just your size. Change, have a drink, do whatever you need to mentally prepare."

Avizeh opens the box which contains a full black burqa. She takes it back into her cell, leaving the smallest crack in the door, afraid it would lock if closed. She changes into the burqa and suddenly remembers what it was like to see the world through a veil. She steps outside where Wahlim and Yasin stand in shalwars and turbans while holding submachine guns at their side.

"What is my name?" Avizeh asks.

"What?"

"Do I get a different name, to protect my identity?"

Mueller chuckles. "You said you'd never been to Kabul, and you disappeared four years ago from a small town far away. Avizeh Fatah is Afghan enough. Besides, you won't be doing any talking; Yasin and Wahlim will be escorting you at all times so don't think of running off."

Avizeh gives him a look that she realizes he cannot see. Mueller retrieves a teleporter from his pocket and hands it to her.

"They'll give you the coordinates. Hide this as soon as you arrive, and don't think for a second you can use this to escape. The battery can only handle two jumps and since your little stunt I've had them all hard programmed to leap back to our base on the second jump; inside if you get the coordinates right, outside if you press the emergency jump button."

Avizeh takes the teleporter and follows Yasin and Wahlim outside. They walk in silence toward the teleport platform. Avizeh turns and looks at Mueller as he watches them march. Yasin holds out his teleporter, showing her the coordinates, which Avizeh copies with the slightest modification so she doesn't appear in the exact space. She shivers profusely as the wind kicks up. Three 'ghosts' appear, displaying three soldiers who roughly correspond to their body size and type.

"Wahlim will go first, then you."

The taller soldier of the pair stands inside his ghost, presses a button and disappears. Desperate to escape from the freezing cold, Avizeh steps into the place of her own ghost and presses the jump button. The world suddenly becomes warm and dark, smelling of mud and dust. She turns and sees Yasin and Wahlim standing beside her in a decrepit brick room with a single portable lantern on a nearby table where another man sits, appraising her.

"Salam, Avizeh," the man greets. "I'm Arman."

"Salam," Avizeh replies, instantly feeling life return to her stiff limbs. The shaking Afghan gazes around the dimly-lit bare room. Wooden boards cover the windows and two carpets cover half of the dirt floor. A large metallic box rests under the table Arman sits beside, which she realizes must contain a large battery as there is obviously no electricity in the house.

"Where are we?" Avizeh asks, careful to fall back into the regional accent, even while speaking English.

"In the northwestern edge of the town, near the mountains. Technically it's under the control of Ghilzai Khan, but this is the poorest of the poor areas; he's more concerned with his core base in the northeast. That serves as the hub where the opium arrives and then heads south into the Wazir Akbar Khan district to satiate the Afghan elite and international drug peddlers."

"Doesn't NATO have troops there? Why not capture his men when they arrive in the Green Zone?"

"We're not after the drugs; we're after the terrorists in the countryside," Arman explains.

"So, what are we going to do?" Avizeh asks impatiently.

"We wait. In a few hours some of our men, planted with a rival street gang, are going to cause chaos in Ghilzai Khan's backyard... we actually told those boys we were going to help them take over Kabul." Arman smiles deviously. "The NATO boys are going to make it a long, protracted battle; push in on the south, east and northeast, always moving forward but never fast enough. We're hoping that will make him pull troops from the west and we can slip through. We're going to have to crash into one of the slum houses right next to his main headquarters. Then we'll use this." Arman raises a worn leather suitcase and puts it on the desk. He opens it, showing what looks like an old-fashioned laptop with physical keyboard and screen. "This little thing that looks like a USB is called an Infiltrator, it can wirelessly connect to any computer, even ones that aren't connected to the internet. That's when you work your magic and we teleport out."

"Okay," is all Avizeh murmurs, more to herself than Arman. *Antarctica, Anar Dara, Las Estrellas and now Kabul. If I hadn't leapt across the world when I was young I might not be able to cope now,* she ponders, realizing that the strange is a normal part of her life. She walks over to take a seat at the table, lets her head fall back and closes her eyes. *I've moved from a frozen cell in Antarctica to a hot box in Kabul.*

"Have you ever done anything like this before?" Arman asks.

"You mean spy work?"

"Not in-the-field stuff; I heard you were green. I mean hacking."

"I've done some basic stuff. I helped out in the base, but never under a timeline, I guess."

"Try to work fast. We leave when you're finished."

After a brief silence, Avizeh asks, "What's Kabul like?"

"It's a shithole," Arman replies. "In between the first Afghan civil war, then the Soviets, then the second civil war, then the US invasion, then the third civil war, it's never had a chance to build up its infrastructure; poor plumbing, no rail, buses that break down all the time and smell like goat shit. But it keeps growing. That's the weirdest thing about Kabul, and Afghanistan as a whole. I've been doing jobs here... well, maybe I'm not supposed to say." Arman grins, flashing long pearl-white teeth in the lantern light. "Kabul's got maybe eight million people in it now and it keeps growing. It's hard to say exactly why, because the city's so divided.

"Personally, I think it's two completely opposite faces of an extremist culture coming to a head. I mean, on the one hand you have the proud, defiant side, that's fallen in love with Afghanistan's ability to repulse superpowers. It gives hope to those who want a purist Pan-Islamic movement without oil sheikhs and ayatollahs, people who want one big, united caliphate, like in the old days before it split apart.

"Then there's the anarcho-libertarian-minded that is in love with Afghanistan that's the polar opposite. This is the Wild West out here. There's no one to stop anyone from doing drugs, starting a clan, or laundering money. There's underground gambling, hell, you can even buy people. Everything goes here, and despite the mullahs who oppose the lawlessness there's no central power to hold people to it. It's like Mecca, Las Vegas and Tijuana all in one package."

"Should I book a vacation here?" Wahlim snickers.

"There's some fun stuff to do here for sure. I heard one warlord in the southern end likes to go to the zoo and pet the animals. Giraffes, zebras, I heard he even walked up beside a hippo, with a gun of course."

Yasin smiles. "That sounds amazing. Close the gates after hours and walk around in a zoo at night with the lights off."

"Oh no, he doesn't wait until then. Sometimes he shows up with his men and they push everyone out in the middle of the day. I swear, as long as you aren't walking outside the US embassy with RPGs and IEDs, anything goes."

"So, what would you do if you became a warlord?" Yasin asks.

"I know what I would do." A big smile spreads across Arman's face. "I would round up my enemies and take them to the zoo and have them marry a tiger. Then for the honeymoon we'd put them in a cage and bang pots and pans together."

Avizeh shakes her head and tries to tune out the men's fantasies. *Clearly, they would be hilarious warlords.*

Halfway through Wahlim's fantasies, a rumble gently shakes the house, followed by an intense series of whistling sounds. "It's started," Arman announces. "Intel will tell us when the west side is clear. Wahlim and Yasin will move ahead. Stay close to me and keep your head down." With those meager instructions given, he lets his head fall back and closes his eyes. He raises his hands as if holding a submachine gun. He points it one way, then jerks it another, clearing out an imaginary room, all while furiously pulling on an invisible trigger. He even pushes his right shoulder backwards, simulating the kickback. He grabs a magazine only he can see and mimes inserting it into his pocket.

"Oh, remember, we can't leave any evidence behind. No magazines, no guns, nothing that might alert the mountain tribes we are coming for them. Our comrades in the fight east might be using the low-tech, shitty weapons that the street thugs use, but we have the real goods, which means we can't leave them behind. Only bullets, and use those sparingly. Shoot to kill, don't hesitate; we have no backup, no room for error." As soon as he finishes, he reloads his invisible gun and continues firing.

The whistle of gunfire approaches them in waves. Soon it is no longer a far-off hum, muffled by thousands of brick and mud shanties, but the clear sound of war rolling towards them like an incoming storm. The arrhythmic *ratatat* broken only by screams gives Avizeh flashbacks to her wedding night. She sees her bloodstained white dress and Razaaq's murderous eyes glaring at her.

A small voice calls, "Clear," in Arman's earpiece and he jumps up.

"Let's go."

The three men grab their guns and head out the front door. The sound of gunfire suddenly grows louder as Wahlim leads them towards it. Avizeh has to sprint to keep up with the men, which is difficult since she can barely see in front of her. She looks up at the brick buildings and notices people standing on the roofs looking down at them.

"Slow down," Arman orders, then paces forward slowly, hugging a wall. "Command, there are people on the roofs watching us. Non-hostile, just for the sport, but some of them might tip off our prey. Create a civilian distraction."

Avizeh walks slowly, panting from exertion. She looks up and watches people looking down at her as the steady rumble of gunfire echoes in the distance. The terrified Afghan notices that there are no police sirens to announce the law come to end the chaos. When night falls here it is the time of the warring clans and the civilian population closes their doors and prays for the daylight to return, except for the brave few who stand above them, watching the fiery combat in the distance while wondering why these armed men and scared girl are moving towards it.

Arman grabs Avizeh's arm and growls, "Don't scream but run with me and look frightened."

An explosion bursts just over and behind them. In its wake, Avizeh hears shouts from the nearby building. She jumps and Arman pulls hard on her arm, urging her forward.

"Hold," she hears Wahlim say through Arman's earpiece and Arman and Avizeh lean against the closest wall. She hears what sounds like a dog whistle, almost imperceptible, and someone screams. The same whistling sound breaks through the chaos and the screams end.

"Clear," Wahlim announces and they move forward.

They march toward the sound of gunfire and Avizeh's heart pounds from exertion and terror. Through an alley Avizeh can actually see fire explode from gun muzzles.

"Hold," Wahlim orders again.

They hug the wall for a long time, listening to the arrhythmic bursts and screams. Avizeh peers down an alley at the battle. An explosion tears through the side of a nearby house, sending dust and bricks tumbling to the street. Arman grabs her and pushes her against the wall.

From inside his earpiece she hears Wahlim say, "We're taking a detour, stay low and run."

Arman lets go of her arm, jogs in front of her and takes an alley to their left while Avizeh follows close behind. They turn right and Wahlim and Yasin flank the front door of a three-story tenement that is riddled on all sides by bullets. Arman stands at the edge of the alley, submachine gun leveled. He puts his hand back, keeping Avizeh inside the narrow corridor. She obeys but peers past him, watching Wahlim and Yasin. The two turn on flashlights mounted on their guns. Wahlim holds up three fingers, then two, one...

Wahlim kicks down the door and shouts furiously as they storm into the building. Screams burst from inside. A woman nearly topples over herself as she runs outside with two little boys no older than six, while a man stumbles after her. Another woman hobbles out, clutching her hunched back in pain. A final man holds a teenage boy's arm over his shoulder and they limp out the entryway and down a side street. Avizeh watches the exodus, hearing the cries in front of her mix with the all-encompassing sounds of battle.

"Clear," Wahlim announces through the comm-line.

Arman pushes on Avizeh's back and they run into the decrepit tenement. Arman closes the door behind them and lights his lantern, then turns to Wahlim and Yasin. "Barricade the front door with everything in the house. Avizeh, let's go upstairs."

Avizeh leaps up the stone steps to the second floor, where she steps into a large room with three mattresses on the floor and a few photos on the wall. Arman enters, crosses the threshold and closes the window. He puts the lantern down and opens up the suitcase, which he puts down between them. He turns the laptop on and opens a program before turning it to face Avizeh.

"We should be close enough to link up with their comps even if they aren't connected to the internet. Genius stuff. And here we can brute force our way into them. Now, here comes the tricky part: your job. Uncover any hidden or encrypted files and download them. Anything you think is related to the opium trade, anything that mentions any connections, anything outside of Kabul, download it. The sooner you finish, the sooner we go home. The sooner they go home." He points out the window. Her gaze darts to the window and she briefly wonders if Clara is out there.

Avizeh tears off her veil and places the computer on her lap. She searches for hidden files, discovers one, then attempts to open it. When that doesn't work she tries to break through, looking for some kind of flaw which might allow for a backdoor. Wahlim enters the room, grabs a mattress and retreats downstairs. The remote computer's code is written in Farsi and non-phonetic script, making the process longer and more difficult. After a few moments, she notices a pattern in the flow of the words and their double meanings. She pulls up a password algorithm, notices there is a Farsi option, enters a few parameters and waits as the computer enters millions of passwords in seconds. Within seconds the first file opens. She glances at it, thinking it looks like a jihadist manifesto but from a brief reading of certain passages and a section that reads, "we call on all brethren, the hard men of the mountains and the farmers in the fields," she guesses that it is code for terrorist hide-outs and opiate producers.

An explosion causes the building to shake violently and the wooden boards on the windows rattle open. Avizeh screams. Arman's eyes widen and he puts a hand over her mouth while giving her a murderous glare. Avizeh calms herself and he steps back. Yellow light intermittently illuminates the spartan room as gunfire bursts in the distance. Arman leans over and closes the windows. Wahlim re-emerges and carries down the second mattress. Avizeh turns back to the computer and continues her work.

The process slows and the young spy doubts if there is anything left on the computer, or if, conversely, her skills aren't up to par when she finds another file ten minutes later. This one is much harder to crack, but she finally manages it. When she opens the file she finds a lengthy series of jumbled numbers, symbols and letters; obviously code for something. *Maybe coordinates? Payments? Maybe both used interchangeably? The file was heavily encrypted so it must be important.*

Avizeh searches again and as she does, Arman states, "If the time comes that you can't find anything else, start copying everything you can. The more we get, the better."

Avizeh nods. A silver moonbeam shines through a crack between the windows, announcing nightfall. Wahlim and Yasin rest in the stairwell, looking down.

Machine gun fire explodes from below and bursts through the floor, tearing apart the wooden table, chairs and mattresses. Avizeh jumps and screams. Wahlim and Yasin run down and start firing. Arman grabs her arm with one hand and the computer with the other. They run to the stairwell and sprint to the top floor. He leads her into the last room and pushes her against the wall. "Keep working, yell when you're finished," he orders. He leaps back to the stairwell and aims his gun down. Avizeh looks down at the computer, which shakes on her lap. With trembling hands she starts copying files as quickly as she can. An explosion from below rocks the house.

Gunfire rumbles beneath her, followed by screams. Dust flies up the stairwell. A second explosion sounds and the house shakes as bricks crumble violently below. A stream of bullets tears through the third floor between Arman and Avizeh.

"Done!" Avizeh screams and closes the computer.

Arman runs to her, puts a finger on his earpiece and yells "Jump!" while pulling out his teleporter. "Hold on to the laptop, do not let go!"

Avizeh clutches it tightly to her chest as the building collapses around them. Arman puts an arm around her waist and enters his code. He squeezes her so tightly she can't breathe.

A sudden silence consumes the world. Arman lets go of her and she sucks in air, instantly feeling the subzero temperatures piercing her lungs. Wahlim and Yasin appear next to them. They turn to their comrades and Wahlim screams. "Holy shit, that was so close! We're not dead, are we, Yasin?"

"This is too cold for hell; I think we made it."

"You know, the deepest circle of hell is a frozen pit."

"The hell are you talking about? It's a lake of fire!" Yasin retorts.

Arman ignores them and turns to Avizeh. "Give me your teleporter." She reaches into her inside pocket, pulls it out and gives it to him with shivering hands. He pockets it, then takes the briefcase from her. "Come on, let's deliver your work to the suits." Arman leads a freezing Avizeh, Wahlim and Yasin towards the officer's building and into Colonel Mueller's now too-familiar office. Once inside, Colonel Mueller stands up and eyes the curious band nonchalantly. The men salute, and Arman walks over and hands Mueller the briefcase.

"I take it the mission was a success?"

"I believe so," Arman confirms. "All went according to plan." Wahlim snorts. Arman ignores him and continues.

"We set up shop next to Ghilzai Khan's hub where we managed to infiltrate his computer. Avizeh pulled over as many files as we could before we came under fire and had to flee."

"I told you not to alert them to our activities."

"Sir, there's a good chance they think it was just an inter-tribal war," Yasin interrupts. "We laid down a series of explosives and blew up the entire building we were in. There's nothing left but rubble there."

Mueller takes a deep breath as he considers their work. "If that's the best the situation offered..." he breathes while picking up the briefcase. "I'll take this to central command. You three are dismissed."

"And me?" Avizeh asks defiantly.

"You can sleep in your assigned bed. Your fate from here on will depend on what information you can give us."

"That wasn't the deal."

"There was no deal, it was an offer. You help us for a chance not to be tried as an enemy combatant. Congratulations, Avizeh, your willingness to help the United States government in its ongoing operations has convinced at least me that you should be granted some form of leniency; beyond that depends on how well you performed. Privates, please escort her back to the women's quarters."

Avizeh opens the door behind her and jogs forward, knowing if she stays a second longer she will throw herself on her superior. The men shadow her as she walks back through the biting cold. As she enters the women's dormitory, the handful of remaining personnel regard her. Their look reminds Avizeh of the Afghan men who watched the fighting from the rooftops: wide eyes wondering what this new disturbance might portend. She looks down and realizes that she is dressed in a traditional Afghan burqa, almost identical to what she was wearing when she first arrived in Fort Powell, except it is black instead of white. Avizeh walks past them in silence to her bunk where she grabs a fresh pair of clothes and heads for the showers.

"Hey," Jaina calls as Avizeh walks by. Jaina stands up and gives her a furious look. "Do you know how much trouble you got me in? You had to know what you were doing was stupid."

Avizeh takes the blows; having just been under immediate threat of death moments ago makes her words meaningless. "I made a bad decision."

"No shit."

"Mueller told me to stay, for Clara's sake. I didn't want to abandon her. She..." Avizeh wants to say she is her first and one of her only friends on the base. "She helped me when I first arrived here and I owe her. But I can't be trapped here; I needed to get out."

Jaina shakes her head. "They're never going to let you out now. I didn't think they would after you'd been here so long, but now that you've done this, now that they've got real dirt on you... and you dragged me down with you." Jaina shakes her head angrily and walks past her.

Avizeh's heart pounds in her chest as she contemplates Jaina's words. She had suspected that they might never let her leave, but to hear that confirmed... there is nothing she can do. She retreats to the women's showers and tries not to think about how she is trapped in an icebox and has lost her only friends.

Chapter Ten
Jessica Brown

Avizeh sits alone in the cafeteria. She hears her name mentioned a few times and catches a few sideways glances directed at her though no one has spoken to her since Jaina's outburst. She forces the food down her throat and steps outside. The days pass peak luminance; to an outsider the slight variance in the blinding glare wouldn't register, but Avizeh can feel the days get slightly colder as the months-long night approaches. As she stands outside she wonders where she can go. She doesn't want to go back to the women's dorms where everyone regards her with mistrust and, in Jaina's case, outright anger. The mess hall and co-ed recreation room are almost as bad. She doubts that she will be allowed to visit Las Estrellas, and even if she is she will have to convince someone to escort her. Asking someone to trust her now is unthinkable.

So Avizeh stands in the cold. She pulls back her hood, pulls down her jacket and removes her goggles, squinting against the snow's glare. A slight breeze kicks up flecks of ice which land on her exposed face. The cartilage in her ears and at the end of her nose begin to freeze painfully and she blinks madly as the water in her eyes solidifies. The cold air freezes the skin on her face even as the sun burns it. Avizeh starts to shake from the cold and the pain. She remembers the summer droughts when she stood on sand hot enough to burn her feet and felt intense pain with every inhalation of burning air.

"Avizeh?"

The startled Afghan shakes, hastily dons her goggles and blinks furiously in an attempt to see again. Through bleary eyes she sees Clara, her short dark hair grown long, her face caked with scratches and dirt, looking down with concern clear in her face.

"Get inside, Avizeh. I'll be back shortly."

Avizeh nods jerkily and runs to the women's dormitory, fighting the freezing feeling that has sunken into her bones.

*   *   *

Avizeh lies in her bed, wondering if Clara hates her and thinking about the last conversation they had. *Did she hate me then? Was I a bratty teenager who was distracting her from real work? Does she hate me as much as Jaina does?* Ever since the mission, Avizeh's anxiety has lessened and even the thought of death doesn't seem so bad, but the pain of being locked in a cage alone and despised still frightens her.

"Get up, we're stepping out."

Avizeh turns over and sees Clara eyeing her impassively. Avizeh does as she is told and dons her snow gear. Clara leads her outside, then past the gate. They walk out a hundred meters before Avizeh asks, "Where are we going?"

"Just away, where we can talk. I heard about what you did."

Avizeh waits for the reprimand.

"Did they tell you I was involved in the assault?" Clara asks in Farsi.

"You were?" Avizeh responds in her mother tongue.

"Yeah, scary stuff there. But you did in a day what I couldn't in a month. I'm proud of you."

Avizeh actually laughs, feeling like an enormous weight on her back lessened ever so slightly.

"Then there's the other thing you did."

"Jaina hates me."

"Do you blame her? You stole secrets behind her back, made her look like a fool for letting her guard down; you made us all look like fools. We've all looked at you like this innocent kid who was victimized by war but now you've shown how capable you are, and Jaina's the one who's getting the blame for it. She's been harshly reprimanded and now has a huge black mark on her record. It's iffy if she'll ever be promoted or transferred to anything. If we weren't so starved for people she may have even been fired. The only saving grace she's got is that she trained you so superbly and even that isn't going to be taken so well."

"I didn't mean any harm, I just couldn't be trapped here."

Clara nods slowly. "I understand. I disagree with you. I think it was wrong..." She takes a deep breath.

"James was with you, wasn't he?"

"That's confidential information."

"He's my friend. Can't you at least tell me if he's alive?"

"He is alive. If he had died it would be public knowledge and I'd be inconsolable. Beyond that I can't tell you."

Avizeh sighs. "What do I do now?"

"Talk to Colonel Mueller, ask him how screwed you are. At least you'll finally know; nothing worse than being in limbo, right?"

"I was shot at."

Clara looks at her as if she doesn't think that is worse.

"Why are you so eager to go out on dangerous missions?"

"Because I want to feel like I'm doing something important. Jaina's job and mine back when I was sitting behind a desk are worthwhile but only because there was someone with a gun out there who was using my info, tracking down the bad guys. When I worked intel I always felt like the middleman between command who ordered things and the people in the field who did them. Don't tell me you didn't feel a little good doing it; a little alive?"

"I suppose so. It's the first time since Las Estrellas that I actually saw someplace new."

Clara smiles. "I hear you were a riot."

"I made a bunch of friends I'll never see again." Avizeh sighs again. "You aren't going to leave me anytime soon are you?"

"If something blows up anywhere in the world where they speak Farsi or Tajik, I will. Barring that, we have some time together." Clara pauses. "As for Jaina, just give her some time. God knows you have nothing but time. Let's head back."

"Clara." Avizeh takes a step towards her. "Thanks for taking care of me."

Clara puts her arms around Avizeh. "It's okay, Avizeh. You don't have to be tough around me. Part of me has always felt bad that you've been stuck here, unable to have a real life. Then part of me remembers that you were married at fifteen, and I think maybe you've had more than your fair share of what the world has to offer already. I wish I could have done more for you, Avizeh. I had no idea you would be up here this long and I wasn't ready to form the family you needed. I want you to know that I care about you, and from now on I'll be looking out for you whenever I can. I'm sorry I didn't do that all these years when you needed me."

Avizeh's head falls into the soft layers covering Clara's chest. Tears fall down her face and pool inside her goggles.

She cries for her mother, who taught her how to smile even in the worst of times. She cries for Laily, who is prettier than her and the joy of the Fatah family. She cries for her brother Aamir, who dreamed of being a footballer. She cries for her baby half-brother Daoud and her three half-sisters Elina, Omira, Ilaaha, who played with her even though their mothers hated each other. She cries for her father who she disappointed first by not being born a son and second by abandoning the family. She cries for a home she remembers as select images and moments while the small universe that was her childhood in Farah fades. She cries for the years spent alone among strangers in a frozen prison. She cries because she told herself she was strong and didn't need love. She cries for a life lost in Anar Dara and a life taken by powers that view her as a tool for their own machinations. She cries because for the first time in years she feels loved, only after she was ready to take her own life, and still thinks she might. She cries because she does not know when she can afford to cry again or be held by another person.

*　　　　*　　　　*

Avizeh waits in the officers' building for an hour before being told by a guard that Colonel Mueller is ready for her. She steps into his office and takes her now-usual seat.

"Avizeh," the Colonel announces.

"Colonel," she says as respectfully as possible, her voice cracking slightly. "I'd like to know what will happen to me."

"Ah. Well, I suppose that's up to you."

"What does that mean?" She tries not to sound testy but it seeps through her tone.

"You've done some incredible things. Both here and in the field. I had Jaina identify all of the dark net chatter you grabbed and the computers you helped her infiltrate. Wow."

He chuckles and shakes his head. "That was a pretty impressive list, even for someone with nothing else to do. And you have field experience too now. That's an impressive record for someone ten years older than you. So, I talked to the higher ups about taking you on as one of our operatives."

He lets that statement hang in the air while waiting for her to respond. "Why would I want to do that?" she balks, exasperation clear in her voice. "Don't try to sell this to me on patriotism."

Mueller laughs. "No. If you keep doing what you've been doing here and occasionally do some field work, albeit usually less dangerous work than last time, I can grant you some perks. A salary—"

"Which I can't spend."

Mueller holds up a finger. "And a month of vacation every six months."

"Vacation? To where? At the Russian science base? Do they have a hot tub?"

"You can't go there; Russia has never been on good terms with us. But there's France, the UK, maybe visit the good ol' US of A."

"You're serious? You'd seriously..."

"I am. We're willing to let you teleport to any country with a US military base or joint US and national base; meaning most countries that aren't China, North Korea or Iran. Once there, you're free to do whatever you please as long as you don't tell anyone what you do, who you are or establish any long-lasting contact."

Avizeh turns her head and scoffs. "You trust me not to run away?"

"No. We watch everything, Avizeh, and if you don't report back to the base in time you'll be sent to a maximum security prison until your death. But this is your one shot at freedom because the option to find you a family or permanently relocate is gone. You know too much and you can do too much. We're keeping you on a leash, but we're letting you choose how long that leash is."

"Freedom." She rolls her eyes. "And if I don't want to?"

"Why wouldn't you? You'd turn down a chance to finally get out of here? I thought that's what you wanted."

"And if I don't want to?"

"Then we send you to a maximum security prison for the rest of your life."

"On what charges?"

"Will the legalese really matter to you when you're surrounded by concrete? Don't tell me you need time to think about this. Just say 'yes.'"

"Yes. I don't have any other choice."

"My point exactly." He waves his arms and smiles as they finally come to an agreement. "We just need you to sign this," he points to a piece of paper on his desk, "and everything I said will be official. You'll even get a new name and an American passport."

"Do I get to pick the name?"

"No. You will be Jessica Brown, born and raised in rural Nebraska to a white father and Mexican mother and any other name you give out will be subject to harsh punishment including revocation of vacation rights, salary, solitary confinement and potential life imprisonment."

Avizeh shakes her head furiously while signing the papers.

"Welcome to the United States Navy Crisis Response Division, Jessica Brown. You'll receive assignments from me. If you want to report upcoming travel, you will have to run it by me as well. I'll have Oden Smith set you up with a computer and give you permissions in the intel room for your work here. On your way out, Max will take your photo for your new ID and passport. Any questions?"

Avizeh stands up and turns to leave to keep herself from

smacking him.

"Jessica," Mueller calls. Avizeh is about to open the door when she realizes he is referring to her. "You forgot to salute me."

Avizeh grinds her teeth as she looks back at him sitting smugly across from her, hands folded over the contract that gives him her life. She raises a stiff hand to her temple, then quickly drops it.

"Needs work, Ms. Brown, but you'll learn in time," he says while waving her out.

Avizeh steps into the lobby still fuming and sees that Max has set up a camera and put a piece of blank white paper against the far wall.

"Hi Jessica, please stand against the wall for the photo," he says so cheerily Avizeh guesses he must be a new recruit. "Smile."

Avizeh tries smiling widely but knows her eyes can't match it.

"A little less, we don't like full smiles in official documents. Distorts the face too much for easy ID."

Avizeh falls back into her usual pout as the camera flashes. "Perfect."

Chapter Eleven
The Holy of Holies

Within a month, cranes and building crews almost completely surround the base. Walls move outward, scraping across ice as new constructions take their place. Despite the rapid expansion of the base in size and personnel, Avizeh feels more alone than ever. Aside from the odd meal with Clara, Avizeh spends nearly all her waking time in one of the newly set-up computer rooms, which remain cavernous and bare, with only a few desktops in operation and dozens of loose cables and wires strewn across the floor. As lonely as she finds intel work, it offers a respite from the suspicious glares she has grown accustomed to.

After nearly a week of working morning to night alone in the unfinished room, Colonel Mueller enters and approaches her.

"Log off Jessica, I have a new assignment for you."

Avizeh turns in her chair, still irritated at her new name. "What is it? Afghanistan again?"

"Not here."

Avizeh locks her computer, puts on her coat and snow

pants and follows him outside in the half-light to the central command building. They enter the main lobby that is the one place in Fort Powell that looks like it wasn't made on a budget and could just as easily be found on a top-level base back on the mainland. The floors are polished oak, and a miniature brass chandelier hangs over the entryway. Mementos of the Navy Crisis Response Division's long history adorn the walls, including one photo of a previous president signing the bill authorizing the creation of Fort Powell. Security personnel stand at ease, looking unbearably bored, as Avizeh imagines their only practical duty is to salute the old generals who pass them by.

"This way." Mueller leads her to the right, stopping to show the guards his ID. "Oh, and hers." He reaches into a pocket and pulls out another ID card. When they finish scanning, Mueller hands the card to her. Avizeh peers down at the photo which is the same as on her Nebraskan driver's license with the title 'Contractor' underneath the name 'Jessica Brown.' The two walk through a body scanner before Mueller leads her down a hallway and to a door on their left, into what resembles a lecture hall with three semi-circular lines of chairs centered around a large screen on the far wall. Inside sits a crew of three people who Avizeh had only seen arrive at the base recently.

"Jessica Brown, this is Jordan Collins," Colonel Mueller motions to a muscular, long-haired blond man with green eyes and a fresh tan, "Omar Holland," a tall black man with a gentle, smiling face and shaved head. "And Brad Smith," a short man with a deep red sunburn on pale skin, round nose and dark curly hair.

Avizeh shakes hands with each man in turn.

"Pleasure to meet you, Jessica," Omar sings as his strong but gentle hand clasps hers.

"Pleasure." Avizeh feigns a smile.

"Jordan, Omar and Brad, you will be Jessica's bodyguards. I can assure you she is one of our best programmers. Have a seat." He waves towards the front row while moving to the far wall. The lights dim and the screen lights behind him.

"Your mission is in Varanasi, India. A few things you need to know before you go: number one, the city is the holiest city of Hinduism. Number two, sea-level flooding has pushed five million Bangladeshi Muslims into the city. Anyone see the problem?"

He had meant it as a joke, but his dour humor left only Jordan snickering. "Sounds like a curry-serving Jerusalem."

"Exactly," Mueller responds. "Except whereas Israel is only so limited, being a small country of so many millions, India is the most populous nation on Earth with one point six billion people and is one of the world's major powers. Its rise has been accompanied by a strong sense of nationalism and distrust of Muslims, who Hindus have fought with for fourteen centuries now. The idea that their holy city could be occupied by more mosques than temples doesn't sit well with some of the kshatriyas, the self-described 'warriors' who are trying to right society. For over a hundred years there have been massive riots in India between Muslims and Hindus but we have evidence to believe that one group, the 'United India Movement,' is intending to take this to a whole new level. We believe they intend to spark a massive purge in Varanasi, hoping it will spread throughout all India. Your job is to uncover the UIM's base of operations and their secret weapons caches. Furthermore, if you can find any dirt on them, or any humiliating secrets, then release them to the public. Our ultimate goal is to prevent a holy war from breaking out across India.

"Tomorrow, the four of you will teleport to a base just outside Philadelphia. From there you'll take a civilian flight from New York to Varanasi, go through customs and tell them you're working with Pine Gap Installations, a front we've set up to give you an excuse to get legal visas without suspicion. From there you will meet up with Indian nationals also working undercover. Once you arrive Aviz—I mean Jessica, will work on the ground with our techies to find any local networks they're using to communicate their plans. The three of you will provide protection for her and possibly infiltrate strategic locations depending on where the most important data might be stored. Once you uncover the UIM's plans, leak them to the public, then teleport out. Any questions?"

Avizeh looks back and forth between the men, then dares raise her hand.

"Yes, Jessica?"

"If the men we are after are Indian nationalists, then won't they be writing in an Indian language? What use can I be?"

"That shouldn't be a problem," Mueller claims, though he doesn't sound sure. "The largest Indian language is only spoken by thirty percent of the population. Most educated people in India use English as their *lingua franca* and if the UIM fashions itself as a true national movement they'll be using English to communicate with far-right sympathizers throughout the subcontinent.

"Any other questions? No? Be in the lobby of this building at seven hundred hours tomorrow. Jessica, I had one of the girls leave you a small suitcase on your bunk with everything you'll need. Also, be here fifteen minutes early tomorrow. Dismissed."

Avizeh stands up and joins Jordan, Omar and Brad as they file out of the briefing room.

"So, Jessica, have you done any missions before?" Omar asks, smiling down at her.

"Yes," Avizeh replies curtly.

"Anything really dangerous?" Jordan laughs, guessing the

answer. "I was in the crumbling Indonesian states for three years. Sometimes you fly by in a helicopter and see entire villages and cities on the coasts half submerged in water from where the ocean rose and the over-developed land collapsed. We were island-hopping from one aid station to another, using them as bases for jungle ops to take out rebel fighters. Scary place. Funny thing was that there was never any united group. There's ten thousand islands and ten thousand kings and our job was to topple one but a week after we left a new one would take over."

Brad puts a hand on Jordan's shoulder. "Save the war stories for the long flight over. I'm sure we'll have more than enough time to hear your brave exploits for Uncle Sam."

Without another word, Avizeh separates from the men and returns to the women's dormitories. She walks the length of the room looking for Clara, who is nowhere to be found. As she passes Jaina's bunk, her old friend glances at her and tightens. Jaina's eyes fall to her book and she spins her chair around, turning on Avizeh. Though the scant odd encounters still sting, the spy from Anar Dara has dealt with her silence for a month and hardened herself to Jaina's rebukes. She walks to the showers, daring a look for Clara. When she can't find her, she tries the mess hall but Clara isn't there either. Avizeh thinks about going to one of the intel stations but it isn't her shift and she thinks she is in enough trouble as it is.

After all, it's because of me that the teleporter charging room now has a guard at all times.

Avizeh walks back to the women's bunk and packs for the trip, eyes flying to the door every time it opens, hoping the next time it will be Clara.

*   *   *

The next morning Jessica Brown returns to central

command, suitcase in hand. A guard inspects her before escorting her to the same briefing room as the previous day. Inside, another man hands her a cell phone and a wallet with a credit card. For the next fifteen minutes he explains the special rules for women's conduct in India. While there are no strict laws, he advises she wear modest clothing and to remain outside arm's length of the opposite sex, especially around religious sites. After her specialized briefing ends, Jordan, Omar and Brad file in and receive their teleporters and coordinates. They march in unison to the teleport bay and stand in their ghosts. With a shaking hand, she presses a button and suddenly stands in a similar-looking military base but instead of snow and ice, the ground around the platform is covered in grass and pine trees loom over the outer walls. A Chinese man in uniform with golden stripes on his arm salutes them, which Avizeh awkwardly repeats while two men beside the sergeant step forward and take the new arrivals' coats. After depositing their winter gear, the sergeant escorts them to a bus and explains that it will take them to JFK Airport.

Avizeh stares out the window, taking in the sights of the country she's sworn to serve but never before visited. Within a few hours they pass over a hill and past a sign that reads, "Welcome to New York" and her mouth drops open. She has seen movies but the actual city awes the woman from humble Farah. She leans over in her seat as they enter Manhattan, lowering her face to the bottom of the window as she tries to look all the way up to the tops of the mammoth towers, though they stretch upward farther than she can see.

"Don't tell me you've never been in a big city before." Omar leans over.

"No," she replies. "I'm from Nebraska; there's nothing much there."

Omar gives her a quizzical look. "Which part of Nebraska?"

"Lawrence. Lots of farms out there..."

"That doesn't sound like a Nebraskan accent."

"It is," Avizeh insists. "Everyone I know talks like this."

Omar raises an eyebrow but otherwise doesn't question her.

The Afghan-turned-American spy wishes she had brought her camera, but she was told she wasn't allowed to take one for some unexplained reason. She tries to commit each vista to memory before the bus pulls into the airport terminal. Once they board the plane, Avizeh takes the window seat, eyes wide in fear and anticipation.

"Ever flown before?" Omar asks from beside her.

"It's been a while."

"Jordan, I think she's afraid of flying."

"I am not!" Avizeh retorts.

"Just think of it this way: the drive to the airport is always more dangerous than the flight itself."

Avizeh recalls the crumbling building in Kabul. Remembering the bullets flying through the floor certainly makes her emotional drama seem small in comparison, but one danger doesn't make another any more bearable. She looks out the window nervously as the turbines begin to spin.

"Too bad the teleporters are stowed in our luggage. In case the plane starts going down we could have been raptured," Brad whispers.

Jordan grins at him. "Even if the plane was going down, a trained pilot could bring it to a managed emergency landing. Nearly all planes that have trouble do that; it would have to be hit with a missile or something for us to actually die."

"Yeah, but what if it lands in the middle of the ocean?"

"Shut up!" Avizeh barks at them.

"Hey Jessica, relax." Omar tries to sound soothing without patronizing her. "I heard you'd been stuck doing intel work for a long while. Must be tedious, being stuck in the cold.

Where we're going it's going to be a balmy twenty-seven degrees and every night we can get curry and naan and do the whole tourist thing." He leans in and whispers, "That's why the three of us are so stoked to be doing this new job. We used to be doing jungle fighting or were part of assault teams. If you've ever seen one of those screwed up war movies where the soldiers get muddy and watch their comrades die in an explosion... well, that was our job. Now? We get to go on vacation for higher pay. Don't tell me you aren't excited to get out into the field, see a new culture and help save the world?"

Avizeh fixates on his claim that they are 'saving the world,' and imagines the operation in Afghanistan that took place after she left. She pictures some of the new recruits who have arrived at Fort Powell teleporting into caves and mountains, tracking down terrorists. She dares hope that there will be peace in her home country. *I could see my family again. Except what if Baba still resents me?* She pushes the thought away and looks out the window.

Suddenly the engines roar and Avizeh's eyes widen from a mixture of fear and amazement as they rise off the ground. She leans back and watches their ascent as suddenly the skyscrapers shrink in the window. The land disappears and the world beneath them is overcome by endless blue. After a few moments of looking out, she can't tell where the sky ends and the ocean begins. A wave of nausea rolls through her and she looks away. Omar notices, leans over and closes the window.

"No point in looking out. We won't be seeing anything but the Atlantic for the next couple of hours until Spain and Morocco pass us by. So, tell me about you."

"What about me?"

Omar smiles widely. "It's a long flight, Jessica Brown. Maybe I should have warned you beforehand, but I'm a talker."

Avizeh gives him a sideways smile that is meant to be inviting but can't mask her feeling of awkwardness. On the one hand she is trapped, as she always is, with someone whose job is to monitor her. On the other, she finally has someone to talk with who doesn't distrust or hate her.

"All right, what do you want to talk about?"

Omar smiles widely. "Tell me what you want to see when you get to India."

Avizeh pauses. "I don't know," she replies honestly.

"Oh, come on, don't tell me you haven't thought about it. I hear it's got everything. Ancient history, art, clubbing. All right, tell me what you like and I'll tell you where we should go."

"Oh, okay. Uhm, I like food," she says, realizing immediately how dumb that sounds.

"Me too. I never miss a meal. The only reason I work out is just so I can eat more. If my gym membership expires I will gain a hundred pounds in a week. I hope you like spicy food, otherwise you're not going to last long in India."

"I do," Avizeh replies, suddenly excited. The food at the Antarctic base was unsurprisingly lacking in flavor and Avizeh's mouth suddenly waters at the thought of eating something fresh.

"So, we get food and lots of it. You must like music, right? Would you want to go to an Indian music concert? Not like, traditional sitars and that stuff, I mean like Bollywood-style. Sound appealing?"

A pang of nervousness stabs Avizeh and a mental image of Colonel Mueller's stern face appears in her mind. "Are-are we allowed to?"

Omar laughs so loudly that a mother and father from across the aisle shoot him stern looks. "Good one, Jessica. Yeah, I sometimes feel they don't want us to have any fun, especially on their dime, but what can they do? Me, I always find a way to make the higher-ups pay for my entertainment. One time when I was in Jakarta, me and a few other guys were assigned to guard the US Embassy. After two weeks of nothing I got bored and went to one of the underground casinos. I hit the blackjack tables and lost a thousand dollars in one night. Well, I grew suspicious, so I watched the table from the bar. The dealer was very subtle but I saw he was using card tricks to scam people out of their money, especially foreigners. Every time a foreigner sat down, like clockwork, they'd win three hands, lose two in a row, then win one, then lose big. So, I did the only thing I could; I told the Indonesian authorities that American intelligence had it on good authority that members of the terrorist group that was haunting Jakarta frequented that casino. They went in and broke up the whole thing. And ya know what? They actually did find some of the terrorists. I got a promotion and was even reimbursed for the two thousand dollars I lost."

Avizeh's mouth hangs open and she laughs. "No way, that's incredible. But I thought you said you lost a thousand?"

"Yeah, well," he leans in, "sometimes I exaggerate," he scratches at his stubble, "but I mean well, and I do very well if I don't mind saying so."

Avizeh catches sight of Brad, who rolls his eyes at the conversation before returning to his book. She suddenly frowns. "Hang on, was... was any of that true?"

Omar pulls back dramatically and leans away from her in his chair. He waves his hands in front of her and says, "What is truth?"

Avizeh laughs while shaking her head, suddenly feeling very foolish. "What is truth? You want to get philosophical?"

"I mean what is truth to people like us?" Omar asks. "Now, if I were to ask you all the questions that I ask pretty girls the first time I meet them: where are you from, do you have any siblings, what's the coolest place you've ever been, what are the odds I'll get an honest answer from you? No, I think you're a lot more interesting than you're willing to say, Jessica Brown."

Avizeh stares deep into Omar's eyes and wonders how he can know her when she has barely even spoken to him. Her lips separate and she wants to say something but nothing comes out.

"Of course," Omar leans back casually, "I could be completely full of shit."

Brad audibly clears his throat.

"But that's the thing about admitting to someone that not everything you say is the truth; ironically it allows you to tell them the unfiltered, honest-to-god truth and they won't believe you. In a way, because I tell big lies every now and then, I'm the most truthful person you'll ever meet."

Avizeh forces herself to look away. She feels like he can peer into her soul and plumb her innermost thoughts just by locking eyes. But at the same time she feels a warmth to him, as if he searches her from a place of caring. After a moment she looks back at him with a smile. "We still have a long time until we get there."

"And I have lots of stories, some of which actually happened," he replies with an ear-to-ear grin.

*   *   *

The automatic sliding doors of the airport open and the Antarctic Americans are greeted by a blast of humid heat accompanied by the roar of engines, cars beeping and a thousand conversations from the masses of people walking the streets. A fair number of them are in English but Avizeh can discern at least a dozen languages as she and her three compatriots saunter towards the cabs where Brad hails a van just big enough for them to squeeze in with their luggage. From the window seat she watches with wide eyes as they near the holy metropolis of Varanasi. Stretching out nearly to the airport's runway fence are shanty towns and huts composed of little more than a few wooden boards for walls and strips of sheet metal for roofs. A million of these little shacks sprawl towards the hundreds of clear-shining skyscrapers that mark the heart of the sacred city. As they near the city the shanties give way to concrete high rises, cafés and university campuses. Billboards advertising energy drinks and Bollywood movies are plastered all along the highway. Avizeh tries counting the number of Hindu temples to mosques as they enter the city. The historic brick-and-mortar temples appear old and worn with blackened walls from a million diesel-burning engines and factories that turn the air a jaundiced yellow above them. The steel-and-concrete mosques, in contrast, look like they have been built in the last couple of decades.

The van passes its first skyscraper and the driver rolls down their windows.

"Smell that?"

Avizeh leans out the window and breathes in. A hundred spices hit her nose and she is transported back to her family's table during the Eid al-Fitr feast.

"Getting onto Raja Bazar is like stepping into my mother's kitchen. There are many good restaurants around here, and they're less touristy than the riverfront, and you don't want to eat there."

"Why?"

"The restaurants get their water from the Ganges. Even filtered I wouldn't trust it. They say it's holy." Avizeh sees his eyes roll in the rear-view mirror.

"Isn't it?"

"I used to live near the Ganges when I was a kid. My family

was never religious but some of my friends were and they bathed in the river. Once, there was a boy born with enormous tumors on his face and one of them was elongated, like a trunk. The priests said he was the incarnation of Ganesh. Then there was this girl who grew huge ears and was very, very fat. Probably had a thyroid condition and irregular hormones. I'm not a doctor, but I've heard them say things like that whenever a new avatar is born. Anyway, the girl was called an incarnation of Kamadhenu. Seems like every week there's some new god or goddess in our city." He gives a coy leer in the rear-view mirror. "If you want to bathe in the holy Ganges I would recommend going upstream a ways, unless you want to turn into a deity."

Before Avizeh can grasp the full meaning of his words the van stops in front of the shining marble façade of a hotel. They unload their baggage and Brad gives the man a large tip. As soon as the cab driver takes off the group turns away from the grandiose building and walks down a side street until they reach house number '34.' Brad knocks and the door opens, revealing a towering dark-skinned man in an orange pointed turban and a long black beard, wearing baggy white leggings and matching cotton shirt.

"Pranam," he greets. "I've been expecting you; please step inside."

Jordan grabs Avizeh's suitcase and they file in. Inside, the walls are covered with paintings of famous Indian scenes: battles waged by Mughal warriors, the Buddha and one painting of red-coated British soldiers marching in line as a diplomat shakes hands with a raja in front of a jungle fort. To their right is a lavish living room with plush couches circled around a massive TV and speaker set. As they enter, three other men dressed in similar clothes to the first, but none nearly as tall as him, stand up and join them.

"Not what I expected from a covert ops base," Jordan notes.

"We've been here a long time, this is like our home."

"Not a bad place for a home," Avizeh remarks.

"I'm Jordan, by the way."

"Omar."

"Brad."

"Jessica," the undercover Afghan mutters, hating the taste of the name on her lips.

The tall Indian shakes hands with each. "Rasul. This is Bipin, Bimal and Indrajit. Come, let me show you your quarters."

The towering Rasul leads the four upstairs. On the second floor he announces, "This is our computer room," as he showcases the large open area with six desktops. "We're tasked with monitoring the whole of northeastern India, so we've got quite a bit of tech. This is where you'll be doing your work. Also," he says while walking over to a closet, "this is where the gadgets are. We have an Infiltrator, which allows for hacking into computers in other buildings."

"I've used that before," Avizeh notes.

Rasul smiles. "Well then we have an expert here. Tell me, do you know what this is?" He points to a box with one flashing yellow light.

"It looks like a router."

"It's actually a re-router. It has an incredibly powerful signal which it uses to connect to another computer and then forces it to connect to our servers. It's pretty much the reverse of the Infiltrator. Aside from that, we have a few assault rifles with silencers, flash grenades and some other weaponry in case things get hairy. Don't lose these though; these are clearly American and the Indian government doesn't actually know we've set up shop here."

"And the bullets?" Jordan inquires.

"Untraceable."

"All I needed to know."

The men share a laugh while Avizeh chooses to ignore the morbid humor and admire the tech before Rasul ushers them up to the top floor. "And here are the rooms. You guys will bunk in here, and Jessica, you will be in here."

Rasul shows Avizeh to her room, which is a five by five-meter cozy suite with teal walls and a painting of an elephant over a queen-sized bed opposite a desk with a computer. Avizeh walks up to the window and turns up the blinds. Outside, the landscape is dotted by skyscrapers and a mosque which just then calls the faithful to prayer.

"Close those whenever you are doing work. Or changing. You never know who might be watching."

Avizeh turns red. "Thank you," she says, closing the blinds again.

"There's an attached bathroom behind that door. I'm sure you'll all be comfortable. Take an hour or so to settle in. Tonight, we can have dinner and I can update you on the situation."

*   *   *

Dinner is buttered naan and spicy vegetable curry which Avizeh relishes after reheated ready-made meals. Jordan and Brad eat slowly and down glasses of water and wine like they have been lost in the desert for days. The Afghan spy tries to hide her smile as she imagines them eating Indian food for another six months.

"I don't suppose any of you are Hindu?" Rasul asks. "This would be the perfect city for you. Or the worst, depending on your persuasion."

"What is it for you?" Omar inquires.

"I think it would be bad karma to look at our Bangladeshi

brethren and turn them away. Well, if you aren't Hindu there are other things here for you. There's lots of good shopping; Indian clothes look very good on a woman." Rasul turns with a smile to Avizeh. "You could always go on a spree when we aren't working."

"About the job," Jordan changes topics, "do you have any leads on the ultranationalists?"

Rasul wipes his mouth with a napkin and shakes his head. "I'm sorry to say but I think this mission will be a bit awkward for you. There aren't any central bad guys or masterminds; usually it's just a handful of spontaneous radicals who stir up the resentment of the destitute and unemployed that's always just beneath the surface. There's so much xenophobia in the world nowadays due to the global climate refugee crisis. Whenever someone goes on a rant against foreigners it's hard to tell which people are just speaking their minds and which are going to pick up bricks and throw them at their neighbors. As such, we have to weed through the thousands of political and religious organizations to find the few that will actually turn the pot over."

Rasul leans back and finishes his last piece of naan. "So, sit back, get comfortable, enjoy the city and hope things don't explode."

"What if we want things to explode?" Brad responds coyly.

"Not me. If nothing could happen for six months I'd be happy," Jordan piped in.

"No chance of that," Bipin interjects. "Good, bad, amazing, terrible, something huge happens every day in India. We're a nation that likes to move."

"And you move with it?" Avizeh asks.

"Do I move?" Bipin stands up and grabs a remote. The speakers blast a Hindi pop song and he suddenly begins to dance. Bipin reaches out a hand to Avizeh. She shakes her head, even as the whole table calls on her to join him. Bipin looks into her eyes. Blushing profusely, she stands and joins him, feeling like an utter idiot but smiling as she does. The song finishes and the men all applaud her. She retakes her seat, placing a hand on her cheek to hide her reddening face. Bipin turns off the music and retreats to the kitchen. He returns with another bottle of sauvignon and pours the deep-red liquid into each wine glass, except Avizeh's who waves away the offer.

"Is this what you do for 'work'?" Jordan asks.

"I like it!" Omar slaps the table to laughs.

"It's what we do to live," Indrajit replies. "Work is always there; you have to live life to the fullest when you can."

"Especially since you never know when it will end," Bimal says. His words hang in the air. Avizeh watches each man's face. Their smiles linger but their eyes wander as each reflects on the lived truth of Bimal's words. She knows everyone has seen vibrant life end without warning, as has she. She ponders her family. *They're refugees now, probably no different than the million people in shanties we passed on the drive here.* Survivor's guilt wracks her as she imagines them crowded into a hovel on the Iranian border, burning during the sweltering days, clinging to each other for warmth at night.

If they made it.

"I don't believe in endings," Rasul opines. "Human beings are self-reflective conduits of action. Even when our hearts stop, our words and actions turn the wheels of a universe which will itself be reborn. The end of one story is just the part of another forever and ever."

"Do you get like this every time you drink because, I have to say, I prefer the dancing," Jordan adds. Everyone laughs at the joke and from a need to remove the weight each so often bears.

"I get like this when others drink; it makes my ideas seem more clever. And there's a good chance you'll forget it once your head hits the pillow. Speaking of which, I assume you're exhausted from your trip. Why not get a good night's sleep before we start work tomorrow?"

At Rasul's invitation the three Americans and their Afghan ward retire to their quarters, leaving their hosts to clean up. Avizeh closes the door to her room and sits down on her bed. She looks at the four walls enclosing her and suddenly realizes the room is hers. Her whole life she has shared rooms with others. She shared a room with her brother Aamir when they were children, then her sister Laily. In Antarctica she bunks with dozens of other women. For the first time in her life she can fall asleep without listening to another person's breathing.

Avizeh pulls back the covers, lies down on the soft mattress and listens to a whole new form of silence broken only by her own rhythmic breathing. She closes her eyes, empties her mind and allows herself this moment of calming isolation.

*   *   *

Avizeh opens the blinds and watches the sun peek between the buildings to the east. The peaceful Afghan watches with amazement as the fiery star rises above the horizon in a matter of minutes rather than months. Her male counterparts disturb her serenity when they noisily begin their morning routines which she can hear through the walls. The mystique ruined by the men's grunts and spitting, she forces herself to look away from the strange normalcy of a natural sunrise. She puts on a pair of jeans, a shirt and a purple and subdued-gold shawl that sits loosely on the back of her hair and descends the stairs to see Omar waiting on the first floor. The two step out of the house and join the morning bustle which meets them as soon as they walk outside. The smell of roasted peanuts and flour cake fill the air from a half-dozen stalls interspersed among carts selling dresses, jewelry and carved goods. The streets are already packed with the sights and sounds of people as Varanasi's millions begin the march from their homes and into the city.

The two special agents casually venture southeast as the smell of sugar, salt and fresh vegetables mix with a stomach-curling stench that smells like pungent sickness and vomit. Within minutes, they reach the crowded shores of the Ganges River where thousands of penitents bathe in the brown and green waters. A naked man with a bindi holds his hands together in prayer, turns his face toward the sky and sinks into the waters. He emerges as a soda can and a plastic TV dinner tray hit his torso before bumping against an empty bag of chips and a discarded coat hanger. A half dozen singing voices calling faithful Muslims to morning prayer resonate through loudspeakers from behind the bathers and Avizeh watches a handful of Hindu *sanyāsīs* grimace at the sound and submerge themselves in the dirty green waters.

"Want to go for a dip?"

Avizeh responds with an incredulous look.

"What? Don't knock it until you try it. You might have a spiritual awakening."

"If you go in then we aren't walking together."

Omar shrugs. "All right, another time."

The pair turn from the river wend head back to the city center, leaving the smell of the Ganges behind, and enter a crowded bazaar. Omar points out an ATM to Avizeh near the entrance to the open square and she walks over to the machine with an aching feeling in her stomach. *I figured out how to use a teleporter, I can figure out an ATM.* She follows the steps written on a faded sticker beside the monitor and requests one hundred thousand rupees. To her surprise, the machine rapidly spits out thousand-rupee bills and Avizeh feels like she won at a slot machine. She pulls out the money, feeling the soft paper wealth in her hands, admires Gandhi's bald head and puts the bills in her wallet.

Avizeh's first purchase is warm naan and a fruit cup which she eats as they wander the market. When they arrive at a string of clothing carts her eye lingers on a beautiful blue sari with gold stitches that is marked with a nine hundred rupee tag. Her eyes widen and she touches the fabric, feeling the soft fabric glide across her open palm.

"You like it?" A woman in her mid-thirties wearing a red sari approaches her.

"Yes, very much."

"It feels even better when it hangs on your curves, and you have just the right curves for this. I'm sure your husband would love to see you in this."

Avizeh glances at Omar. "Oh, he's not my husband."

"Oh? Well in an outfit like this, I promise you a husband wouldn't be hard to find."

Avizeh doesn't think she is looking for a husband but even still she buys the blue sari along with a purple and teal one, a pair of shoes, a dozen socks, a light orange shawl and a pink gagra choli dress. Everywhere she goes the vendors look at the bags she and Omar carry and show her their friendliest smiles. A woman her own age offers to paint her hands with henna and ushers her into a seat next to a cart filled with paintings of the Taj Mahal and the Red Fort.

"You know, you're supposed to haggle," Omar chides Avizeh. "I suppose price tags are non-negotiable in Nebraska but where I grew up, everything that wasn't in a store could be talked down to half price."

Avizeh just smiles, enjoying the frivolity that Varanasi offers. *My money is worthless anywhere but here; might as well spend it.*

"You have beautiful hands," the henna artist says as she adds a spiral below her wrist. "Have you ever had henna before?"

"Yes, once…" Avizeh thinks back to the night she had been kissed by Razaaq Hirat beneath the marriage tent. "But it was a long time ago."

"There, now you're fit for a wedding."

Avizeh looks down at her arms, admiring the recursive dark-brown spirals. She remembers the last time she was tattooed. She pushes aside the memory, raises her head in time to see the artist staring at her in silence, and she wonders how long she had been lost in thought. "Thank you," she says and hands her four thousand rupees. "Keep the change."

"Bless you." The artist bows her head as Omar rolls his eyes at Avizeh's lack of negotiating skills.

They leave the bazaar loaded down with six sets of clothes, a scented candle and a small Om wood carving and head back to the house to drop everything off. Avizeh changes into the blue sari and they trek northeast of the Ganges looking for street food, settling on chicken kebab skewers and rice as they walk down tight alleyways. Midday prayers cut through the bustle by the time they finish their walk through the wondrous city.

"Well, now that we've got the lay of the land, any ideas on where to look?" Omar inquires.

"Well… this ultranationalist, fundamentalist religious stuff usually comes from the elites; the wise opportunists preying on the desperate poor. The northeast is filled with segregated slums, with the slums belonging to the Indians and the new sheet metal and scrap houses belonging to the Bangladeshis. Just southwest of them are a bunch of old temples that rich men with gold Rolexes and trophy wives visit. If any violence breaks out, I'd guess it would start there and then move north."

The imposing spy nods. "That's as good as any guess. There are some restaurants all around them; can you set up shop with your laptop and do it discreetly enough that no one will be able to tell what you're doing?"

"I think so. You and the other guys be sure to be obnoxious though and make everyone think we're dumb American tourists."

"That I can do. One time I drank a third of a bottle of absinthe in York—"

"Shouldn't you be saving your stories for later?"

"So I was in York, this tiny little village in England, very quaint, the whole town is surrounded by medieval walls which you can jog on, and I did when I needed to work off my hangovers. Anyway, I was at this bar that served absinthe, drank way too much and didn't get a girl—not my fault, just bad pickings that night. I decided to go back to the hostel. I am fall-over drunk and I think I might have even been hallucinating a bit. I thought, 'what if some group of guys sees me? They could take advantage of me and jump me.' So, I decided to look menacing, so the whole way back I put on this angry glare, a sort of, 'don't mess with me' face. But the thing about drinking so much absinthe is that I couldn't help but smile. So, all the way back I had my face scrunched up and my eyes darting forward with this giant grin on my face; I wish someone had taken a photo of me, I must have looked like I just escaped from the loony bin."

Avizeh bursts out laughing.

"Then, this one time in Glasgow I was wearing a blue sweater that my mom knitted for me. Word of advice: never wear blue or green in Glasgow. Blue is the color of the Scottish flag, the Scottish people, Protestants and their soccer team which they are violently in love with. Green is the color of Ireland, the Irish immigrants, Catholicism and their own soccer team, which they are equally insane about. Well, my friends and I were on a pub crawl when we got lost looking for our next stop. We cross the River Clyde into the Irish territory like drunken morons, and stumble into the nearest pub. Well, the bar is full, everyone was wearing green, it was about the time that everyone had too much to drink and the Irish Celtics were playing against the Scottish Rangers. As soon as I enter, a few people turn to me and drop silent, then more, then the whole pub just looks at me and my friends. I catch a look at the screen and somewhere in my booze-addled mind I realize what's happening and knew what I had to do. I grabbed the front of my sweater and ripped it open and yelled, 'Celtic pride!' The whole bar burst into cheers, glasses were raised and someone even bought me a drink. I even went home with a red-haired lass. Shame I had to lose the sweater but I learned a lesson that day."

Avizeh laughs the whole way back as Omar regales her with five more stories of drunken misadventures which he cleverly managed to turn around.

*   *   *

The four special agents repose at a table in the second story of an imitation French café overlooking a busy street. Avizeh takes a sip of hot chai as she waits for lamb biryani in the strangely peaceful restaurant. In the opposite corner of the room a young man reaches across the table and holds hands with a doe-eyed beauty who smiles widely with pearl teeth and thick lips in a scene worthy of a Bollywood poster. At the table next to them, four older gentlemen with rich but casual dress and the mannerisms of doctors discuss their trip to São Paulo.

Avizeh tears her gaze from the lively scene and returns to

her computer. She is in direct range of three Hindu temples and two mosques. She scans through their computers but finds little other than tax records and a list of songs and sermons. She is about to save their donation lists when she feels a stab of guilt. *Should I be taking a list of all the personal donors? This seems intrusive, and even if violence is hidden in these sermons, who's to say that the donors are in any way knowledgeable of what their local priests are doing?* Despite her revulsion she saves all the files, knowing that if a religious riot or terrorist attack occurs she will end up sitting across from Mueller again trying to avoid life in prison.

"That's why I've never gone snorkeling again."

"That doesn't sound like a shark." Jordan smirks.

"It was a shark! I know what I saw!" Brad exclaims.

"You said you saw a big blurry shape."

"What else could it have been?"

"A rock? A drop in the sea floor…"

"It moved!"

"You were bobbing up and down in the waves, how could you tell?"

"I swear, it was a shark, and when I swam back someone else said they saw a shark."

Jordan waves a hand incredulously. "You saw a rock, pissed yourself…"

"Don't you know what to do when you see a shark? Punch it in the gills, you'll be fine."

"You would never be able to punch a shark hard enough to save yourself. Everyone says that but you can't. Do you know how fast fish swim underwater? The fastest you could make your fist go is half, maybe a third as fast as on land. That would be like a gentle breeze to a shark. The only way a punch could work is if a shark came right at you, fin sticking out of the water like in *Jaws*, and then raised its head above water to bite you head on. If a shark comes at you from underwater, which it would, you would get your leg chomped off before you could do anything."

"Jessica, what do you think?"

Avizeh looks up from her typing. "Baby. I could fight off a shark." The table erupts into 'ohs!' followed by laughter at Brad's expense.

The lamb biryani arrives and the table finally quiets. After finishing, Jordan leans in and asks in a conspiratorial manner, "Find anything?"

"I'm almost done here, but there isn't anything, unless it's in code, which I can work on back home since I downloaded it all."

Omar nods. "Okay, guess we'll just have to go out to eat again. We'll all be fat by the end of this mission."

While the men talk about what sea animals they could fight off, Avizeh breaks into the Iranian immigration services database and pulls up a series of four files on her family. Her chest tightens as she looks at the photos. Laily was always a pretty child but now she is a beautiful young woman, whose uncovered face shines. Her mother gives a worn look to the camera. She looks wearied and uncomfortable at having an uncovered face. She wears her hijab tight and low on her forehead so that not a single strand of hair is visible. The next photo is of her Baba. The aging patriarch displays the bitterness of an unquiet life. She reads in his visage the loss of the power and prestige that would have come from her wedding to Razaaq Hirat and the shame of his second wife's departure. Last is Aamir. He stares back through the camera. His is not a face caught in time but a living expression of male Afghan youth. He is an avatar embodying the acceptance of uncertainty. He cannot decide his country, his occupation or his future. He gazes placidly on a world on fire with the uneasy reassurance that everything is temporary on this Earth. As the wind remakes the desert, nations, ideologies and entire peoples disappear at the slightest breeze.

Avizeh looks at each photo, tears welling in her eyes. She discreetly turns her head and gently brushes her face with her napkin. She steals a look at the other men. Despite sitting opposite her, Jordan and Brad don't notice, so engrossed are they in one of Omar's stories. Omar gives her a sidelong glance and she realizes that he sees her sudden pain. Even as the other two are content to ignore their shy techie, he discreetly watches her. She turns away from him, uneasy that someone would devote so much attention to her, especially now that she is ignoring Mueller's dictates to not be a human being and looking for her family.

Avizeh finds the phone number to the refugee camp and commits it to memory. She closes the laptop just in time to hear Omar say, "and the baboon got away with my passport."

*　　　　　*　　　　　*

Every morning to midafternoon, Bipin, Bimal and Indrajit work in the intel room looking for anything dangerous on local sites while Rasul spends most of his time coaching Avizeh, who is by far the best programmer but mostly ignorant of Indian politics and subcultures.

"Don't use keywords like, 'deportation,' 'Bangladeshi' or 'Muslims' or anything like that; you'll end up with a million comments, either pro-tolerance or against it, none of which are likely to be our targets. Use words like 'Hindutva,' 'sepoy,' and 'Sangh Parivar.' Terms like this would be no doubt in any manifesto we find, alongside 'Mughal' and references to Western imperialism."

Despite his help, there is little concrete evidence for an immediate terror attack, other than a few anonymous pamphlets that have been ejected into cyberspace and passed on, attached as a word doc to nearly every Hindi and Telugu movie on local pirate servers. Avizeh, Jordan, Omar and Brad spend two weeks going out to one restaurant after another and find nothing. It isn't long until Jordan and Brad become disgruntled and claim that their outings are a pointless waste of time and money.

"Well, if you two would rather stay in, order a pizza, watch an action film in English and pretend you're back in California, I'll take Jessica out," Omar offers to the defeated soldiers who acquiesce without a fight. That night Avizeh puts on her pink sari and walks with Omar to a restaurant on the Ganges. The entrance to the restaurant is located on the opposite side of the river and boasts dozens of candles burning incense, successfully overpowering the pungent smell. The two manage to get a window view of the Ganges which looks surprisingly romantic in the dark. Avizeh stares at the beautiful ghats as the last pilgrims emerge from the water and return to their homes. A shadowy landscape interspersed by a million lights strewn across the living expanse that is the holy city beautify the night.

Avizeh is about to pull out her laptop when Omar reaches across and puts a hand on hers. "Don't. We've worked for fourteen days straight; fifteen if you count the travel over here. You deserve a break."

Avizeh gives him a worried look. Even on the other side of the world she fears Mueller, but... *He is thirteen thousand kilometers away and this is one night. I deserve one night.*

"Okay." She smiles, and places the bag at her feet, just as a waitress walks by with tea.

"Have you picked up some of the language yet?"

Avizeh shrugs. "Bits and pieces. Nothing that wouldn't immediately make me stick out as a ferengi... foreigner."

"Right." Omar laughs. "Yeah, I haven't caught anything, but it sure feels good to be here. The people feel so authentic, so friendly."

Avizeh nods slowly. Alongside religious studies, she had grown up learning Pashtunwali, the code of conduct for all Pashtun peoples. Its first tenet was Melmastia, hospitality, and the requirement to give shelter and food to any visitor regardless of their race or religion. The third tenet was Nyaw aw Badal, the code of revenge, which stipulated that any wrong must be rectified in the blood of the offender or his nearest kin, and that no time passed could ever forgive a slight to honor. While Pashtuns had been taught to always show kindness to others it was in large part to avoid the inevitable wrath that even a minor slight might cause. Avizeh wonders how much nicety Indians offer to create karmic balance for their acts of 'justice.' She sips her tea and admires the skyscrapers around her, doubting such moral codes survived the transition to modernity.

"So, how'd you get into this line of work, Jessica?"

The feeling of landing on an ice floe beside a barking seal returns to her. She remembers the conversation Brad and Jordan had about the shark and wonders what would have happened if she punched an orca. "It was kind of sudden. To be honest, I didn't feel I had much of a choice, but now I'm here."

"I can relate. I'm the sort of person that can't let a problem sit. With so much craziness in the world, I had to sign up for the marines just to give myself some sense of control over it all. I know I don't really fit in with the army type, but here I am. You seem the same."

"I do?" Avizeh asks, suddenly self-conscious.

"You don't ever feel," Omar leans in, "like this whole job is like wearing a scratchy set of clothes that don't fit you right?"

"I do, absolutely," Avizeh replies eagerly as she stares into his inviting eyes and wonders how he can know how she feels.

"So why do you stick to it?"

"I..." Avizeh pauses. "I'm not sure what else I can do."

"A techie like you? Oh," he leans back in his chair, "right."

"What?"

"Well, whenever you leave it's not like you can put everything you did on a résumé. I doubt the government lets people claim they worked at Fort Powell, for security and all. Might be a bit hard to sell yourself if you ever left the job."

Avizeh breathes in, glad he came up with an excuse for her. Normally Avizeh is in a constant state of low-level panic around others as she tries to recount each specific lie she needs to tell them to remain safe. Omar accepts that everything she says and does has a legitimate reason, and he often fills in the blanks for her better than she can herself. Even though she cannot give any details she feels more open with him than anyone except Clara. "It is what it is. I tend not to think about the future."

"Oh, but that's where the best stuff happens. Colonizing Mars, dropping through wormholes into other universes with squid-people with cauliflower for brains, that's the best."

Avizeh snorts. "I doubt any of that's going to happen."

"But you don't know. Did you have any idea two months ago that you'd be sitting in a ritzy Telegu restaurant in the holiest city in the world, overlooking a river that opens to the spirit world, dressed in a movie star's gown looking like the most beautiful woman in the world opposite a man who can only be described as the Mozart of inebriation?"

Avizeh's mouth opens in an ear-to-ear smile as she laughs. "I sense another story."

"Not tonight," he replies with a small smile. "You've been so quiet since we got here. I feel like in all our walking I've explored everything but you."

"What do you want to know?" Avizeh replies, mentally

preparing to lie yet feeling relaxed and open beside the smiling man opposite her.

"Well, I'm not going to start by asking your deepest, darkest secret. That's for after some wine. Tell me, what do you do for fun?"

"I watch a lot of movies... I like movies from all over the world. I don't mind reading subtitles. I like books too, and I'm getting into photography."

"Oh yeah? Taken any photos of the city?"

"I don't think that's allowed," she whispers.

"Oh psh. Call it research and you could take pictures of people in changing rooms. Not that I've ever done that, of course."

"Of course."

"Back to you. Those are some pretty nice hobbies. What's the coolest thing you've ever taken a picture of?"

The Afghan woman in a Bollywood star's dress thinks back to the Antarctic landscape and when Clara pointed out her way using the stars. "I took a picture of a family of penguins once, up at the base. But then my camera broke."

"Bad luck. I was in Paris once and my camera broke right as I visited the Tomb of Napoleon. Worst time ever. Still fun though. Have you ever been to France?"

Avizeh shakes her head.

"Learn a little French before you go. If you try they love you. The phrase I used was, 'C'est belle, non?' That means, 'Isn't it beautiful?' As soon as the person next to me asked, 'quoi?' meaning 'what,' then I could insert any noun I'd want. 'Le ciel,' 'le tableau,' 'le jour,' 'le ville,' or 'toi, madame.' That last one worked really well, and I got some good stories out of that. From there the conversation would just roll along and they might even switch over into English. That's the trick: people hate being 'forced' to speak your language, especially the French, but when you try theirs, maybe say a few cute words, then they'll decide whether or not they want to talk to you and if they do, then they'll switch over into perfect English."

"I'll remember that. So, what was Paris like? Is it as beautiful as in the movies?"

"It lives up to all of it. Going from Montmartre to the Palais Royal to Notre Dame was like walking from one painting to another. There was this feeling that you were a part of something, and everyone was in a dance, constantly trading partners. It was as if everyone was looking for a connection of some sort; romantic, philosophic, and they were just waiting for some person to find them and put the link together, but it all felt like you were meant to be there. It was very different from most places. Thailand is beautiful, so is parts of London, but everything and everyone in those places felt like they had it all figured out, and meeting you was a happy interruption of their lives, but Paris had this feel like it was a party waiting to start for when you got there.

"And the wine was amazing. Best wine in the world for a few euros a bottle."

"I sense a drunken adventure..."

"This one time..."

Omar insists on a bottle of wine with their meal. Despite her initial protests Avizeh consents to one glass, just to see how it tastes. A look comes on her face as she drinks alcohol for the first time.

"Not to your tastes? I imagine it'd be a little different than what you're used to back in Nebraska."

Avizeh smiles and shakes her head. For the past two weeks she's eaten the spiciest food without so much as flinching while Jordan and Brad down pitchers of water during every meal; meanwhile she struggles to sip at the wine. She begins to feel warm and tells herself it must be the korma. Dessert is mango qulfi, a type of thick frozen ice cream.

"This is the best thing I've ever had," Avizeh says between mouthfuls. She gazes out at the Ganges and wishes she brought a camera to capture the blissful moment. She looks at her dish, then at Omar, closes her eyes for a second and dedicates the moment to memory.

Omar picks up the check and waves away her attempts to pay her share. "With your haggling skills we'll end up paying for everyone here." The dozen candles in the entryway are halfway burned out when they depart. He leads her away from the traffic-heavy roads and through side streets and alleys. The city is bathed in faint golden light from the odd streetlamp shining between buildings, reminding her of Antarctica during nautical twilight, a month before permanent dusk, two months before the whole sky surrenders to the stars. She looks up, wishing she could see the different starscape above them and know she is truly somewhere else.

The Afghan woman looks over at Omar with a faint smile. Her whole life has been one of isolation and secrets, none more dangerous or secluded than her own feelings. Her whole life she has been discouraged from sharing her emotions and wishes, which she was told were either dangerous or a nuisance depending on who she has spoken with. For the first time she is with someone who actually cares about her and wants to know that beautiful part of her that she has boarded up. Part of her is bursting to tell him who she really is, how she isn't an American spy but a captured Afghan from Farah, in a desert not too far from where they are. She already knows the words and can taste them on her lips, more real than the wine and qulfi.

Two blocks from their safehouse, in an alley filled with hanging plants on the patios of wealthy houses, Omar catches her hand. "Hey, stop for a moment." He puts his other hand on her hip and looks down at her, smiling.

"I had a really great time with you tonight, Jessica."

"Omar, I have to tell you something. My name—"

Omar leans in and kisses her. His soft lips press against her, and she smells cologne on his neck. Avizeh hardly moves. She likes the feel of lips touching her, hands touching her, after being so alone for so long to have another human being to demonstrate affection. But...

She tries to kiss back but feels like she is doing it wrong. She sees his eyes are closed and so she closes hers too. He places a hand on her lower back and gently pulls her body into an arch pressing against him. As he does Avizeh wonders if there is something she should be doing with her hands. She puts them on his hips and immediately thinks, *No, that's wrong*. Omar reaches into her with his tongue and she instinctively gags.

Avizeh puts a hand on his chest and pushes him back. Omar looks down at her, his eyes sensitive to her sudden rejection.

"All right then. You have to admit: the dinner was fantastic."

Avizeh nods awkwardly. The walk back to the safehouse is mercifully short, and she is thankful that he chose not to kiss her until they were nearly back.

Chapter Twelve
Mission Accomplished

Avizeh spends the next two weeks going out to restaurants in rotation with the men, though Jordan and Brad aren't nearly as interesting and they fall into a routine silence. Rasul escorts her one night and regales her with stories about growing up in the mountains bordering Nepal. She grows to like him but every time he calls her 'Jessica' she is reminded that she isn't meant to have any meaningful relationships with anyone. After a week of mutual avoidance Omar escorts her to dinner. He laughs, jokes, and everything is like before. Then one night he doesn't come back to the house. Near midnight Avizeh stands in the entryway while the men lay back on couches watching a Bollywood action film as if nothing is wrong.

"Hey, do you guys have any idea where Omar is? It's so late, I think something's happened to him."

"Relax. There's nothing happening to him that he didn't want," Jordan answers.

"What does that mean?"

Jordan glances over at her just as two rivals jump from their elephants and punch each other in midair. "He texted me and said he won't be back tonight; he found some girl." Without another word Jordan turns back to the TV to watch the nonsensical and epic confrontation.

Avizeh leaves them to their movie, returns to her room and forces herself to sleep. Lying in bed, she watches the sunrise, now accustomed to natural days again. She feels a pit in her stomach around midday, not because she is jealous; just the opposite. Avizeh doesn't feel any hurt, betrayal or even anger towards the other woman, nor desire for Omar despite his muscled body and handsome face. She feels nothing for him.

Is there something wrong with me? Shouldn't I feel something? Shouldn't something have kicked in when he was kissing me? It just felt like getting licked by an old dog. But how can that be, for someone as experienced as him? For a second Avizeh wonders if despite Omar's bluster he just isn't as much of a man as his jovial boasts imply, but when he returns that morning with a swagger in his step and immediately jumps into the shower she knows he is everything he claims.

"I'm going on a walk. I have my phone with me and it'll be constantly sending my GPS location to my comp upstairs," she says to Brad without waiting for a response as she steps out in a magenta sari with a bright olive-colored shawl.

The young Afghan exits the house and looks over her shoulder, half-expecting someone to rush out and follow her. She takes a few cautious steps and waits for voices to call after her. To her amazement she is left to walk in public without a chaperone for the first time in her life. She feels a sudden thrill at the anonymity of being lost in a crowd. Then she catches sight of a CCTV camera and remembers that her phone is transmitting her location at all times. Privacy is an antiquated word like 'chivalry' or 'wheelbarrow,' a concept belonging to a lost age. Anonymity is an illusory feeling in a world where every lens is an eye and through technological evolution the primal male gaze evolved into Big Brother. Yet, she hopes that even All-Seeing Eye might turn a blind eye to indiscretion so long as her actions don't challenge his authority.

The Afghan agent walks to a cluster of tight roads where peddlers sell phone cases and SIM cards in front of telecom shops. She walks past a man offering her two sparkling glitter cases for, "the lowest price in Uttar Pradesh, guaranteed," and into a telecom emporium advertising pay-per-minute phone plans. She thumbs through a rack of cheap plastic offerings and picks out the lowest-tech specimen she can find, a relic that can only make calls and texts with no internet browsing or smart features. She takes her selection to the counter where a balding man looks at her with disinterest. "Can you put three hours on it?" she asks. The teller opens the phone, plugs it in to a computer and mechanically does as instructed, looking as if such a small purchase is barely worth his time. He growls out the price and Avizeh hands him a wad of cash and says, "Keep the change," before turning away.

What am I doing? Is this worth it? As soon as she thinks that, Avizeh gives off a sad laugh, seemingly the only kind she is capable of. *What do I have to lose?* The displaced woman tries to find an area where she can be even more lost. She walks until the sidewalk cracks and iron bars mark the windows of shops with graffitied signs. She pulls out the burner phone and enters the number she memorized.

Avizeh navigates an automated system until she's prompted to wait for an operator. A starving dog approaches her then scampers away when it realizes she has nothing to give. Two men watch her and she walks towards a group of women on a nearby corner. She walks without direction while trying to appear like she has a purpose. An hour passes before a female voice asks her in Farsi who she wants to contact. "Laily Fatah," Avizeh replies, then recites her date of birth and Iranian-issued refugee ID number.

"Who should I tell her is calling?"

"Tahmina Saidova."

"Wait one moment," the aid worker replies.

The moment drags. Avizeh sweats from her hour-long walk.

"Avizeh?" her sister's voice calls through the phone.

Avizeh stands paralyzed upon hearing her beloved sister speak her real name. "How did you know?" Avizeh laughs while stifling a sob.

"The only Tahmina I know was an awful girl who threw rocks at me when I crossed over into her family's plot. Until you chased her away."

Avizeh laughs, genuinely, the first time in a long time. "You remembered. You were five years old then."

"It's one of my favorite memories of you. Women don't get many opportunities to show their strength in Anar Dara but you took every opportunity you could. It made me want to be brave like you."

Avizeh places her chin on her chest. "How are you?"

"Safe," Laily replies.

"And... do you get enough to eat?"

"More than before," Laily replies. "It's not great... but we're alive. And safe. We're applying for refugee status. Mom is hoping we could be resettled in Germany or France. Could you imagine? But that'll take a while; maybe a year or more, if it goes through. In the meantime we're in a camp. But you already knew that."

"Do you have something to do? Can you get an education? Can Aamir work or—"

"Avizeh, tell me about you. Ever since the wedding night, you've become a ghost. I haven't known a single thing that's happened to you, even though you seem to know exactly where we are. I thought I dreamt the night you came back but Mom and Aamir remember it too. Where did you go?"

Avizeh puts the phone on her shoulder and turns her head to look at those around her. She feels disoriented and suddenly unsafe.

"Avizeh?"

"I can't say," she replies.

"Why not? Why call if you won't talk?"

"I wanted to know that you're safe. And Mom and Aamir. And..." She lets the word hang. "Baba resents me."

"No," Laily insists. "He's... what can you expect?"

Avizeh bites her lip. "I suppose I can't expect anything."

"That's life," Laily replies, the meaning of the words far deeper than any a thirteen-year-old should say. "I can't talk for much longer, there's one phone for a thousand people. Do you want me to tell them anything for you?"

"Tell them I'm safe. That I love them."

Avizeh hears a half-muffled voice on the other end of the receiver. "Tell me you're okay."

"I'm okay," Avizeh says, unsure what she means.

"When will I see you again?"

Avizeh pauses. She takes a deep breath. Then the line goes dead. She closes her eyes. *This is a victory. My family is safe and cared for. So why do I feel so hollow?* She mechanically walks to a trash bin and throws the phone inside. She is too overwhelmed with emotion to process anything. Instead, she pushes her thoughts aside and walks back towards the city, hoping for something that will distract her from her inner torment.

Avizeh meanders towards the Ganges while remaining far enough away that she can't detect its pungent reek. As she wanders past the city center she hears the call to prayer sound from a mosque beside her, and stops to listen to the chant. The song is in Bengali but she recognizes the meaning and flow of the words. She wraps her shawl around her hair and climbs up the imitation-marble steps. She enters the building which is beautifully decorated with slender ivory-colored pillars and geometric shapes coating the ceiling in the Persian fashion. She walks over to the women's side where nearly forty congregants are on their knees and joins them in the namaz. Avizeh takes a spot in the middle of the room beside a woman who appears to be her age. As she looks around at the women she feels like she is finally, truly anonymous, that for the first time in a long time she isn't being observed and she isn't an outsider.

Avizeh bows and opens her mouth, though nothing comes out. She knows the words but doesn't say them. She knows the mantra's meaning but the recitation feels like nothing to her. It has been so long since last she prayed. She thought she might have yelled to God when she was on the ice floe; if she did then that was the last time.

Well, hello. I know this is a holy city, but I was taught this is the wrong one. Or is it? How is my family doing? Did I do something wrong? I don't feel guilty. I didn't feel wrong for taking the teleporter, even though stealing is a sin. I didn't feel wrong for sneaking away to be with my family. I don't really feel ashamed or self-hating, just confused. I'm not sure I can be anyone's friend. I'm told I can't have any friends. Is that why I didn't kiss Omar back? Because I'm afraid? But I feel nothing for him. Is there something wrong with me? Did my heart never grow the way it was supposed to?

Avizeh peers down at her own hands which rest on the prayer carpet. *These thoughts should make me sad, but getting them out just feels so cathartic.* She looks up at the ceiling and loses herself in contemplation of the intricacy of the details. The forever-receding nature of the design reminds her of the henna swirls. Her mind wanders and she contemplates the empty space between each shape in the ceiling, imagines the distance between each curve and line of the spirals on her hands. She dreams she witnesses the infinite everywhere all at once, as something majestic and enormous but also infinitesimal and insignificant. Now she sees how the space between her home in Anar Dara is both a world away from Fort Powell and a blink of an eye. The mosque she kneels in is both hundreds of kilometers from Anar Dara, yet she can see her family gathered in Farah's own mosque, with similar Persian-style reliefs, kneeling in prayer for their lost daughter. A sudden peace overwhelms the woman from western Afghanistan as distance and time vanish, leaving only her thoughts and feelings in this singular moment as she kneels wrapped in silk sari and shawl. *They are safe, as am I. That has to be enough for now.* A deeply contented half-smile forms on her visage and she thanks the universe for calling her inside this night.

Avizeh waits until a few other women leave before excusing herself. She walks down the street and lets her gaze rise to the sky. The light pollution and smog blots out every star, leaving an infinite void. A meaty hand appears around Avizeh's mouth and simultaneously a sharp pain shoots through her neck. She tries to scream but the sound dies in her throat. Darkness like the void above spreads through her vision and the feeling of peace is replaced by fleeting panic before unconsciousness takes her.

*   *   *

The world is blackness. Avizeh lies prone on cold concrete with her arms and legs tied. Above her, two men are speaking a language she has heard recently but cannot understand. She gags violently and realizes that she has a rag in her mouth. A harsh laugh greets her as heavy bootfalls approach her, their sound echoing. Two fingers press against her head and Avizeh stiffens. A strong hand grabs her left breast and squeezes. Avizeh jerks backward and gives off a muffled scream. She bumps into something that groans and she wriggles away, panicking as a lewd laugh sounds from above her. Someone mutters in a foreign language, then ends with, "Filthy whore," in accented English.

The first pair of boots walks away before another follows them, and the sound of the door closing crashes through the darkness. There is a 'click' and the voices disappear. Avizeh pants, suddenly feeling light-headed as she inhales her own warm breath. She lets her head fall down to the cold concrete floor and closes her eyes. She fumbles for her pockets and searches for her phone, only to find them empty.

You've been captured, but the phone's GPS will lead the men to me. Except... did I struggle? What if it fell out of my pocket outside the mosque? What if they threw it out in an alley? There are so many ways the trail can go cold... How long have I been here? Who's captured me? Was it ultranationalists who captured me because I was praying in a mosque? Human traffickers? How much longer will they hold me before asking for a ransom? Will they ask? Would the US pay it? That could lead to questions, and I'm not supposed to exist...

For the first time since the crumbling building in Kabul, Avizeh fears for her life. She frantically struggles against her bonds but they hold strong. They feel like plastic clasps that police use: the kind that won't come undone with any amount of pulling or biting. She tries to shake the bag off her head only to realize it is tied with a pin to the back of her dress. She gives up her struggle and sniffles meekly.

What choice could have saved me from this? Should I have kissed Omar back? Should I not have disobeyed Colonel Mueller? Should I have hidden from the firefight and waited for my husband Razaaq to return? Is he still my husband? We were never divorced and I vowed myself to him. Am I a widow? Did I sin when I left him? Is all this my punishment?

Avizeh cannot accept blame for her plight, no matter how her mind reels. No part of her believes this is her fault, but dark thoughts tumble through her mind as she tries to rationalize her predicament. Minutes turn to hours or so she imagines; just like the skies in the Antarctic base, the permanent darkness removes all sense of time. She begins to feel faint. Her breathing stills and she hears a painful, muffled crying from her left. Avizeh squirms away from the person but he or she, she cannot decipher which, still bawls. She closes her eyes, opens them and closes them again, realizing there is no difference.

A heavy, wet thud echoes from the next room. The door opens with a familiar 'click' sound. Boots march directly towards her and she stiffens. Avizeh's bag lifts. She looks up and sees a fuzzy dark shape above her as her eyes adjust to the light. In a moment Jordan comes into focus. He puts a finger up to his lips and pulls out his knife. He cuts the restraints on her hands and legs, then pulls the rag out of her mouth.

"Thank—"

Jordan puts a hand on her mouth and shakes his head. He grabs her hand and helps the shaking woman to her feet before leading her to the door. As they move towards the exit, Avizeh looks over her shoulder and sees thirty other people tied up on the floor in the small room, some moving, most still as corpses. Jordan tugs forcefully on her arm and pushes her out of the room.

"Eyes up," he orders, but it is too late; she has seen the bloody body. Jordan puts a hand on her back and pushes her forward through the hallway towards an open door to the outside. Omar steps between them and the door, a rifle with silencer pointed to the floor.

"Do you guys have this?"

"Yeah we do. Take her home." Jordan turns to Avizeh.

"We're close to the base, Jessica. Cover your face with the shawl and don't speak. We'll be home soon. You'll be all right."

Numbly, Avizeh does as she is told. The pair walk to the door and out into a busy intersection just as the sun rises between a pharmacy and a Pakistani restaurant. A rickshaw passes them and a car blares its horn as it flies down the road. The smell of warm naan mixes with the heavy brown smog above them. Behind the haze, deep purple thunderheads roll towards them from the south, bringing with them the season's first monsoon.

*   *   *

Avizeh watches the sun slide down between skyscrapers. Her head rests on her knees while her arms cross in front of her. Weeks ago this room filled her with joy as a place that was finally hers. Now the four walls oppress her; they become just another prison whose belongings are temporary distractions.

There is a knock at the door. Avizeh does not respond, instead preferring to watch the cityscape.

"Jessica? It's Omar, can I come in?"

She takes a deep breath. She turns, letting her feet hit the floor as she faces the door. "Yes."

Omar steps inside. His visage is placid, far from the sympathetic and conciliatory looks everyone else has been giving her. Normally the young Afghan prefers truth over condescending compassion but as he towers over her she is not sure she can handle it. The imposing marine grabs the desk chair, places it opposite her and sits down.

"I got an order from Colonel Mueller. You're being sent back to Fort Powell for psychological care."

"What better place to unwind than the Fortress of

Solitude?" Avizeh bites back.

"You've got some fire in you. Must be that youth. That's a good thing; defiance is a great healer—"

"Spare me your wisdom or your stories."

The two lock gazes. She appreciates that he can hold her icy glare, that he can become the object of her hate. It feels good to hate someone else when all you've done is hate yourself.

"I put in a good word with Mueller, though Rasul's report means a lot more. He says you accomplished more in a day than his people could in weeks."

Avizeh pauses for a long time, gathering the strength she needs to ask what is truly on her mind. "Why didn't you stop them from abducting me?" She nearly chokes on the word 'abducting.'

Omar's look doesn't change.

"They weren't amateurs. They must have removed my phone on the way to... my GPS was gone and in a crowded city like this they wouldn't be easy to track down. One of you was following me."

"To see where they were going," Omar replies.

Avizeh blanches. The air catches in her breath and she feels the blood drain from her.

"Once you were knocked out, our field operative could fight with them, during which you and innocent bystanders could be hurt. Further, it would raise suspicions by the Indian government, possibly jeopardizing our place there. It was the safer option for everyone to follow them to wherever their hideout is and infiltrate it later."

Avizeh's breath suddenly comes back to her. Her chest heaves rapidly. It bothers her how he can return her gaze with such practiced calm.

"Was it you?"

"Does it matter?"

Emotions and angry words tumble through her. "Did you let them kidnap me because I wouldn't kiss you back?"

For the first time Omar's face cracks. He winces at the blow but he doesn't look away. "If I said 'no' would that be better or worse?"

Avizeh wants to retort that it would be better but then she thinks on it and realizes Omar could be the sort of man who would sacrifice his love to complete a mission. Maybe he already has.

"Why can't you just answer my questions?"

"Because my answers wouldn't be the truth."

"Then tell the truth!" she yells, exasperated.

"What truth?" he replies.

Avizeh gets a strong urge to hit him. "What truth? The truth, why is this so hard? Or is this just who you are? Just a liar whose every story is some fiction."

"And you aren't doing the same, 'Jessica Brown'?"

Her breath catches in her throat.

"You can't tell the truth either. Everything you've told me about yourself is a lie."

"That's not true! Some things are."

"I'm sure you believe some of what you said. But you're new to this career, I can tell. You still want things to be 'true' and 'false.' You need to let go of that; trust me, it's so freeing. When you do, then anything you want can be true. All those fanciful stories I tell, who's to say they didn't happen? You wouldn't know. And if you told me you won a ticket to go up into space but had to cancel because you were scheduled to meet the Dalai Lama, would I know? You can be anyone you want."

"Anyone but myself."

"No. Being yourself is the most dangerous thing in the world."

"More sage advice from a character actor?"

Omar lets silence fill the room before he asks, "Who were you calling on that burner phone?"

Avizeh freezes. Sweat breaks out on her face.

"Someone you weren't supposed to," he guesses. "You're lucky it was me tailing you that day. I haven't reported it yet."

"Will you?" Avizeh gasps.

Omar shrugs. "Doesn't concern the mission. When you leave, I'll be reassigned. It won't affect me." He stands up, towering over her. "Think about what I said, Jessica Brown. In this profession you can live the lie you choose or have someone else choose it for you. Might as well make it yours. That's the closest to truth we can ever come to." He shrugs. "If you still care, that is."

Chapter Thirteen
Modesty

Humid heat gives way to deathly chill as Avizeh reappears on Fort Powell's teleportation bay. Her first sight is of a bundled-up Colonel Mueller standing beside a thin woman in her mid-forties with long curly blonde hair and thin glasses who Avizeh recognizes as Dr. Sarah Kiernan, one of the base's two psychiatrists. Dr. Kiernan walks up to her and puts a hand on her arm, which Avizeh shrugs off angrily.

"Come on," Mueller instructs her and the two follow him to his office. Inside, Mueller says, "You performed well, Jessica. Rasul tells me you accomplished all that he could have hoped from you. Given what you've just been through, we can consider this first six-month period over, even though we're cutting it a bit short. You'll have a month off, the first week of which you will spend here taking counseling sessions with Dr. Kiernan."

"Is that mandatory?"

"Yes. One hour of therapy sessions minimum every day for one week with Dr. Kiernan, then you can take your vacation, pending her approval. Now, did you have any questions for me regarding your first official mission?"

Avizeh stares him down. "Who kidnapped me? Did they turn out to be who you were looking for?" She wonders if she even cares.

"You're not in that field of operations anymore so that's confidential."

Avizeh rolls her eyes. "You can't even tell me who those bastards were? If they even had anything to do with why I was there? Did I even change anything?"

"You are safe here so that information is irrelevant. As for your success in the operation, I've reported to my superiors that you have done an excellent job, so you have." He places his hands together in front of him, waiting for her next question.

"Can I leave?"

Mueller nods, prompting Avizeh to stand up and reach for the door. As she does, Dr. Kiernan rises to follow her. "I was hoping to start therapy today," she says in a voice that sounds genuinely concerned. Avizeh slams the door behind her. The decommissioned spy marches into the women's dormitory, jogs down the aisle of beds and runs into the bathroom where two women shower. She exits the dormitory and searches the mess, then the intel room. Finally, she returns to the dormitory and approaches a woman at her computer.

"Hey, do you know where Clara is?"

"She's gone."

"Gone? Where?"

"Some mission. She didn't say where and I didn't ask."

Avizeh feels a hole open up in her stomach. She checks Clara's computer and her own bunk, looking for any note or message Clara might have left, but there is no trace of her.

*   *   *

The couch is softer and more comfortable than anything else in the barracks, Avizeh muses as she sinks into it. She reminisces on those relaxing days in Varanasi when she would plug away on her laptop chasing down cyber criminals while watching Indian soap operas before one of the Americans complained and switched the channel to sports. That makes her think of her walks through the alleys, the phone call and her prayer in the mosque.

The awkward kiss.

And the basement.

"I'm glad you showed up, Jessica. I know you must be pretty rattled from the event two days ago but it's best to just talk it out as soon as possible after a bad thing happens to you. After traumatic incidents people start developing bad thinking patterns, including blaming themselves and obsessing over every negative thing, often real but mostly imagined. Our psychologies are strange and complex things; the brain wants to know the source of its pain, and will inadvertently invent reasons for why it, or in this case you, are hurting. But sometimes there is no good reason for our pain. Sometimes things just happen and we can't let individual bad moments live on and become a reason for us to be miserable when there is so much joy to be had. How have your thoughts been?"

Avizeh glances aside. She tries to think about that question honestly but her thoughts tumble over each other, one after the other and her focus moves from one idea to the next until she has a headache.

"It's okay, take your time."

"How much do you know?"

Dr. Kiernan doesn't so much as flinch. "What would you like me to know? Or is there something you don't want me to know?"

"Don't screw with me." *Do you even know my real name?*

Avizeh is burning to ask but she knows she can't; that's another government secret.

"Jessica, I think you're turning your frustrations at your situation and yourself on me. Which is fine, I have thick skin; but you're not going to get anywhere unless you start talking."

"I just want to know what you're allowed to know," Avizeh replies slowly.

"Everything. But maybe there's something they don't know about you, or maybe I do know something about you but you want to put it in your own words."

Avizeh wonders how much is 'everything;' it could be nothing, or less than nothing. Perhaps Mueller's secretary has invented an entire fake biography for Jessica Brown. Maybe she was a cheerleader and high school valedictorian before her boyfriend cheated on her, thus turning her away from silly things like romance and on to national service. She thinks back to the mosque. *Was I really connecting to God then or just putting everything in my own words?*

"I hate my life. I don't like getting up in the morning. I'm trapped in a cage with people that hate me. My only friend, Clara, is off on a mission and may never come back because she's insane and likes throwing herself in danger. My other friend, Jaina, hates me. And I have to work for people that make me do dangerous and sometimes immoral things and I don't even get to know what my work leads to, or if it does good or not. And I'm so alone." Her voice quavers as she says that last, dreaded word. "I almost never hear from my family and I'm afraid I never will again. Even if I could I'm not sure they want to hear from me. And I'm trapped in this position and no one can help me, and I'll have to do this, and keep living in this cage until I die, naturally... or in a basement."

She gasps and turns her face downward.

"So, how is talking about this going to help?" Avizeh fires

back with her now-usual bite, holding back tears.

"I've diagnosed a lot of people and those that show no emotion are the ones who have lost all hope. I know what you're going through hurts but it tells me that you still experience deep happiness and still want to. Tell me, what was the last thing that you did that made you happy?"

Avizeh shakes her head and looks aside. "I walked the alleyways of Varanasi alone. I felt free. It was warm, and I was beautiful. I was wearing a magenta sari... I guess Varanasi is the first time I got to choose my own clothes, I think ever. Growing up, my mother would dress me modestly, and here it's nothing but winter coats. That was the first time I got to choose..." She lets the word roll around her mouth. "I got to choose," she repeats, liking the words, "what I wanted."

"And you got to learn more about yourself; what you like?"

Avizeh nods. "I liked that. I knew I was being monitored but there was some freedom there. I got to go where I wanted, do what I wanted. And it was warm."

Dr. Kiernan smiles. "Did it remind you of home?"

The woman from Anar Dara meets the doctor's eyes, wondering if 'home' refers to Afghanistan or Nebraska.

"No. It was humid and crowded; it was better than home. I got to lose myself there in the crowds."

"So, you enjoyed Varanasi?"

"Yes..."

"Most everything you've told me about what's bothering you has nothing to do with what happened in Varanasi. Are you avoiding talking about it because it's too painful? Because sometimes—"

"No, that's not it..." She stops and contemplates how best to put her feelings into words. "Danger is becoming normal for me. When I was in Kabul I was being shot at in a collapsing building. Then I got locked in a basement in

Varanasi. I lived both times."

"They didn't hurt you?"

Avizeh shakes her head.

"In any way?"

"No. I was rescued before they could do anything. They just trapped me in a room with a bunch of other people... what happened to them?"

"I don't know. I'm here for you."

And if I ask Mueller I'll get just as much information but without the feigned concern.

"Do you miss your family?"

Avizeh looks away.

"Jessica?"

"I do, but..."

"I think you know what you feel. Even if you're confused, trying to put it into words can help."

"I... I don't know if they would still consider me part of their family. I've been away so long. I haven't observed any of our customs. I ran away from home one night." Avizeh's voice catches in her throat. She glances at Dr. Kiernan, who gives her an understanding look. The beleaguered spy takes a breath and continues. "I miss them; I grew up with them, I remember talking with them, living with them, depending on them. But I think the people who I remember are different than the ones I grew up with. I know I am."

"Do you feel them with you still? Do you care about their disapproval?"

She sees her father grabbing her, trying to force her into the car, seeing in his eyes she is his bargaining chip to regain his old life. "I don't know. I just have no one anymore. I'm completely alone. There's no one I can trust but myself."

Dr. Kiernan pauses. "Have you thought about where you're going to go for your month-long leave?"

Avizeh shakes her head.

"May I suggest somewhere nice? Somewhere safe and boring where you won't have to worry about getting shot at or attacked?"

"Where would that be?" Avizeh snorts, trying to think of a place she has visited where she wasn't in danger.

*   *   *

The young Antarctican from rural Afghanistan hums "Happy Birthday" to commemorate turning eighteen as she eats alone in the mess hall. She hopes that Jaina will talk to her, or, miraculously, Clara might return. Neither happens, and her birthday passes like any other day except slower. After a week of thirty-minute sessions Avizeh is given a clean bill of psychological health, though she is told to work on her positive thinking. She stands on the teleport pad, backpack full of clothes and a teleporter in her hand. She closes her eyes and presses the button.

Wispy clouds appear in a sky that seems so much softer than before. She looks down and sees a Caucasian man in American sergeant's uniform standing beside a Taiwanese sergeant. After a short greeting, she is ushered into a building where she drops off her coat and has her passport stamped. From there a short bus ride takes her into the urban heart of Taipei.

Avizeh steps off the bus onto a street surrounded by five-story buildings with shops on the first floors and a few odd fruit stands between them as towering skyscrapers paint the background. Despite the enormous buildings around her the street is mostly empty, save for a mother pushing her two kids in strollers and a man in a brown suit who bites down on a mango as he saunters past her. The whole area around her is unnaturally calm, so much so that Avizeh nearly jumps as two girls laugh next to her. She looks over her shoulder and sees them emerging from an alley; not a dark or foreboding alley, not even a bamboo-strewn alley that might be someone's home as in Varanasi, but a clean little side street that looks like it leads somewhere exciting. Avizeh suddenly feels an urge to get lost and she takes off down the passage. Wind chimes tinkle in the light, crisp breeze from a fenced-in miniature backyard. The other side is a narrow street as the modern architecture gives way to apartments with Parisian balcony facades engraved with Mandarin characters. She spies another alley and races toward it.

The narrow passage suddenly explodes with voices and Avizeh nearly steps into a burst of steam as a man lifts a lid on a massive pot of boiling water on a bar top. All across the bar, men with chopsticks lower pieces of raw beef inside pots before retrieving the cooked pieces. A dozen stalls selling fruits, spices and raw meats surround her. She suddenly realizes how hungry she is and takes an empty seat at the bar between a man in a black suit and a woman her age with short-cropped hair, jeans and a blue T-shirt with a Japanese band logo plastered across the front.

A barman with a thin goatee eyes her, gives a slightly worried look and says in stilted English, "You want rice?"

Avizeh nods. "Yes please. And beef, like that." She points at the big pot the group of men are dipping into. The server nods and brings out a bowl of rice and a plate of raw strips of beef. He retrieves a small pot of water and places it on a stove in front of her and turns it on before placing a cup of water in front of her and a pair of chopsticks before turning to other customers.

The Afghan spy-on-holiday gazes down at the chopsticks. She has seen chopsticks in movies but never encountered them in her time in Farah or at Fort Powell and wasn't sure if they were real or not. She is familiar with the concept of chopsticks but always thought them an oddity and even wondered if they are still used by East Asian cultures or if it was just Hollywood's way of making the region seem more exotic. To her dismay chopsticks are real. She looks over at the men who handle them so effortlessly. *They don't even have to look at them while they eat!*

Avizeh picks up her chopsticks and tries to emulate the way the man to her right holds them. She lowers the sticks to the sticky rice and tries rolling a ball but accidentally flicks some rice out in front of her. She hears a feminine laugh from close to her as she does. The young Japanese woman to her left puts a hand over her face and turns her almond-colored doe eyes away innocently, though she can't hide the smile spreading across her cherubic cheeks. Avizeh looks away from her and back to the man on her right, who mercifully ignores her. She decides the meat strips would be easier to control and with a deftness that surprises her, manages to grab a piece, which she lifts slowly and delicately. Her hand shakes as she places it over the bowl. Her fingers slip and the beef falls to the bottom of the boiling plate.

Avizeh looks down at the small dark spot in the boiling pot. *This isn't over yet. It still has to cook... but for how long?* After a few moments of waiting as the beef shrivels, Avizeh reaches in with her chopsticks. Now the meat is slippery and it seems to dance around her chopsticks. She watches as the meat continues to shrink between the bubbles. Frustrated, she puts one chopstick in each hand and tries to fish it out, when two sticks shoot out from her left, grab the beef strip and put it on her plate.

Avizeh turns to the Japanese woman who smiles with her eyes, her mouth full. She swallows and remarks, "I couldn't watch anymore, it was too tense."

"Thanks... for fishing it out, I mean."

"Want me to show you how they work?" Before Avizeh can

respond, the Japanese woman brings her hand up and says, "Hold them like this. The bottom stick never moves, only the top one. Practice clicking them together. Just like that."

Avizeh lowers the instruments to her rice bowl. She tries to ball the rice up but only manages to raise three grains to her mouth.

"You're a pro!" she cheers. "I bet you could do this blindfolded."

"I think I'm going to starve; I'm here another three weeks."

"Oh well, not everything needs chopsticks. You should get triangle rice; it's just like what you've got but you eat with your hands. Then you'll really fit in. These," she waves with her chopsticks, "hole-in-the-wall traditional restaurants are only visited by old geezers and tourists looking for 'the real Taiwanese experience.' Meanwhile all the real Taiwanese are at the convenience stores getting hot dogs, chicken curry and apple milk."

"Are you some sort of expert here?"

"Yes! I've been here three days but I walk fast and I know how to read Chinese. A little. Signs usually have English beneath them. I've seen a lot of the city, now it's just, I dunno, see temples and caves and bother natives. Any of that sound fun to you?"

"All of that sounds fun to me."

"We should do some adventuring together! I've been getting bored walking around by myself. I don't know anyone else here since Ikumi bailed on me. She's such a flake, always has been ever since she first got interested in boys. We can grab some food you can actually eat, then head out to the mountains. By the way, I'm Mikasa."

"Jessica."

"Nice to meet you, Jessica! You can tell me all about yourself on the way."

Avizeh doubts that and eyes the enthusiastic woman

suspiciously. "Really? You'll travel with me, just like that? What if I'm a crazy person?"

"Pshhh, what are the odds that both of us are crazy?" She laughs. "The most interesting thing about travel is meeting new people. Everyone's so serious and adult here."

Avizeh chuckles, drops her chopsticks, hands the confused barman a wad of Taiwanese dollars and follows Mikasa down a labyrinth of alleys that lead from one plaza to another where hundreds of businessmen weave around busloads of tourists and tiny lanes where students and poor laborers live in half-submerged houses beneath monolithic towers of modernity. Along the way Mikasa explains that she is a native of Sapporo on the northern Japanese island of Hokkaido, 'where it's too cold for the yakuza.'

"I never fit in there. I'm too bubbly and it's so dour there. Everyone I know is either growing a suit and being responsible and boring or leaving for somewhere fun like Tokyo or Osaka. I can't do either; I didn't get high enough marks to get into a university and living somewhere that isn't freezing is expensive. But every now and then I get to travel, which is why I'm here," Mikasa explains while leading Avizeh down another side street. "This way, the metro will take us to a bus station, which will take us up to the mountains. So, what brings you here? I don't suppose you have family? Where are you from again?"

"America, in Nebraska. No, I don't have family—"

"Nebraska? I've never heard of it. Is it anywhere near New York? I want to go there some day."

"No, nowhere close to that," Avizeh thinks, though her American geography is not great and she isn't sure.

Before long the two are on a bus headed southeast out of Taipei. After a few minutes of watching the skyscrapers turn into fields and forests, Mikasa turns to her and asks, "What music do you listen to?"

"A lot of electronic. Lots of Persian pop."

"Do you have any I can listen to?"

Avizeh pulls out her phone and Mikasa hooks in her earbuds. Avizeh plays a song by an Iranian pop star singing about crossing a desert that was so hot the sand became shards of glass all so he could chase a beautiful woman only to find out she is a mirage. The song ends and Mikasa gives her new friend a look like she ate something too sour.

"You listen to weird shit, Jessica."

"What's weird about it?" Avizeh asks, slightly hurt.

"What can that song make you feel? It's so mellow."

"It doesn't make me feel anything... it's mostly for just, I don't know, relaxing and tuning things out."

"That's not music. Music is supposed to overwhelm you. Here, listen to this."

Avizeh puts her ear buds in and nearly jumps back as a man screams as if he is being tortured. The high-pitched scream turns into a guttural roar as guitars whine to an arrhythmic drumbeat and mournful cellos. When the song finishes Avizeh looks over at Mikasa who is in the middle of a subdued head-banging.

"Hell yeah!"

"I don't get it."

"You're not supposed to get it. Music is supposed to make you feel, even if what you feel is wrong. You must have felt something."

"Only confusion. Maybe terror."

"Okay, try this one. I'll turn on the subtitles."

Mikasa pulls up a video of an all-female group of Japanese singers dressed as bubble-gum pop stars but with machetes who are stabbing anime mascots, a few of which Avizeh recognizes.

"Well, what did that make you feel?" Mikasa asks expectantly.

Avizeh can only laugh.

"What? What is it?"

"You listen to some weird shit, Mikasa."

An hour flies by as the two share videos, desperately searching for some music they might mutually appreciate, while the bus scales the mountains, moving from tiny towns to remote hamlets. They approach the outskirts of a picturesque village complete with paper lanterns and wooden houses when Mikasa motions for them to get off. The two march up a narrow road surrounded on all sides by thick vegetation where only the odd truck passes, when Avizeh spots an overgrown dirt path leading to a winding trail up towards the summit of a nearby hill between two mountains. The two follow the path and very quickly Avizeh begins to pant as she realizes that her confinement at Fort Powell hasn't done her body well. She remembers how she avoided the gym because it was always packed with half-dressed, sweaty men and curses herself for her modesty.

"Come on, slow-poke!"

"What are we looking for?" the panting Afghan named 'Jessica' barely manages to force out between breaths.

"Adventure!"

"What," she gasps, "does adventure look like?"

"I don't know. It's not an adventure if you know how it ends!"

Pain courses through Avizeh's legs, her chest heaves and she feels that every time her foot hits the ground it will stick there and she won't be able to lift it again. She grits her teeth and trudges forward, refusing to let Mikasa get ahead of her. After coming up to an even area, the world suddenly cools and Avizeh wonders if she hit a second wind. Mikasa abruptly stops and peers to her left. Feeling as if she is on the verge of collapsing, Avizeh baby-steps up to her strange new companion. In front of them, just visible beside huge palm trees, is a cave entrance whose lip is roughly two meters above where they are standing. Mikasa glances at Avizeh. Without a word, she walks towards it.

"Give me a boost."

Avizeh kneels and cups her hands in front of her. Mikasa places a slender foot on them, grabs the lip of the cave and climbs inside.

"Whoa!" she exclaims, her call echoing long afterwards. She leans over and reaches out a hand to Avizeh, who strains to pull herself up. Mikasa reaches out again and Avizeh just manages to grab the lip and struggle over it. She forces herself to stand and sees the cave extending at least six meters before narrowing.

"Isn't this cool?" Mikasa pulls out her phone and turns on her flashlight. The Afghan woman follows the light and watches a small stalactite drip water on a tiny mound at her feet. Mikasa turns her flashlight towards the back of the cave, illuminating a downward curving ceiling with only a small opening, less than a meter tall but around three meters wide, in front of them. Mikasa steps forward and kneels.

"Shall we?"

Avizeh looks up at the rocks around her.

"Don't tell me you're claustrophobic?"

Avizeh is afraid but she decides the best option is to move forward as quickly as possible before her fears can catch up to her. She kneels and crab-walks forward behind the strange woman. Mikasa's flashlight flies back and forth ahead of her as they dive deeper into the all-encompassing darkness. The small tunnel drops to the right and they sidestep deeper into the cavern. Avizeh forces herself forward, feeling the rocks scrape against her bare legs. She looks up and in the shaking light sees the ceiling almost touch her nose. There is an immense darkness in front of her and she pauses to retrieves her own phone which she holds in front of her and sees the cave expand enough that they can stand. Avizeh moves forward into the open area, rises to her feet and shines the light around her. The cave's ceiling is at least six meters high and twelve across. So many stalactites drip and echo that it sounds like rainfall. At the end of the cave and to the right is a drop-off that leads deeper into the mountain. Mikasa stands up beside Avizeh and looks around, mouth open.

"Wow... I'm hungry. Care to eat?"

Avizeh smirks at the seamless transition from awe to hunger, but is quietly grateful for the breather. The two sit down and Mikasa puts her phone on the ground and plays a death metal song, which echoes ominously through the caverns while they eat their triangle rice.

"This is the coolest thing I've done in a while," Mikasa muses as her eyes peer deep into the shadows. "You're all right, Jessica. And I like how you pronounce my name; not like other Americans. We had some foreign exchange students from California at my school. White people talk so slow and enunciate everything. It makes English easy to understand but they say things wrong. They kept calling me 'Mi casa,' which I learned is Spanish for 'my house.'"

Avizeh grins. "I know how you feel. Everyone pronounces my name 'A-visa,' you know, like 'a visa,' for traveling."

"They pronounce 'Jessica,' 'A-visa?'"

Avizeh's rice catches in her throat.

"Your name is 'Avisa'?"

"I shouldn't," Avizeh stammers.

"No, don't lie to me! We've been together all day and I don't even know who you are? At least tell me your real name."

Avizeh eyes the phone, which emits a guttural scream accompanied by fast-paced pounding drums. "Turn off your phone."

"Why? It doesn't have service, we're in a cave."

"Turn it off anyway."

"It's going to get really dark."

"Turn it off!"

Avizeh seizes Mikasa's phone and takes out the battery. She does the same with her phone and the world is enveloped by blackness.

After a moment of listening to the dripping around them, Mikasa breaks the silence. "Are you going to kill me?"

Avizeh sighs. "No. And my name isn't Jessica; that's my fake identity. My real name is Avizeh Fatah. I'm an Afghan but in service to the United States Navy Crisis Response Division."

"No way!" Avizeh can imagine Mikasa's incredulous face in the darkness, huge eyes enlarging.

"It's true. I work for the US government at Fort Powell in Antarctica. I'm a computer expert; I help them track down terrorists all around the world before the soldiers teleport in and kill them."

After a pause Mikasa asks, "Are there any terrorists in Taiwan? Who are you tracking down? Can I help?"

"No and no. I'm just on vacation."

"Wait a minute, you said you were Afghan? Isn't that a place the US doesn't like? Why would they let you work in their most important base?"

"It's complicated."

"That's just another word for interesting."

Avizeh feels her own moist breathing in the dank cave's chill air. Even in the darkness she feels eyes on her and her heart races inside her chest. Without thinking she lets the words tumble out as the secrets that have tortured her for years spill into the recesses of the dark rock. She recounts the massacre at her marriage, the ice floe and the orca, over a year of boredom while trapped in legal limbo, the teleportation and discovery by Colonel Mueller, the return to a ruined Kabul and a brief mention of her time in Varanasi, minus the awkward kiss and the kidnapping. There is a profound silence and Avizeh wonders if Mikasa scampered off, fleeing from the dangerous woman beside her.

From the near darkness Mikasa nearly shouts, "You are the coolest person I've ever met! I don't believe in fate but this is fate. You are so awesome, Avizeh Fatah! What a cool name. Avizeh. That's almost Japanese, since it's one quick sound, only it's more exotic. I wish I were as cool as you."

"Really? You think I'm cool?" Avizeh's cheeks warm and she thanks the darkness for hiding her embarrassment.

"What other person can compare? You've had so many adventures, chasing terrorists, having a nightmare wedding. I am so jealous."

"Thanks, nobody's called me 'cool' before... and I don't have much in the way of friends."

"Well then I'd be happy to be your first friend! I have some cool friends; one does his own pottery and makes his own dishes and cups and paints demonic cats on them, but you're way above him."

"Thanks," Avizeh breathes, a sudden warmth overtaking her.

"Hey, will anything happen to me if I hang out with you?"

After a moment of silent pondering, Avizeh replies, "I don't think so. As long as I keep reporting to my superiors and we don't share any electronic information, no email or texts or phone calls, they won't have anything to trace us. But if you write down your info on a piece of paper sometime we can communicate... on my next vacation in six months. But until then I have a year's salary which I can only spend now if you want to do something."

"What?" Mikasa nearly screams. "What are we doing in a cave? Let's go live it up!"

*   *   *

The two emerge blinking from the cavern as they are bathed in the dim light of a red sun hovering above purple clouds. After consulting her phone Mikasa leads them back to a village where they follow a series of paper lanterns down a cobblestone walkway to a two-story traditional bathhouse. The curved red tiles and paper windows are new and pristine but the wooden beams appear centuries old. The smell of pine mixes with incense sticks in the chill air and the sound of wind chimes accompanies the soft rustling leaves.

"The smell's amazing."

"It's just crisp forest air." Mikasa looks sideways at her. "Oh yeah, you've never been in a forest before, have you, Jessica?" She says the name with a wink.

"No... I could get used to this."

They enter the bathhouse, stepping into an enormous open room with oaken floors and pillars that are bathed in a golden light. Four large staircases are spread across the grand entryway and there are over a dozen deep turquoise-painted doors on both floors. Avizeh watches the half-dozen Taiwanese patrons when her eyes fall to the beautiful calligraphy of the hand-drawn signs, and notices that there's no English script to be found. Mikasa walks up to the counter and speaks to the concierge in what Avizeh assumes is Mandarin. After a moment in which Mikasa sounds unusually calm and polite, she turns to Avizeh and asks, "Should we get separate rooms?"

"Yes," Avizeh replies.

"Okay, that's going to cost ten thousand Taiwan dollars for the night with the bath services."

Avizeh reaches into her backpack and pulls out a wad of money.

"For you too; I prefer not to use a card or anything

traceable."

Mikasa's eyes widen as she takes the money and passes it over to the concierge. She says a few words and receives two sets of keys and two towels. Mikasa bows and turns back to Avizeh.

"I made sure we have rooms on opposite sides of the hotel. You're 234, I'm 201. Drop your stuff off, then meet me over on the left side; that's where the women's bathing pools are."

Avizeh nods and walks up the antiquated steps to her room. The room is slightly larger than a closet with a small bed in the corner with a flat-screen TV on the far wall and a painting of a mountain range over the bed. The Afghan-American-Antarctic spy on vacation tosses her backpack on the floor, opens her window and gazes out on the forests that cling to the sides of the mountains. She closes her eyes and commits the view to memory. When she finishes taking her mental picture she removes her coat and grabs a one-piece swimsuit and towel. The suit has an attached skirt on the bottom but Avizeh is still a little embarrassed at how much it reveals. *No one will be looking at me anyway,* she reassures herself and leaves to join Mikasa, who she finds waiting on the first floor outside the imposing far doors.

"Come on," Mikasa eggs her on through the doors and to the left, down another door and a short hallway into a changing room with small, open cubbies. Mikasa puts her towel down on the bench in the center of the room and undresses. Avizeh's brow furrows as she looks for Mikasa's swimsuit.

"What are you waiting for?" Mikasa remarks while turning to her traveling companion, now fully nude.

Avizeh blushes. "Oh, I thought..." She gazes down at her swimsuit.

"No, it's an all-nude spa. See, what you do is you hold your 'modesty towel' like this when you walk around," Mikasa holds her towel below her belly, "and once you get into the baths you wear it on your head like this. Koreans like to tie it on both sides, so it stays on." Mikasa attempts to tie the towel to her head but only succeeds in messing up her hair. "Oh well, it doesn't matter. The point is, no one will see your lady parts. And it's just us girls anyway."

Avizeh stands still, feeling very warm and a little light-headed.

"I'm sorry, is this too much of a shock?"

"No, no... I can do this."

Avizeh puts her swimsuit down and begins to undress while Mikasa turns away. She puts her things in one of the cubbies, grabs her modesty towel and holds it in front of her like a server at a restaurant.

"There you go! Now just relax: this is what we're here for."

Mikasa gives her a cherubic, eyes-closed smile before turning and leading her out. The traditionally-raised Afghan woman forces herself to keep her eyes up as she steps into the courtyard. Avizeh has spent much of her life in a full burqa then over two years in concealing winter gear to ward off the negative fifty-degree Antarctic chill. Now she walks out to open, steaming pools with a dozen naked women holding only a small towel that doesn't even reach across her wide hips.

Oh, what beautiful trees. Is that an owl I hear? I bet there's a lot of wonderful wildlife in this forest. I wonder if the rocks around the pool are artificial or real. They look real. Oh, that woman's getting out and she can't find her towel. Oh, and another woman's stood up to help her look for it, and my, what pretty stars are out tonight!

Mikasa steps delicately into the water. Avizeh puts her legs in and raises the towel slowly, making sure she is submerged before lifting it onto her head.

Her Japanese traveling companion leans back and sighs.

"This is amazing. The warmth all around and the chill air on your face. The water feels heavy, you know? Like you're just sinking in, almost like a mud bath."

Avizeh nods and one end of the towel slips off her head, dipping into the water. Mikasa laughs, reaches out and lifts the towel end. "Peekaboo."

Mikasa lets go and the wet end flops on the side of Avizeh's face. "Oh hey, look up."

Avizeh puts a hand on her head and follows Mikasa's gaze.

"Look at all those stars. Have you ever seen so many before?"

Avizeh laughs. "Only everywhere. Have you ever seen pictures of the Aurora Australis? I got to see those almost every night during the blackout months. It's incredible; the Milky Way above you, the aurora dancing around, like a cosmic, liquid, neon snake. And I got to see the Milky Way every night growing up in the desert."

"Of Death! Sorry, it just sounds like a fairy tale."

Avizeh smiles widely, finally feeling relaxed. "So, you're a city girl?"

"More than you. But I don't want to be. I want to get out to some mid-sized town. I have this dream..." She looks away and then back to the stars.

"What? Tell me. What's your dream?"

"It's not going to happen."

"Hey, tell me."

Mikasa closes her eyes. "I want to open up a movie theater in northern Hokkaido that's also a restaurant. I had this plan to show foreign films and serve traditional cuisine from whatever country the film takes place in. So, if a Bollywood film was playing there'd be curry and rice, and if we played 'Les Chansons D'Amour' there'd be crêpes, and if we played a Spanish film there'd be tapas."

"That sounds like the coolest thing ever."

"I think so, but it will never happen. People are dumb and like explosion movies with men who wear sunglasses and tight pants. Not many people watch films with plots and ideas."

"I do. I love films. I've even seen 'Les Chansons'."

"Really?"

"Yeah." Avizeh remembers not to nod as she drops her hand back into the water, her towel finally balanced on her head. "Over the last few years my only connection to the outside world was movies. I've seen... I don't even know how many. Have you seen any German films?"

"No. You?"

"Hundreds. It's my favorite scene, even more than French. French is so melancholic, every character and every scene is an existential crisis. German cinema is great because it's so nouveau in spirit, if not style, it feels free and open to interpretation. I don't know how to describe it. It's as if even though there's a story going on, you can make it about anything."

"Like abstract?"

"No, it's like when you're listening to music to help you fall asleep. As you're drifting off you're not thinking about anything related to the music but it's there. It's all in the subconscious. I always liked German cinema because it made me feel like I could be there in that world. I've read a lot of reviews online. Most people think it's slow-paced compared to American films but I like it."

"Recommend me a film."

"'Die Bayerische Heiligtum'. There's no way I'm pronouncing that right. Just look up 'The Bavarian Retreat'. It's about a woman who gets lost on a hiking trail and stumbles into a cabin that her family used to vacation in when she was young... it made me think of home. About reinterpreting objects and memories to reflect how someone changes too."

"What would you eat with it?"

Avizeh laughs. "I wasn't thinking about that. Um... what do Germans eat? Meat and beer."

"No, that's Americans. Or English. Some Western place. But meat and beer sounds really good."

"Don't give up on your dream, it sounds amazing. Even if it's not very profitable, do it for you, and because it matters."

"If only the world worked that way."

"Have you ever taken a big risk on someone before? You say people won't give it a chance; why not give them a chance?"

"You have a lot of faith in people for someone who's been through all you have."

"Maybe I'm just feeling good because I trusted you and so far it's worked out great."

Mikasa smiles widely. She leans back and puts the end of her towel over her eyes. Avizeh does the same, feeling more relaxed and at peace than she's ever felt. Images from her childhood return to the woman from Farah. Happy memories of playing with Laily in the shade of the house and being gently rocked to sleep by her grandfather return to her. She remembers the taste of raw honey and her mother's freshly baked bread, and her father pointing up into the heavens and naming the stars and telling her which ones she was born under and what that meant for her life. She remembers her teacher Mr. Hossin bringing her to the front of her small class and announcing to everyone that she had received the highest grade. Beautiful recollections of joy, discovery, pride and familial warmth flood through her as if a font suddenly opens and the hard exterior she has built for herself bursts. Ever since arriving at Fort Powell her memories of her childhood were painful; memories of regret, fear, humiliation for herself and the times she brought shame to her family, until she convinced herself that her family hated her, even Laily and her mother. Now, finally alone with her thoughts, her stomach filled with fresh food that hadn't spent a month in a freezer, her nostrils filled with clean air that smells of pine needles, wild grass and wet stone, her body suddenly relaxes. Sitting beside a friend who knows who she is and cares for her even more because of that, Avizeh looks back at her past and feels a smile spread across her face. She even chuckles to herself as the soft towel over her face reminds her of a burqa. She asks herself how she ever came to be filled with such self-hatred and delusions about her past and her beloved family when Dr. Kiernan's words come back to her.

"I'm glad you showed up, Jessica. I know you must be pretty rattled from the event two days ago but it's best to just talk it out as soon as possible after a bad thing happens to you. After traumatic incidents people start developing bad thinking patterns, including blaming themselves and obsessing over every negative thing, real but mostly imagined. Our psychologies are strange and complex things. The brain wants to know the source of its pain, and will inadvertently invent reasons for why it, or in this case, you, are hurting. But sometimes there is no good reason for our pain. Sometimes things just happen and we can't let individual bad moments live on and become a reason for us to be miserable when there is so much joy within and so much more we're capable of. How have your thoughts been?"

Avizeh breathes deeply, feeling the warm water press against her skin. *I have spiraled into a self-destructive pattern of thinking. But it didn't start because of the basement in Varanasi,* she winces as she dwells on that painful memory, *or the firefight in Afghanistan, or even Colonel Mueller imprisoning me. My wedding night started it all. Watching the armed men arrive in Farah while my frightened relatives could only say 'yes' to their every demand. The mullah asking me in private if I accepted*

Razaaq Hirat as my husband so that there would be no hiccups in the ceremony, when a proper Muslim wedding would have had him ask for my acceptance in front of my family. Then the firefight erupted. Blasts of light in the dark. Screams. The soldier I thought might save me and died in front of me. Razaaq threatening to kill me. The leap onto the ice floe and the orcas. It all started then. I've been a frightened girl, jumping at whatever friendship was offered, taking to small hobbies like knitting, watching movies, and programming, all to avoid coming to terms with what happened. My whole adult life has been stilted because of that. But that doesn't have to continue. Even if I am never legally tolerated or independent, my mind can be free.

There's never been a reason I can't be happy that I didn't create myself. But tonight, I choose to be free.

Avizeh cannot tell if the hot, wet drops that trail down her cheeks are sweat or tears. From beside her she hears Mikasa say, "Come on, let's get out before I get pruney."

Avizeh grabs her towel, stands up and lowers it in front of her. She looks over at the dozen women bathing in front of her and wishes she has a second towel as she turns away from them and follows Mikasa back to the changing rooms. Avizeh's eyes trail down Mikasa's back, then back upward as she watches the ends of Mikasa's dark hair cling to her slender neck. Beads of water tremble on her perfect skin with every step. Mikasa puts her towel down on the bench. Avizeh does the same and takes a step towards her, feeling her chest rise and fall rapidly, hearing her heavy breathing betraying her. Mikasa meets her gaze and Avizeh feels herself falling into her eyes. Avizeh leans in and kisses her while placing a hand on her warm, wet hip. Mikasa slips her tongue into Avizeh's mouth and she lets out a soft moan. Avizeh's hands caress Mikasa's warm, soft body. As one hand massages Mikasa's breast the other pulls on her lower back, arching the Japanese woman's form into hers while their soft lips touch and Avizeh quivers at how natural it feels, as if this is something she has always known how to do and has always been a part of her. She reaches down, longing, burning to touch her. Mikasa catches her hand.

"Not here. My room. 201."

Avizeh nods and rushes to put her clothes on.

*   *   *

The blissfully exhausted lovers awaken slowly to the sound of morning birdsong. Avizeh's head gently bobs with Mikasa's every breath as she listens to her soft heartbeat. Her whole life she has felt the need to hide who she was. Now she feels like this is exactly where and who she should be. Mikasa smiles and places a hand under Avizeh's chin and pulls her in for a kiss. The sun rises above the tree line by the time Avizeh pulls herself away from Mikasa.

"What do you want to do today?" Avizeh asks. "Stay in? More of this?"

"You are insatiable. Have you never been with a girl before?"

"I've never been with anyone before. You have?"

Mikasa nods. "Boys and girls. But mostly girls; they're better. I guess Japan is more open than Afghanistan."

"Don't say it so loud."

"What? You took the batteries out of our phones and pulled out all the cords in the room. I don't think anyone's listening."

"Still..."

"You liked it?"

"Did you hear me last night?" Avizeh laughs.

"I think everyone in the building heard you." Mikasa smiles and runs a hand through Avizeh's long hair. "Well, I need to get out. You still have lots of money, even after paying for all this?"

Avizeh nods.

"Let's go get a big fatty breakfast, then go clothes shopping; I want to get a cheongsam so I can impress my friends back at home; I always thought they looked prettier than kimonos. Then we can get a big lunch, something something, then back to this."

"Okay," Avizeh kisses her and stands up. She reaches out to help Mikasa to her feet and barely resists kissing her again. "You can be so distracting," she grins as she forces herself to look away so she can get dressed.

*   *   *

Avizeh sleeps more peacefully than she has her entire life. Flashbacks to gunfights and memories of isolation in a frozen cell disappear. Within a day Avizeh and Mikasa develop in-jokes and references as they recede into a universe they create for themselves. Avizeh loves the way Mikasa's beautiful, smiling, almond eyes gleam whenever she looks at her. She loves how Mikasa holds her like no one else in the world has for years. Every night when Avizeh closes the hotel door behind her she can't suppress a conspiratorial grin before she launches herself at her lover. Every day spent with Mikasa is a miraculous adventure and every check-in call made with her superiors is a reminder that it will soon come to an end. Three days before Avizeh is due back she sits near a fountain in a vibrant green cheongsam, her hair done up in a bun with flowers, beside Mikasa in matching red with golden dragon inlay, holding a plate of noodles in her lap and a fork in her hand.

"Screw chopsticks."

Mikasa grins and deftly finishes off the last of her noodles with the hated instruments. "You know you'll have to learn how to use them if you ever visit me. There's no way I'll tell people I'm dating someone who doesn't know how to eat the right way."

"I can't visit you. At least, not in Japan. It would be too obvious that we have a long-lasting relationship."

"What does that mean? Are we... breaking up?"

"No, never." Avizeh's eyes widen as her heart races. "I mean... what I meant to say is that if I met you in your hometown, someone might watch you. They may have already caught me talking to you here. If they know I followed you back to your house they might get suspicious."

"What do you think they'd do?" Mikasa appears more excited than worried.

"I don't think they'd do anything serious. Just watch you, monitor you, and use you as a bargaining chip against me. I don't want them to know about us."

"So, what's the plan?"

Avizeh pulls out a small notepad and a pen.

"Well, that's old fashioned."

"Write down your email address and your phone number. I can't give you anything I'll use; I'll have to always make new accounts when I talk to you. In six months from now, give or take, I'll get another vacation, and I can see you then, and I'll have enough money to pay for everything. But we should decide where we want to go tonight."

"Let's go to Moscow!"

Avizeh shakes her head. "I'm only allowed to go to countries that are friendly to the United States."

"Well, that cuts it down a lot. There's Europe and some other cold places... Australia!"

"Okay. We have to pick some place to meet."

"Perth. Six months from today."

"How about a week past that? I'll email you and tell you when I can see you and where exactly we can meet up. Make sure you'll be there a full month because I might get waylaid. Sorry I can't be more precise."

"No, I understand, you have secret James Bond stuff to do. You even have the same initials." She winks. "Have I told you, you're the coolest person I've ever met?"

Avizeh wants to lean in and kiss her when her eye catches a CCTV camera and she decides against it. "When we meet up let's go somewhere in the wilderness. Somewhere where cell phones don't work and we can be alone. Maybe I can convince the aboriginals I'm one of them and we can go to a sacred site."

"You think you can pull it off?" Mikasa smirks.

"I'd probably have more luck than you."

Avizeh meets Mikasa's eyes and longs for one more kiss. "I don't want to say goodbye."

"But alas, this is what we must do." Mikasa stands. "Nice to meet you, Jessica Brown," and kisses her on the cheek. She looks at Avizeh for a second longer than just a friend would before turning away and disappearing into the night market.

The next three days are an act. Avizeh visits museums, temples and other famous sites alone, pretending that she isn't just killing time. She lays in bed thinking about Mikasa's body occupying the empty space next to her to help her fall asleep. On the third day she checks out of her hotel and returns to the military base in Taipei. After checking in with the onsite US advisor she is left to change into her winter clothes, pull out her teleporter and disappear.

Chapter Fourteen
At Arm's Length

The sky is a pitch-black void broken by small silver twinkles while the far horizon gleams blood red, tinting the plains of ice and the dark steel walls of Fort Powell a deep crimson. After arriving in the beginning of the six-month day and living under the three-month twilight Avizeh is now a creature of dawn and dusk. Barring her missions, which might as well be on another world, the sun will always be just below the surface.

Clara still hasn't returned. Avizeh asks about her and hasn't even been allowed to know whether she is still alive. It is only after leaving Colonel Mueller's office that she remembers James is missing too. The week before Avizeh is set to leave for the next mission, she summons all her courage and walks the short distance from her bunk to Jaina's where Avizeh finds her knitting purple mittens.

"Jaina."

Her eyes shoot up to meet Avizeh's. She doesn't have hatred in her eyes or mistrust—just a placid acceptance.

"I need some air and I'm not allowed to go outside the base alone. I was hoping you could accompany me. Unless you're doing something important."

"I'm not doing anything pressing," Jaina notes without getting up.

"I'm going on another mission soon and I might not make it back. Like Clara and James, you might never hear about me again."

"That's the job."

"Can we have this conversation outside?"

"Are you serious?"

Avizeh doesn't move. Jaina takes a deep breath, mutters, "Whatever, kid," puts her knitting needles and yarn aside, stands up, dons her winter clothes and escorts Avizeh out past the base's perimeter. After a few minutes of silent trekking, Jaina notices Avizeh has stopped walking.

"I looked up the aftermath of my last two missions; not just what was in the civilian news, but what's been passed around in reports up here."

"Unless we're specifically tasked with providing intel on it, we don't share stories of where we've been," Jaina snaps. "That'd be a violation of confidential information."

"I was in Afghanistan for the first mission." Avizeh ignores her. "I was tasked with tracking down an opium dealer. I was told that the US would use the intel to track down terrorists in the mountains, except the opium hasn't stopped flowing; it's just passed hands from the dealer that was in power to one that works with the US and he has even more control of Kabul than the previous warlord did with more opium shipments.

"Then I was in Varanasi, India. I was told that the work I was doing there was to prevent ethnic violence. Instead, after I left, some of the info on the ultranationalists was released to the public, tainting the relations between the Indians and the Bangladeshis. Now there's a religiously-motivated murder every day.

"Everywhere I've been sent it isn't to keep the peace or win a battle; it feels like it's just to keep these different groups tearing each other down. I feel as if what I'm doing is wrong and the people who give me these missions know it. It's as if down the line we get these little pieces of one giant puzzle and we're never told how they fit with every other piece but we're told that if everyone just did as they were told and put them together they'd all add up to impenetrable national security. But I can't have faith in that, not when everywhere I go more violence breaks out as soon I finish a mission."

Jaina eyes her, expressionless. "Why are you telling me this?"

"Because you must have had a moment like this before."

Jaina doesn't so much as flinch. "We all do. What you end up doing is a lot different than what you signed up for. It's like this with every job. This is the same but on another level." Her words are impassive but Avizeh can hear her softening, a tinge of regret tinting her speech.

"And you're okay with this?"

"What choice do I have? What, whistleblow? Go rogue? You aren't thinking about that, are you?"

"I have been a little. I don't know how, but I think it might be a good thing."

Jaina's eyes widen in shock, then narrow as she measures how serious Avizeh is. "Why the hell are you telling me this?"

"Where I grew up, nearly everything was forbidden to us women. To tell another woman a dangerous secret was to tell them you were their friend and you cared for them. You were putting your own security in their hands in order to get closer to them."

Jaina tries to hold the same placid look but Avizeh can see in her eyes a concern that she hasn't seen in over a year. "Up here we keep friends at arm's length. You never know how long you'll have someone or what you can or can't tell them.

Remember the people in Las Estrellas? Remember I told you about the woman I've talked to for years?"

"Yes."

"I saw her last week. She asked me what was going on in my life. I told her my son was finally graduating from high school and that I was going to see him on break. I even smiled when I talked about him, told her about what he liked, how he played the piano and how he was applying to grad schools to be a chemist."

"I didn't know you had a son."

"I don't... and he never graduated." There is a slight hiccup in her speech and Jaina looks away.

Jaina isn't nearly as practiced at being cold and reserved as she thought. Not like me.

"Shall we head back?" Jaina switches back to her impassive voice.

Avizeh nods and the two march back to base. She realizes that Jaina just admitted that they are friends, but it is a different kind of friendship than when she was a child and harmless. They might be friends but Jaina will never trust her again.

Chapter Fifteen
Land of the Free

Avizeh sits inside Colonel Mueller's familiar office with a feeling of deep-set resignation as she is briefed on her upcoming mission.

"Your next assignment will take you state-side. Since you are so familiar with the Infiltrator, we're sending you to the US to track down an underground organization known as 'The Vanguard.' They're a hacker group that's launched cyber-attacks on our facilities, predominantly the NSA, the CIA and FBI. We've tracked down a few but they seem to be a loosely connected cabal, like a hydra of sorts."

"But you think there's some connective tissue between them and you want me to find it?"

"Exactly, but if the best you can do is round up a few, maybe that will help put some of the pieces together. We're dropping you off in New York City with an escort. From there, spend a couple of days searching and find what you can. If nothing is promising, move on to the next city and the next, and so on. And don't just hit the big cities; if you monitor an inordinate amount of traffic in a mid-sized or smaller place, that could be a sign of underground activity."

"That's it? You want me to spy on American citizens just like that? Isn't that unconstitutional?"

"No one's challenged it before."

*   *   *

The bus from inland New York rolls lazily towards the city which looms above them on the horizon. Beside Avizeh stands Nathan Branch, an ex-marine dressed in brown slacks and a light blue t-shirt. He is a charming man, late forties with a bald head, a wide grin with laugh lines and the beginnings of a pot belly. He has a lot to say about fish, and catching fish, and what to use to catch fish, and what time to go out to catch the fish. When Avizeh asks how to cook fish he responds, "You'll have to ask my ex-wife."

In the city Avizeh does what all tourists do the first time they visit New York: she tilts her head straight back and tries to make sense of the towers which look like massive pillars that hold up the sky. After a few seconds in which Avizeh realizes her brain will never piece this manmade mystery together, she leads Nathan to a nearby café. She buys an overpriced coffee and scone and invades the privacy of anyone linked to the four thousand hotspots in range. She connects to each and runs a search for computers with high levels of activity, takes their IP numbers and compares it to the NSA databases that collect all internet activity. None of the people near Bowling Green are guilty of any cybercrime, though she spots what she thinks are a few dozen cases of embezzlement.

When she finishes her work in the downtown area they catch a subway and move up Manhattan, midway past Central Park where they step into a half-full Italian restaurant and she recommences. Unlike her previous bodyguards, Nathan chooses not to disturb her while working. Instead, he pulls out a large hardcover detective novel with a picture of a noose dangling from a tree on the front cover.

"Why don't you use e-readers?"

"I like pages."

Avizeh is just about to leave him to his antiquated habits when she remarks, "You know, physical books are bad for the environment."

"I'll use it as toilet paper when I'm done."

Avizeh chuckles and leaves him to his mystery.

*   *   *

New York is a dead end as far as the Vanguard are concerned. Avizeh finds a few servers that are either attacking government and financial institutions or hosting viruses from other sources but nothing on a sophisticated level; nothing a government-level firewall can't fight off. She reports them to her superiors and is told they would 'deal with it.'

"Our next stop should be Philadelphia," Nathan confers Mueller's orders. "Once we pass that we can head into smaller towns, ones which probably haven't been looked over too well by other officials."

Their course set, the quiet pair board a train south and repeat the process. A week of stopping in cafés, bistros, restaurants and bars for quiet labor pass. By the third day Avizeh decides to use the gym and swim laps in the hotel pool. *I don't want to look like a whale the next time I see Mikasa.* On the sixth day Avizeh notes that the book Nathan is holding has a different cover, this one of a half-shadowed sinister-looking woman entering into the office of a smoking private detective.

*　　　　　*　　　　　*

For the next four months the pair move south through major cities and small towns alike. Avizeh uncovers dozens of hacker organizations and forty servers that manage fraudulent e-currency. She flips through over a hundred thousand people's lives but there is no sign of the Vanguard anywhere between New York and their current location in Asheville, North Carolina.

They are sitting in yet another café when Avizeh decides her eyes are too sore to continue and she turns off her computer. She takes the battery out of the laptop, then removes the battery from her phone. In a low voice she says to Nathan, "Do you think they exist?"

"Who?"

"The people we're after."

"Why wouldn't they?"

"Because I can't find a trace of them anywhere." *Because the Vanguard is the perfect excuse to invade Americans' privacy.*

Avizeh decides to quickly change the topic to something that isn't potentially subversive. "This American food is always so heavy."

Without looking up from his book, Nathan suggests she try eating fish.

*　　　　　*　　　　　*

The Afghan spy from Antarctica is sitting in a Mexican restaurant barely reading the code out of the corner of her eye while she looks at the people around her. *I wonder if this is all as frail as Colonel Mueller insists it is. If I don't complete my mission, will Asheville, North Carolina turn into Kabul overnight?* She knows better than to voice her concerns to Nathan, who is content reading a thriller about a female detective who just got out of an insane asylum and is hired to solve a new case. Avizeh watches as her laptop scans one of the fifty computers in range. Her eyes widen just for a second. A program scans a seemingly harmless personal computer, with personal e-mail address and saved passwords to a Facebook and YouTube account, when she notices it has a large, deeply hidden encrypted file. She opens it and finds a word doc with a thousand lines of code.

Avizeh reads through it trying to determine its purpose.

"Ready to go?" Nathan asks, finishing.

"Order dessert, my laptop is acting slow."

Just as the sopapillas arrive on the table, she determines that the code is meant to delete an unlimited amount of personal photos and videos and the accompanying script might just be strong enough to get through a government-level database. Avizeh examines the text a second time just to be sure. Once she can confirm her suspicions, she turns off her computer.

"Okay, let's go."

*   *   *

Avizeh tells Nathan she is going to the hotel gym before sneaking outside and walking to a hole-in-the-wall phone store in a strip mall with no security cameras. She buys a new phone in cash, putting all false data in the customer sign-up sheet. That night the two visit a hipster coffee shop that serves Vietnamese food and Avizeh is happy to find the suspicious computer still in range. She pulls up the hidden file, retrieves the code, then waits for Nathan to go to the bathroom. As soon as he does, she takes a series of photos of the code with her burner phone.

The next morning Avizeh takes a walk past the hotel. She looks down the street, hoping she timed this just right. She pulls out her burner phone, with the full code written out from the screenshots she took, and sends it to the IP address of an NSA-run computer. Family photos begin to appear on her phone, video files, bank account listings, emails.

A message pops up saying, 'Deleting 1 of 9,491,475,377,398,383,445,578 files.'

Avizeh puts a hand on her mouth. She pulls the battery out of the back of her phone, knowing that somewhere the entire private history of every person in the United States is suddenly going to be private again; for a while at least.

A garbage truck noisily pulls up to the house just left of where she stands and Avizeh walks towards it. The garbage man lifts a nearby bin, calls, "Morning," to her and throws the waste into the back of the truck. As he replaces the bin, Avizeh walks past him and throws the phone into the open back.

*   *   *

"Come on!" she prods Nathan, "I'm starving, let's get food!"

"Okay, there's a nice bistro two blocks south—"

"No, the only good food is around Aston Park. Let's go!"

As soon as she sits down, Avizeh has her computer up and running. She finds the computer where she got the virus and copies the data to her laptop, then deletes the file on the suspicious computer. Next, she pulls up another computer in the area with white supremacist manifestos on it, makes a hidden file and puts the virus in it. Avizeh immediately reports the second computer to base, highlighting the suspicious code, while saying, "I found this dangerous code and subtly altered it so it wouldn't work in case the user tried to enter it. Here is a screen cap of the original. As you can tell, this is serious stuff."

Avizeh tries to keep her breathing level as she imagines

the entire security and intelligence apparatus of the world superpower whirling in a pool of chaos and fury at this unprecedented digital meltdown while she sits in a 1950s Americana diner waiting for French toast. Not five minutes after she returns to her hotel, a knock sounds from the door. She looks around at the walls, again feeling like she is trapped in a box. The knocking continues loudly and urgently and she gets up and walks to the door. She nearly jumps as Colonel Mueller stands before her in a gray suit, which seems too casual a thing for him to wear.

"Step back, let's talk," he says in a low voice. She does as she is told and sits on the far twin bed while he takes up a position on the near one. Avizeh breathes in, remembering the day she was caught with the dead man's teleporter. She eyes the stringent colonel sitting augustly across from her and realizes she can't remember Mueller ever leaving Fort Powell even for vacation. He has always been synonymous with the base itself, as if he is a specter haunting the southern rim of the world. His sudden ability to appear wherever she is makes her tremble.

Mueller reaches over and pulls the cord out of the phone on the bedside table. "Is your mobile off? Your laptop."

Avizeh takes the battery out of her phone and laptop.

"You did good work, very good. You're the first person to catch a Vanguard agent in... a while. They're a reclusive bunch, always hiding behind these techno-rocks, proxy servers, I don't know what the hell. But you did well. Unfortunately, not before they were able to unleash a massive virus to the NSA servers."

"Will they recover?"

"Oh yes. Mostly everything they had on file can be recaptured in a few weeks. But can you imagine if a terrorist was planning an attack today and we knew nothing? That's the thing about being a guard against the barbarians: you always have to man the wall, even if nothing's happened for years, the one day you sleep in might be the day a whole horde comes barreling down on civilization."

Avizeh struggles to regulate her breathing as it doesn't come to her naturally around the Colonel.

"But you caught the culprit. And that's one more win for democracy."

Avizeh summons up the courage to ask, "If I may ask a question, Colonel Mueller, why are you here?"

"Because these things need to be said in person, especially just following a massive security breach. I've been in non-stop communication with a host of different big-name players. They're all impressed by your work." He leans in and for the first time gives her what she thinks is an attempt at a friendly smile.

"Remember that door? The one that leads to your freedom? It's opening again. Jessica, how would you like to leave Fort Powell and make this your permanent job? Touring around the United States looking for cyber criminals? No more gunfights, no more mobs or strange foreign diseases. You'd get to live in the first world in luxury. You'd have to travel a lot but since you'd be in one country and you'd be going through the same areas every so often you could even make permanent links, have some friends, maybe even a love interest. He'd have to be government-approved of course, but you'd have a life. How does that sound?"

Avizeh looks into his eyes, wondering if he is serious. He seems to be, and regardless she can't remember a time he has ever told a joke.

A real life? I haven't had that since... no, don't say 'in over two years.' The real answer is never. I wonder what a real life would be like. A real life? A real life... The phrase seems hollower each time she silently repeats it.

You could have real friends who never know anything about

you. Your name would be Jessica Brown. What about Mikasa? Could I ever see her again? Is this my chance or... they would watch her every second. Her file would be one of the innumerable ones on a database accessed by thousands of agents. Every thought written down, every idea spoken, every word whispered would be monitored, recorded and examined. The better I do at my job the more they'll watch me and everyone around me. And if I do worse they might take away privileges. I might never see her again. He says that the door to freedom is opening, but that door to a life imprisonment will never close, will it? Or maybe they're the same thing.

"Can I have some time to think about it?"

Mueller's fake smile cracks and the frown that has always been underneath reappears. "I thought you would jump at the chance. Isn't this offer what you've always wanted?"

"It's a lot to take in all at once."

Mueller grimaces but the answer seems to placate him. "Good work, all the same. Do you think you've found any other Vanguard in the city?"

Avizeh shakes her head. "That's the only one. You were right about them being disparate. I figure Nathan and I will check out the rest of the city just to be safe, then leave for Knoxville."

"Okay," Mueller says as he stands up. "Think about the offer."

He pulls a teleporter out of his pocket, enters the coordinates and vanishes.

*   *   *

Nathan knocks on the door and asks Avizeh if she wants to go out. Still shaking, she tells him that she needs to "process some data," and has to stay in, which is enough to get him to return to his room and his latest book. For a long moment

Avizeh sits on the edge of her bed, staring at the opposite wall. Images and sounds cascade in a disconnected kaleidoscope through her mind of everything she has and everything lost. Her mother, father, Laily, Aamir, Clara, Jaina, James... Mikasa sitting beside her in her red cheongsam with golden dragon inlay, almond eyes smiling. That moment was the most beautiful of her life and the most haunting. In that moment Avizeh knew that her traumatic life hadn't permanently stunted her ability to love and be loved. That moment Mikasa's eyes told the woman from Farah that her next wedding will be flowers, sunlight and joy. That moment Avizeh held back from kissing her as she felt the presence of the American military and Colonel Mueller in every camera and suspicious glance. That was the moment when Mikasa became another stranger as she walked down the night market. Avizeh realizes that she is bouncing up and down as her feet tap nervously against the carpeted floor. Tears stream down puffy cheeks and meet under her chin before falling onto her t-shirt.

Avizeh continues to stare at the same spot as if the wall has all the answers she is looking for. From behind the wall she hears two children screech to the sound of popping bedsprings. An older male voice nearly shouts at them and a gentler, woman's voice tries to calm the entire room. Still bouncing on her heels, Avizeh looks out the room's window as lazy clouds float across the sky. Shouting continues through the far wall and Avizeh stands up and pounds on it, more out of restlessness than anger. In response a heavy thudding so loud she thinks the plaster might crack booms from the wall as the man's voice calls, "Why don't you shut up or I'll call the front desk!"

Avizeh puts her hands on her head. She grabs her laptop, pulls up YouTube and browses Japanese metal videos while turning her volume up to 100, hoping to drown out the dysfunctional family next door and her own thoughts.

Before she can press 'play' a command prompt appears on her computer with a line saying:

Safe comp?

Avizeh sits back and stares at the message.

0 she replies in the negative.

The command window disappears. Avizeh looks around madly, eyes scanning the walls just as the children next door begin to cry. She walks to the window and looks out at peaceful, downtown Asheville. She walks over to her phone, wondering if there is some sort of message for her and finds nothing in her texts, notepad, calendar or any other app. She walks back to her computer, waiting for something to happen. She stares at the screen for ten minutes, with shaking expectancy. When nothing happens she pulls up every document she has to find any hidden file that might have been altered. Despite twenty minutes of meticulous searching she finds nothing.

Avizeh returns to her Japanese metal, though the hellish screeching suddenly takes on a more ominous tone. *Apparently, Colonel Mueller isn't the only one who can appear at will.* She looks down at the comments section and sees that the top ten comments all say 'Hello. Come home, Spruce Eagle.' Avizeh reads the message over and over. She jumps up, walks to the door and peers out of the peephole. She steps outside and looks down the hall, seeing no one. She walks over to the next door and puts her ear to it. Nathan's snoring is so loud the door vibrates. With her guard sleeping and the world security apparatus busy repairing itself, Avizeh finds the courage to walk down the stairwell and out the door. She purposefully leaves her phone back in the room and doesn't know exactly where the intersection of Spruce and Eagle is, though she suddenly remembers a Japanese restaurant in the area and lets her stomach lead her east.

Asheville is a city that boasts a small town feel even in its skyscraper district, which Avizeh likes. Normally it feels peaceful, like an intimate community removed from the larger world, but between Mueller's unexpected arrival and this new intrusion she is very aware that the wider world and its problems are too big not to be everywhere at once, even in this tiny, sylvan city. Avizeh's stomach doesn't betray her and soon she finds herself at the corner of Spruce and Eagle.

Four people stand on the corner: two black women talking to each other, an elderly tan-skinned man, and a six-foot-tall, clean-shaven white man in a light blue sweater vest and glasses with trim dark hair. The crosswalk's walk sign flashes and the first three take off down the block. The tall man looks down at Avizeh and holds her gaze for a few seconds before turning away. She walks up next to him and waits. When the light turns again the two cross the street together. The tall man turns down a smaller street and Avizeh follows and, when he approaches a bar with a 'closed' sign in front, pulls out a set of keys and opens the door before turning to her.

"Cell phone?"

"Of course not."

He smiles. "Brave. Are you sure you want to follow me? You can still turn back."

"Are you going to do anything to me?" Avizeh asks without fear in her voice.

"That depends on what you tell me, Jessica."

The man opens the door and motions for her to step inside. Avizeh walks past him and hears the door close and lock behind her. He steps forward, his heavy feet pounding loudly against the wooden floor, and leads her past the bar and into the back room. The room is completely bare, with a single light illuminating three other men and a woman. One of the men, who sports countless freckles on his cheeks and unruly orange hair, walks directly up to her.

"I have to do this," he says as he starts patting her down. He reaches into her front pocket and pulls out her billfold, looks through it and starts taking out cards. One of the other men grabs a security wand and waves it over the billfold, then her.

"Nothing. You are interesting," the ginger remarks.

"Am I?"

"Let's start with introductions first," the tall man announces. "I'm John."

"Sam," the ginger introduces himself.

"Bruce," a portly man with trim brown hair and glasses calls.

"Uma," the dark-skinned woman says. "You must be Jessica. Jessica Brown..."

Sam the ginger smiles. "Fake name?"

"Yes, but so are yours."

Sam looks suspiciously at Bruce. "How do you know? Do you know us?"

"No, I haven't been spying on you personally. It's just your names are the same as the stars of the main actors from *Pulp Fiction*. John Travolta, Samuel Jackson, Bruce Willis and Uma Thurman. Sorry, Uma was obviously fake." Avizeh glances back at the ginger. "You seriously thought you could pull off Sam Jackson?"

'Sam' grins sheepishly and looks over at 'Uma' for support.

"In any case, Jessica," 'John' interrupts from behind her. "We are very curious about you. You had the chance to catch me and seriously hurt the Vanguard but you didn't. Our man on the inside told us that the virus was sent from a different computer unrelated to us, though we don't know who."

"I sent it, from a burner phone I destroyed. Then I copied the file, hid it in a white nationalist's computer and blamed it on him. I figured he's a really bad guy, he deserves what's coming to him."

Sam nods to the others with a mixture of gratitude and amazement at her gall.

"We have to ask; how did you find out about us?"

"I'm part of the top echelon of special ops intel. Our laptops have special Wi-Fi extensions called Infiltrators. They can connect to any computer within fifty meters, even if they aren't connected to the internet."

Uma turns to Bruce, eyebrows raised. "High-tech..."

"Yeah, wish we had that," Bruce whispers back.

"Well, we'll just have to factor that into our operations," John notes, though his uneven tone betrays his nervousness. "Why were you spying on us?"

"Because I've been assigned by the US government to find Vanguard members and alert agents who will arrest them. Actually, I just had a meeting with someone who offered me the job full-time. Usually I do intel stuff all over the world, but apparently 'traitors' are worse than terrorists."

Silence overtakes the room before Bruce says, "So, you're deep on the inside. How deep?"

"I work with the United States Navy Crisis Response Division in their Antarctic base at Fort Powell."

There is another pregnant silence as disbelief flashes across every face.

"Holy hell, you're right in the thick of it. And you have access to literally everything?" Bruce puts a hand on his head. "Every black operations, every dirty military secret, all hidden on offline servers thousands of kilometers from everything and you're here."

"Are you sure they exist?" John interrupts. "We had been spying on them until one of us was caught; then they went offline."

"I've seen it," Avizeh interrupts. "Hell, that used to be my job up there: looking at intel on everyone in the world on servers not directly connected to the net."

The room falls silent with the dread implication. "Well, you're exactly the type of person we've been looking for but never hoped to find," Uma explains. "So, why are you helping us?"

"Or appearing to," Sam interjects. "This could be an elaborate trap."

"Let's assume it's not," Avizeh replies. "I want to help you because I think what I've been doing is wrong. Spying on people, holding all their thoughts and memories on a file. When I sent out the virus do you know how many files they had? Ten sextillion files. English isn't my first language so I had to look up the word for it; I had never seen a number that big before. They have everything; every picture, video, phone and video conversation, every peer-to-peer exchange. Everything anyone has ever done in or around anything electronic that's more complicated than a microwave is on file. And I don't think that incredible power is often used for good. I've done missions abroad and I'm beginning to think at least a few of the powers that be aren't trying to stop the world from burning but just to control the blaze and make sure everyone gets burned but them. I don't want to be a part of that anymore which is why I need your help. I don't know how to leave."

"What do you mean?" John asks. "You can't retire? They won't let you become a civilian?"

"It's complicated," Avizeh replies. "They have dirt on me. I'm trapped. It's this or life imprisonment. Or death, I suppose whatever they feel like."

"Well, you might not like our strategy then." John glances at his three compatriots. Their silence communicates their approval and he continues. "You mentioned they have ten sextillion files? We want to release every single one of them to everyone."

Avizeh's mouth drops open. "Why? I thought the Vanguard was all about privacy and ending total surveillance. You want to release everything?"

"If English isn't your first language I'm guessing you're not American. And if I might assume, I'd say you're not from any first world country, so let me take another guess and say you don't know how the security state evolved. It has gone through a lot of battering and a lot of whistleblowers, but it's only gotten stronger. The sad truth is that Americans, British, French, Germans; they all know what their governments are doing. They know about the torture, they know they are all on file and someone at a desk in Pennsylvania or Utah gets to flip through all their bank accounts and their personal messages, they're aware of everything. But they won't stand up to it because they're afraid of being targeted individually. You work in the Crisis Response Division; you know that a battalion with guns can appear at any door in the world within a minute. For all those reasons, the people of the first world do nothing. They're content being quietly violated as long as they aren't obliterated. Now imagine: what if every single personal secret in the world was unleashed? What if every Congressman's emails detailing his under-the-table money and extramarital affairs were released to the voters? What if the minimum wage employees of every company got to go over the credit card and purchasing history of their managers? What if every time a cop shot an unarmed civilian the email exchanges between officer and their superiors covering it up made its way into the public domain? That's the only way to finally free the people of the 'free' world. How can the government blackmail anyone when everything is public?

"Furthermore, one of the security state's favorite tactics is finding out what illegal things people have done; our law system is so comprehensive even using someone's Wi-Fi without permission is a crime. Then what the government does is if they suspect someone of developing a radical agenda or joining a terrorist organization they use their old crimes as justification to lock them up without ever having to prove they were dangerous. Do drugs once in high school to fit in and ten years later when you share a cup of coffee with a white supremacist preacher, that charge will come back and you'll disappear into a prison cell and be labeled a felon and effectively removed from society. But what if every criminal record was made public? What if everyone got to find out about their bosses' criminal records, their lawyers, the police officer arresting them, the judge convicting them, the pastor condemning them? Would the labels 'criminal' and 'felon' still be used to crush so many people in our society when all of us would fit the bill to some degree?

"That's our strategy. We've already set up servers all around the country, the world, hell, we even have a few drones with jury-rigged high-powered Wi-Fi hotspot generators that can host the data from the sky. We have a system in place that's so extensive the government couldn't remove the data unless they shut down the whole internet. Everyone would be able to access all data and once everyone becomes a victim then people will finally be empowered to fight against any organization that would make a system like this, because when everyone is a victim then the government will have no power over their citizens."

Avizeh looks up and meets John's gaze as she judges whether or not he is serious. She turns to the other three and sees in their faces the look of true believers.

"I don't know," Avizeh replies. She realizes a second later that she said the same thing earlier under very different circumstances. "I have met a lot of people who were willing to hurt innocents in the name of the greater good."

"We understand," John speaks for all of them. "Here, take a minute and memorize these sites," he says while handing her a piece of paper with the names 'Holly's Pet Supply Shop' and 'Everything Cats.'

"We communicate through product reviews. A rating of five out of five paws means you want a meet-up. We can determine your location if you just leave a review."

Avizeh memorizes the sites and returns her gaze to the man towering over her. "It might be a while before I can contact you; if I do. I'll be working around the US or abroad for the next eight months at least."

John visibly tightens. "When you get back then. Use those links anywhere in the country. We have people all around, but especially in Boston."

Avizeh nods. "Well..."

"Well, that's it," Bruce says from the corner. "Pleasure to meet you, Jessica."

"You too Bruce. Sam. Uma," she says, oddly amused that they all have fake names, though they at least got to choose theirs.

John opens the door he has been guarding and the two walk to the old bar's exit where he unlocks it and ushers her out.

"Five paws out of five. We'll be looking."

*   *   *

Avizeh doesn't bother bringing her laptop as she and Nathan relax at a bar in Nashville. The lights are low and a man in a cowboy hat is doing a halfway decent Johnny Cash cover. Their food arrives and she picks at her chicken salad while Nathan finishes the last few pages of his latest crime thriller. He closes the book and puts it down on the table and cuts up his enormous steak.

"Where did you serve, again?" Avizeh asks.

"Western Iraq, Eastern Syria, parts of Kurdistan."

"What was it like?"

"Hot," he says before taking another bite.

"See any action?"

"Lots."

Avizeh sighs and looks down at her food. She thinks of Omar. *His stories were probably lies but at least they were entertaining!* She isn't hungry but figures she should finish before she has to live off re-heated base grub.

"Did you have to kill anyone?"

Nathan looks up. "It's not like in the movies. You can't always tell who you got or who the guy next to you did. I would say I killed between two and six."

"Are you proud to have served?"

"Yes."

"More than this?"

He shrugs. "It's a job."

"So, serving abroad was just a job?"

"Mostly."

Avizeh quickly grows frustrated. His short answers are unappreciated as she is being torn between two extremes and desperately searching for a voice of reason in a world gone mad.

"Do you have a family?"

"An ex-wife, not sure if that counts, and a kid. He's off at college, first year."

"If you could be my bodyguard, or the bodyguard of some techie, or be back in the Middle East, what would you be doing?"

"I'm here because I'd rather be here. I'm done with firefights and the like."

Avizeh shakes her head and returns to her plate. She didn't even come close to asking him about patriotism or whether he thinks what they and the government are doing is morally right or even permissible. In Afghanistan nearly any topic could be dangerous; blasphemy and slander in particular were real crimes with deadly consequences. As such, Avizeh learned to be subtle and could talk about the weather or food and covertly tell someone what she thought about God, fate and sexuality. Nathan is a true American, of the blue-collar, white, hetero, male variety; the kind who has grown up with the ability to spit in the wind and not get hit. Subtlety and double-meaning fly right over his head, but the one thing she can tell about him is that what he does is far more a personal matter than any national calling, and that is telling. He either chooses not to talk about patriotism and national interests or chooses not to care.

Disillusioned or disinterested, Nathan reminds her of her uncle and many of the other men in her village. One thing the warlords had managed to do in Farah and throughout the whole of Afghanistan was kill any national or religious zeal of the common people. Everyone she knew had some desire to live in peace and free of influence from their more powerful neighbors or Western powers, but supporting one political party or faction could get you killed by another and if someone was foolish enough to speak out against a powerful politician or warlord, everyone who valued their head took two steps back until the inevitable happened. Strange how the world she now inhabits, which is completely different in some ways, is exactly the same in others, as if the only universals are strife and chaos, while friendship and love are rare, hidden treasures. And now the Vanguard wants her to unleash a level of chaos that the modern world has never seen before.

Avizeh closes her eyes in consternation as she tries to choose one of the two terrible paths laid out before her. The talented singer steps down from the karaoke machine and two drunk girls perform a horribly off-key rendition of Gretchen Wilson's "Redneck Woman" to the screeching bachelorette party at the next table over and Avizeh abandons far-off moral quandaries, suddenly pining for the silence of Antarctica.

Chapter Sixteen
Between Two Extremes

Upon her return, Colonel Mueller gives Avizeh a last briefing on her progress in America. He is more curt with her than usual, apparently disgusted that she won't immediately do exactly as he wishes. When pressed, she tells him that she has her vacation coming up and will think about it then. After that he practically shoves her out the door.

Clara still hasn't returned to base and Avizeh doesn't even bother asking anyone about her whereabouts, despite the gnawing pit opening in her stomach. To her surprise, Jaina takes a seat next to her at the mess hall and the two actually have a friendly chat. *At least I have one friend up here, even if she's a friend at arm's length.*

Avizeh tries to imagine what course her life will take depending on which decision she makes. She could accept Mueller's offer and track down the Vanguard and other anarcho-libertarian hackers. By tracking them down she could finally live in peace, never afraid of hunger or violence again. Eventually she could even retire and have a normal life. *When I'm an old crone, but that is a better deal than any I've received before.*

The other option is to heed the Vanguard's call and try to remake the world. Yet, Avizeh harbors doubts about the true effects of their grand scheme. *What if every person got to read the personal diaries and communications of the people they have a crush on? If everyone in the world knew everyone's internet and purchasing history would that really create a more harmonious society? What about all the employees who bad-mouthed their bosses and fellow co-workers? What would happen to them? If every petty criminal who stole to feed their families had their information released, how could they ever get a job? What if every teenager or child who was questioning whether they were gay or transsexual had their confessions released to their hell-and-brimstone parents? What if everyone who was cheating on their spouse had their secrets revealed to their families? Perhaps there is such a thing as too much truth.* On top of all that, the Vanguard's choice would mean either life imprisonment or execution, with torture a definitive possibility.

The one thing they claim to be able to give her is a clean conscience, but the method they are hoping to use wouldn't just remove the walls around the state and big business; it would have the effect of undressing everyone in America and beyond, leaving every previously-covered blemish open to all. *Isn't secrecy meant to protect just that? Isn't secrecy's purpose to protect the weak against the strong?* The more she thinks about it the more Avizeh thinks that the Vanguard are less like idealistic freedom fighters and more like self-fanaticizing social outcasts looking to use their skills in the most grandiose and destructive way possible.

After eating, Jaina and Avizeh part ways. While her ginger confidante trudges to the intel room, Avizeh realizes that she has nothing to do but wait. Standing between the mess and the women's dormitory she looks up at the half-red sky and wishes for a clear moral choice. *God give me a sign, if you're there. If I knew what was right I would do it, but I don't. Am I good regardless of which decision I make because of my intentions? Or am I damned by either choice? Or is this limbo I'm living in and you are just my own silence? That's what God is, right? God is how we interpret the silence.*

Avizeh closes her eyes and slows her breathing. She thinks of Mikasa and sees her eyes-closed smile as she sits beside her at a bar. Avizeh feels Mikasa's hair as it drapes across her shoulders while they kiss. She sees her body beneath the water as she bathes next to her. Suddenly Mikasa is sitting next to her, shoulder to shoulder in a small bus on a bumpy road and Avizeh is completely at peace. She has a friend who knows her secrets while accepting her. She loses herself in a crowd of people. She has a destination and a clear purpose that she is moving towards. A scream tears through the bus. Drums played by a man who must have four hands pound in rhythm to a screeching guitar all while a wailing ghoul cry out beside it. Avizeh looks over and Mikasa is making devil horns and bobbing her head.

Avizeh smiles and remembers the list containing Mikasa's personal contact information when an image of the websites 'Holly's Pet Supply Shop' and 'Everything Cats' alongside a review with five paws appears beside it. The Afghan spy shakes her head and decides it's time to step out of the cold.

*   *   *

Avizeh stands on the platform with a suitcase in her left hand and teleporter in her right. She closes her eyes, wary of the vertigo that comes with sudden displacement, and presses the button. The air is suddenly lighter and warmer, and the sound of wind and ocean waves mix with the echo of distant cars. Avizeh opens her eyes and sees the familiar sight of an American sergeant standing next to his local counterpart, this time an Australian. She enters a barracks and trades her winter clothes for jeans and a blue t-shirt before hopping onto a bus to Perth. Avizeh searches for the nearest internet café, sets up a new email account and emails Mikasa a message saying, "Here waiting, every day 1pm-4pm by the Bell Tower." As soon as she finishes she deletes the account and leaves.

Avizeh figures Mikasa can't make it to Perth from Japan in time to meet her within a day and spends the afternoon touring the city, discovering where all the museums and historic places are located without actually going inside in case Mikasa is interested in them. At noon the following day Avizeh heads over to the Bell Tower and waits outside the Atrium for Mikasa to arrive. Her stomach growls after waiting for two hours and she purchases a turkey sandwich from a street vendor. Four-thirty comes and Avizeh's eyes scan the crowds for Mikasa. Six o' clock comes and Avizeh forces herself to march back to her hotel.

The next day Avizeh walks the riche district of Perth, admiring the ranch-style mansions colored pink, blue and a dozen other gaudy colors. Just after noon she returns to the tower and waits until sunset. She returns by eleven the next day, and the sandwich vendor preemptively asks, "The usual?" as she walks by. The following day Avizeh decides to go to the beach before heading back to the square. When she arrives she nearly doesn't recognize Mikasa in oversized sunglasses and wide-brim yellow sun hat.

"What took you so long?"

"Mikasa!" Avizeh's eyes light up. Under her breath she adds, "There are cameras everywhere here. Play it cool."

"Sure thing, Jessica." Mikasa smiles back.

"So, what shall we do first? There's lots of beaches, and museums..."

"Let's rent a car and go out into the desert!"

Avizeh smirks, cursing herself for not visiting the museums when she had a chance.

"You made me want to see stars."

"Okay," Avizeh leans in again, "but how about we take a bus out to somewhere small, then we rent a car from there? The more convoluted our trip, the harder it is to track."

"Whatever you say, Jessica."

Avizeh walks over to the vendor and grabs "two of the usual" before setting off. By evening they arrive in Northam and Avizeh hands a huge wad of cash over to Mikasa who returns from the nearby *Enterprise* with a blue Jeep which the manager assures them would meet any off-roading challenge.

"Have you ever driven off-road before?"

"Psh! I've hardly driven. It's all mass transit in Japan and I can't afford a car. That's why this will be extra exciting."

Off-road adventures have to wait as they are still too near to civilization. Avizeh points out a cheap motel and secures a reservation under a fake name. As soon as they are inside she throws her bag in the corner, pulls the blinds and walks over to Mikasa. She grabs Mikasa's oversized hat and tosses it aside. The glasses come off next, revealing Mikasa's beautiful deep-brown eyes. Avizeh leans in and kisses her.

Avizeh groans. "Do you know how long I've waited for this?"

"As long as I have."

*   *   *

Lounging in bed and a long brunch delays their departure until eleven when they take to the road, windows down, wind blowing in their faces, radio on full blast as they speed out into the bush.

"This is really the middle of nowhere," Mikasa muses after

three hours of driving. "Does it remind you of home?"

"Which home?" Avizeh replies.

"You know what I mean. It's been a while since you've lived in Afghanistan, right?"

"It has. This is nicer."

"There's lots of things here that can kill you. Snakes, spiders, scorpions, crocodiles, sharks, jellyfish, stingrays—"

"As long as the people won't bother me, I'm not worried."

"Really? Does that mean you'll help me catch a scorpion?"

Avizeh gives Mikasa a look that she hopes she can see through her oversized sunglasses.

"I hear scorpions don't kill, they just hurt a lot. Wouldn't it be so cool to have a pet scorpion? I think that's the only cool thing that you don't already have, Avizeh."

"Do you really think a scorpion would do well in Antarctica?" Avizeh laughs at the thought.

"Hmm, I didn't think about that. It'd probably be really, really pissed and try to sting everyone. Maybe we should catch a spider instead."

As night falls they pull into another motel around Newman. The next morning, they take off early and within an hour they arrive in the Little Sandy Desert when Mikasa suddenly swerves off road, tearing through a landscape of orange dirt interspersed with patches of green grass.

"Tree!" Avizeh calls out.

Mikasa just barely dodges the lone white sentinel. She laughs nervously and looks over at Avizeh, who tears her hat off.

"Are you actually angry?" Mikasa tries and fails to look hurt through giggles.

"Drive better." Avizeh bites her tongue.

"I'm sorry... Do you want to drive?"

Avizeh pauses. "I've never driven before."

"Well, then this will be a great learning experience, as long as the traffic doesn't kick up."

The vacationing American spy gazes at the empty lands around them. She smiles and nods while Mikasa brings the Jeep to a stop. Avizeh steps outside, walks around the car and takes Mikasa's place.

"Okay, so it's in four-wheel now so you should be good. You're going to want to only use one foot. Right's the gas, left's the brake. And... this is the wheel."

The excited Afghan puts her foot down gently.

"Avizeh, the next tree is one hundred meters that way and it's a little to the right. You can go faster."

She smiles and urges the Jeep forward, enough to feel the wind through her hair.

"Faster!" Mikasa cries and Avizeh presses on the gas and they tear across the open landscape.

*   *   *

A week of hiking and driving through the Australian deserts eventually leads them to Katherine, a small town almost entirely concealed by an impenetrable forest of palm trees. Mikasa parks the Jeep, now thoroughly caked with dirt, and the two step onto the outside patio of a small café.

"I think I'm ready for a hot shower. Care to stay here a few days?"

Mikasa nods. "This is not a bad place to lay low. Could use more air-conditioning though."

A perky, short, blonde-haired waitress who looks just barely in her teens steps up beside their table.

"Hello, I'm Amanda, what can I get for you?"

"Espresso, with—"

In the middle of Avizeh's sentence a shocked look comes across Amanda's face. "One second!" she says while running to the lawn next door. Stunned, the two girls turn to watch their runaway server as she rushes towards a parrot with a red breast, blue head and green back in the middle of stumbling awkwardly across the lawn. Suddenly, it topples over and lays still on the ground. Amanda picks up the parrot, which hardly struggles before falling asleep, and walks back to the restaurant, cooing. She grabs a cloth from an empty table and gently places the bird on top, pulls out a cell phone and has a brief conversation before returning to their table.

"I'm so sorry about that."

"That's okay," Avizeh interrupts. "What's wrong with the bird?"

"Oh, this happens every fall. The parrots eat fermented berries which gets them drunk. They can't fly, they fall out of trees and then they stumble about, poor things. We send them over to the local hospital, which takes care of them until the hangover passes."

"Are there lots of parrots around here that do that?"

"Oh yeah, there's more birds than people here, which is why a lot of them are missed. Most of them recover, but when a bird goes a day or two without eating it can be dangerous to their health. There's only one person I know who volunteers for full time bird patrol, otherwise the people of Katherine have to keep our eyes open for them; it's what makes this little town special."

The two women order their drinks and as their server departs Mikasa gives Avizeh a coy grin. "As soon as we finish drinking we need to go on bird patrol."

Avizeh nods. "We can be just the heroes this town needs."

"And we'll be going so slowly even you can drive, Grandma."

Midway through coffee and scones a burly older man with a straw hat and long beard pulls up in his pickup truck in front of the café, grabs a birdcage and walks up to the parrot, where he scoops the sleeping bird into his callused hands and gently deposits it inside.

Avizeh lays a twenty-dollar bill on the table and the pair stand up and chase after the man.

"Excuse me?"

The bearded man turns to face Avizeh.

"Hello, my name's Jessica and this is Mikasa, we heard about your bird problem. I was wondering if we could help."

"Well, hello. Name's Mike." He reaches out with his free hand. "You have a car?"

Avizeh nods to their Jeep while shaking his hand.

"If you're serious about helping out I'll show you to the hospital, who to talk to, and I'll give you a few tips."

Mikasa sits in the driver's seat and the two follow Mike down the road. The hospital on the edge of town is barely three minutes away but the palm trees and brush are so thick Avizeh feels she could still get lost trying to find it again. Inside, Mike introduces them to a nurse named Ellie who serves as the unofficial 'bird specialist' of the day.

"It's hard to catch the sick birds since the vegetation is so thick; I doubt you'll see many just stumbling about the ground. If you see birds in trees who aren't singing, they could be sick. Watch those carefully a few minutes because they might just fall out."

Avizeh nods and steps out beside her partner, ready to go on bird patrol. She drives slowly through the residential areas, looking up at the trees, and after a few minutes they pass a flock of parrots. Avizeh parks the car and they step out and watch them when Mikasa pulls out her phone and takes a picture. Avizeh gives her a look. Mikasa groans and takes the battery out of her phone.

"I just wanted a quick one of the birds. I didn't want a picture of you anyway." She smiles.

After ten minutes of listening to birdsong, the two return

to the car and circle the town's tiny suburbs. After driving through the entire town six different times Mikasa yells, "Stop!"

Avizeh slams on the brakes and the dirty blue Jeep, which had been cruising at four kilometers an hour, comes to an abrupt halt. The two leap out of the car and run up to the nearest tree. Perched on one of its low-hanging branches a lone parrot teeters, its eyes fluttering open and closed, when suddenly it leans forward. Avizeh runs to intercept it, arms outstretched. The tiny bird falls and she deftly catches it in her hands. She gazes in awe at its brilliant plumage as it looks up at her and tries to struggle clumsily before closing its eyes.

"Oh my god, that was amazing!" Mikasa walks up and runs a hand across the tips of its wing feathers.

The two return to the car where Mikasa takes the wheel while Avizeh gently strokes the bird's head. Within minutes they arrive at the hospital where Avizeh hands the bird over to Ellie, who takes it to a small room filled with cages. She puts the bird inside one with a bowl of fruit and the sleepy bird nibbles at the food before falling over.

"I've had a few hangovers like that before," Ellie observes. "He'll be all right. Good job."

Bird patrol lasts another three hours and only one other bird is saved, albeit in far less dramatic fashion, before the two decide to call it a night and pull into a B&B, feeling like heroes.

*   *   *

Avizeh lies beside Mikasa, drenched in sweat, panting, eyeing Mikasa, who smiles, eyes closed. She kisses her cheek, then her lips.

"You're insatiable."

Avizeh kisses her again before resting her head on Mikasa's chest.

"I only ever feel free and like myself when I'm with you."

Mikasa runs her fingers through Avizeh's hair.

"When I'm with you, my life is an adventure, and I never know what we'll do next, but that's what makes it fun." The Afghan spy turns to look at her lover. "Do you feel the same way?"

"I do. I've traveled and met all kinds of people. Friends, lovers. They're all fun, but after the first few days their flaws come out and the excitement and affection begins to fade." Mikasa brushes a lock of Avizeh's hair aside. "You're the one person in my life that never disappoints me."

Avizeh smiles, her eyes watering.

Mikasa breathes in deeply and her eyes lose some of their luster as her face takes on a somber complexion. "Will it always be like this? Six months pass and then we have a couple weeks together? There's no way you can get away?"

Avizeh runs her hand along Mikasa's cheek. "I don't think so."

"What does that mean?"

"It means anything I do to try to get away could put you in danger, and I don't want to do that... because I love you."

A long moment of silence hangs between the two. Avizeh gazes at Mikasa, who looks out towards the window.

"I..."

Avizeh feels her breath catch in her throat as she waits for the next words.

"You know I feel the same way about you, but I'm not sure I can keep on the way we are. I want to be with you, settle somewhere and start a life with you. What we have shouldn't be a fling every six months; it can't be."

Mikasa takes an audible breath. Avizeh tries to read her eyes, the way her chest rises and falls, but Mikasa's being has suddenly slipped from her and she becomes mysterious and unknowable. After what feels like a silent eternity Mikasa turns to meet her gaze. "I've been close to a lot of people but I've never felt the same about anyone. But what future do we have? You're wonderful Avizeh, but…"

"I love you," Avizeh repeats.

Mikasa opens her mouth but no words come back. She lays her head back on the bed and closes her eyes, leaving her lover to ponder the all-encompassing silence.

*   *   *

They hit every red light on their way into Melbourne and every time they do Avizeh yearns to seize the moment and say something but each moment passes and they keep moving towards the inevitable 'goodbye.' Avizeh sees the rental car parking lot as they near the airport and her insides disappear. Mikasa parks the car and looks over at her partner. Avizeh opens her mouth and waits for the words to come. Before she can think of anything, Mikasa opens her door and steps outside. They turn over the keys and ride a crowded bus to the airport.

Surrounded by hundreds of people rushing around them, Mikasa turns to her and announces solemnly, "Thanks for the fun times, Jessica."

Avizeh reaches out as if to hug her, then catches sight of a security camera. "See you in six months."

Without so much as a backward glance Mikasa steps through a revolving door and out of sight. The second she disappears from view, Avizeh's insides go cold. She takes a step forward and looks through the glass, trying to see her. Part of her screams that she should chase her, stop her from getting on her flight. But she already told Mikasa she loves her and apparently that wasn't enough.

"You're wonderful Avizeh, but..." repeats in her mind a thousand times. She imagines Mikasa going to a bar and meeting someone else. Avizeh imagines growing older, visiting a city and waiting for Mikasa to appear only for the sun to set, leaving her alone.

"You're wonderful Avizeh, but..."

Her words were so similar to what Clara said the first time she left. "I care about you Avizeh. But..."

Avizeh realizes that this is her life. Every friend, every love will always be held at arm's length. *I'm not just trapped in a cage; I'm trapped in a cage alone.*

Avizeh puts her hands over her face and weeps.

*   *   *

Why is it that the safest choices I can make make me feel sick, while my most dangerous are the only ones that feel right? Does anyone else feel like I do? Does everyone, but no one admits it? Do we all have the same desires and sympathies, yet always fail to connect with anyone because of intractable barriers put up by society? Why do I always have such high-minded thoughts right before making terrible decisions?

Jessica Brown waits until dark to slip out of her hostel. She walks down a series of narrow streets, walks up the stairs of a small apartment complex and pounds on a random door. A strikingly thin blonde woman in her mid-twenties wearing a tank top and short shorts answers. Before the woman can speak Avizeh holds out a large wad of cash. "I need to use a computer for an hour or so. Can I use yours?"

The woman stares incredulously from the money back to Avizeh. "What do you need it for?"

Avizeh reaches into her jacket and pulls out another wad of cash. "Is this enough that I don't have to answer your question?"

The woman's eyes widen, her eyebrows shoot near the top of her head and her mouth drops. "You're not like, a terrorist or anything? I'm not being racist, I have lots of indigenous friends, I just mean, it's a bit odd."

"I'm making a big cryptocurrency transfer but I want to avoid taxes by using another computer. Don't worry, I won't even use your computer's IP. I'll use a VPN, log into a proxy server, access a zombie comp, then repeat the process until the whole thing is untraceable."

The woman looks at her blankly and Avizeh realizes she probably doesn't know how to do anything more complicated than share selfies. She rolls her eyes, reaches into her jacket again and pulls out another wad of cash, holding forth enough money to cover the meager apartment's rent for the next five years. "Take it or I'm going next door."

The flummoxed woman stands still until Avizeh makes to move. She grabs Avizeh's hand and says, "All right, come in, come in." The woman introduces herself as, "Brandi," and leads Avizeh through a living room whose décor is best described as a mix between tactful hoarding and chaos theory. A unicorn plushie rests on a coffee table beside sketches of the cityscape. Old pillows of all different colors are strewn haphazardly across a new couch. Posters of old movies and indie bands cover nearly every inch of the wall.

"You didn't tell me we were having company." A brunette emerges from a bathroom, her wet hair tied up in a teal towel.

"She won't be here for long, she just needed, um, something," Brandi replies and hides the money behind her back while pulling Avizeh forward. Brandi pushes her guest into a tiny room littered with posters of boy bands on the walls and with barely enough space for a twin bed, desk and wastebasket. Dim dirty-yellow streetlight filters through a window overlooking a dirty alley. "It's not much but with rents s'high I'm lucky to have it."

Avizeh ignores her and sits down at the computer. "Can you enter the password?"

Brandi leans over and accesses the computer, still eyeing her guest suspiciously. "Anything else?" she asks, though she hardly sounds accommodating.

"Just privacy," Avizeh replies. "You don't want to be here anyway; it's all just lines of code."

Avizeh waits until Brandi closes the door before she begins. She scrambles the computer's IP and runs through a series of proxy servers like she said she would. Then, instead of running an e-currency scam, she opens up a video chat window and waits, utterly breathless. A minute passes without answer. Avizeh takes a deep breath and calls again. Another minute passes with no response. Frustrated, she leans back in the chair and puts her hands on the side of her head. She grabs a pink, frilly pillow from the nearby bed, presses it against her face and screams. Mentally and emotionally spent, she drops it to the floor.

"What do I do?" she says to no one. She sends a video request again. This time it is almost immediately answered. A handsome youth with stunning hazel eyes, night-black hair and dark stubble across his face returns her gaze with a surprised smile.

"Avizeh!" he cries. "My beautiful sister!"

The displaced Afghan laughs and cries at the same time. "Aamir! Wow, you look... really good."

"I know." He smiles and strokes his incoming beard.

"I bet you drive the Iranian women crazy."

"I do," he replies with a bit of a laugh, "but I have to mind my manners, you know? We're still refugees and all."

"Oh yeah? Is that official now?"

Aamir nods. "We got our papers and everything five months ago, which is a relief, since it means Father and I can work and Laily can go to school. I hear her school's not the best, but compared to what we left behind."

The two share a laugh. "Are you liking Mashhad? You always said you wanted to move to a big city."

"I didn't think I'd be broke. Look at this, I have to share a bedroom with Laily. We hardly have anything and she still makes a mess." He grins and waves at a small pile of clothes on the floor. "And she sheds too. Hair everywhere. It's like having a cat. You never did that."

"I wasn't allowed to show my hair!"

"But you can now, wherever you are. It looks good long. I like seeing you smile too."

Avizeh's eyes water and she changes the subject away from herself. "So you're having a good time?"

"Yeah, you know it's not a palace but we're all alive, together and safe. For a long time none of that was certain. We were in a camp for nearly a year and there was always a chance we were going to be deported back. That was incredibly scary. I'm thankful we all made it."

Avizeh nods. "I am too."

After a brief pause wherein the two wait for the other to speak, Aamir says, "Do you want me to get the rest of the family?"

"Are they all home?"

"It's the weekend," Aamir replies, "and we're too broke to go out and do anything." He pauses for a moment. "Do you want to talk to everyone?" He emphasizes the last word.

There is a pause and Avizeh takes a breath. They look into each other's eyes and know each is thinking about the last time they were together, when her father grabbed her before she fought him off and disappeared. "Yes, you can tell them."

Aamir gives her one last sympathetic look, stands up and opens the door. "Hey, everyone come over here, I want to show you something."

"I don't care about football plays, or which club you're fanboying over today," Laily retorts.

"What is it?" Their mother acts the peacekeeper.

"Just get in here," Aamir says. He bends down and picks up a sea-green hijab with shining faux-silver trim and says, "Laily, get in here or I'll use this to blow my nose."

"Don't you dare, you prick!"

"Language!" her father calls out. "How can you find a quality husband if you act so crudely?"

"I'm about—" Aamir lifts the hijab and opens his mouth as if stifling a sneeze.

Laily jumps up and leaps after Aamir. He drops the hijab and puts his arms up defensively as she thumps him wildly. Suddenly Laily catches sight of the screen. "Avizeh!" She nearly screams and runs to the desk. She nearly bursts into tears at the sight of her long-lost sister. Watching her choke up brings tears to Avizeh's eyes.

Laily has changed so much since the last time Avizeh saw her. She wears her long night-black hair down past her shoulders. Unlike Afghanistan, in Iran women can expose their face and can wear loose-fitting hijabs in public. Her soft face is more defined as she develops from a pretty girl to a beautiful woman. As far as Avizeh can tell she is nearly as tall as Aamir, who is now just shorter than her.

Behind her sister, their mother steps into the room. Unlike her more liberated daughters, the matron of the Fatah family covers every part of her body, save for her shocked face. Finally, a thin, gaunt man steps inside the doorframe. Her father betrays no emotion as he looks upon the screen from the far end of the room.

"My baby, how are you? Are you safe?" Her mother starts to cry just looking at her.

Avizeh bites her lip to keep from bawling. "I'm fine, Mother," *not entirely a lie,* "I'm so glad to see you all safe and doing well."

"But what about you? I haven't seen you in two years! Where did you go?"

Avizeh realizes she hasn't thought of a lie, and she knows *it's a long story* won't cut it. "I got picked up by Americans. I've been living as a refugee too," *again not entirely a lie* she tells her conscience. "I can't say where I am now but I'm nowhere near where you are. I wish I could see you."

"I want to see you too, my baby girl. Is there any way you can come here?"

Not unless the Ayatollah and the US President suddenly become BFFs. "No. I had to risk a lot just to talk to you. This isn't my room, as you can probably tell." She waves at the posters of young men walking on beaches trying to look mysterious. "Not my style."

"I should hope not," Laily replies, "their music is terrible. Do you still listen to Persian pop?"

"Of course," Avizeh replies, "but you're closer to the scene than me. Have you been able to go to a concert yet?"

"I want to, but tickets are so expensive. I have friends—"

"Of all the things we could be talking about!" her mother interrupts.

Avizeh smiles, wishing they would talk about simple, unimportant things. She watches the three crowd around the camera while her father looms in the background, unsure of what he should say or do. Her mother notices and turns to him. "Hadad, come here and see our daughter."

"I can see her," he replies.

A knot clenches in Avizeh's stomach. For so long her father had been an imposing figure in her life. His once-imposing frame seems frail, his proud eyes tired. Defiance wells up in her as she sees the same posturing and demand for respect in him as in Colonel Mueller. "Hello Baba," she uses the familial, even childish address, trying to squeeze some compassion from his hard veneer. "I've missed you."

"Then you shouldn't have run away," he replies evenly.

To Avizeh's surprise Aamir turns to him. "Is this what you want to say to your daughter? She could have been dead for all we knew and now she is alive and you rebuke her?"

"She should be with us instead of wherever that is." He waves at the screen.

"I did come back, but you tried to sell me away," Avizeh replies. She watches her father tense. "Remember? When I returned you grabbed me and said you would give me to Razaaq's replacement."

"At least we could have remained in our home, instead of living here like caged animals."

His words cut Avizeh deeper than she thought possible. The rest of her family waits breathlessly. Her mother looks suddenly looks so tired. Aamir and Laily appear on the verge of yelling at their father, but Avizeh speaks first, unwilling to share her suffering with anyone else. "Is that what we were doing before, Baba? Living?" She meets his gaze and sees him recognize a strength he never knew she had. "A murderer came to our village with a gun and said he wanted me and you let him take me. Americans started a fight and tore our home to pieces. Then his followers robbed our family of everything we had left. I risked my life to come back and be with our family and the moment you saw me you tried to give me away without even knowing if I would be safe or if it would even help you."

The shadow in the far corner of the screen takes the beating without the slightest show of emotion. His stubbornness galls her to no end. "I never abandoned my family. You abandoned me." Avizeh watches him tense. She means for the words to hurt. She would needle him in any way she could just to pry some emotion from him. Beneath her venom she wants to know he cares. Yet, she still loves him as only a daughter can love her Baba.

Avizeh lowers her eyes and lets two teardrops fall on her jeans. "I don't hate you," she says and looks up. "You tried to do what you thought was right. You tried to be a strong figure and keep us all together. But the world is bigger than you. You couldn't stop them from taking me the first time. You couldn't stop Fahima's family from taking her away. You tried to do the best you could and it didn't matter." She squeezes two more tears out, which trail down her cheeks as she thinks about how she bore out her heart and said the most meaningful words anyone could speak, 'I love you,' to Mikasa. *It didn't matter then either.* "But we are where we are now. The world won't be any kinder to you if you keep hating me."

Avizeh watches her family through the screen. All eyes turn to Baba. Slowly, he turns and walks out of view. Avizeh closes her eyes and bites her lip. She takes a deep breath and wipes her eyes, feeling sick of shedding tears that change nothing. *Stubborn ass,* she thinks of him and most everyone.

"Avizeh," her mother speaks from across the world. "I'm proud of you. I don't know what you've been through but you are a survivor. I've prayed for you every day, thinking you were dead or barely clinging on. But you have grown so much, becoming beautiful and wise. I will change my prayers and ask Allah to let us see each other again one day. Now I know that no matter what, you will be all right."

Avizeh meets her mother's look and gives the slightest smile.

"I love you too Avizeh," Laily joins in. "I've always admired you. You'll have to tell me all about what you've been doing some time though. I bet it's quite the story."

Avizeh actually laughs, confirming her suspicions.

"Miss you sis," Aamir says. "I'd much rather share a room with you than Laily." At that she playfully pushes him and

Aamir holds out his hands towards her as if to say *see?*

"I miss you too. I am so happy knowing you are all safe," Avizeh replies. "I..." She pauses. She doesn't know what she means to say, though she feels she cannot emotionally take much more. "Thank you," is all she says.

Her family pours out a stream of love and Avizeh smiles while fighting back tears. They talk for what feels like an eternity and hardly any time at all. Avizeh hears footsteps beside the door and imagines Brandi resting her ear on the other side. She decides to wrap up the conversation and bids them a heartfelt 'goodbye.' She wants more; absolution, guidance, reconciliation with her father. As is usual in the lost woman's life, nothing is simple. The glass is always half-full. Every sweet has a bitter aftertaste. Every answer leads to more questions.

Avizeh stands up and turns off the computer. She wipes her eyes one last time and exits the room. Brandi and her roommate are sitting on the couch and turn to look at her.

"I couldn't connect properly, so nothing happened." Avizeh decides to calm her worries before she leaves. "You can keep the money though, I don't care." She passes by and grabs the door handle.

As she leaves she hears a shrill voice ask, "What money? You finally have my share of the damn rent?"

Chapter Seventeen
Choices

Avizeh stands on the teleportation platform feeling the cold steel in her hand, eyeing it like the door handle to her prison. She expects another week of mostly silent torture upon her return to Fort Powell and a birthday spent alone. All the while Colonel Mueller will hover in the background with his offer of 'freedom,' and threats if she doesn't take his offer. One second she is sweating as she stands in a thick winter coat in midday sweltering heat and the next she feels subzero chill turn the sweat on her face into flecks of ice. Avizeh turns her eyes downward to the blinding snow and walks back to the women's dormitory. As she enters she spots Clara sitting at her desk.

"Clara!" Avizeh nearly shouts and sprints down the rows of beds before leaping at her long-lost friend.

Usually reserved, Clara smiles and wraps her hands around Avizeh's thick coat. "Avizeh, it's been a while."

"A while? It's been more than a year."

"Hmm, it has, hasn't it? How've you been? Last time we talked you were in a bit of a tight spot. How is that going now?"

Avizeh responds with a defeated look.

"I understand. At least you're here."

Avizeh shrugs and makes an 'it-could-be-worse' face. "How about yourself? When did you get back?"

"Last week. I've just been making myself comfortable. I think I'm going to have another down period here, like the old times. It should be at least a few months before I head back out."

"How's James? Is he back or out in the field?"

Clara blinks and her face tightens. "That's confidential."

"It feels like he's been gone a long time, longer than our usual tours. Even an extended one like yours."

"I'm not allowed to say," Clara murmurs.

Avizeh wants to press her but realizes that the heart of Fort Powell is the last place they should break the rules and talking about him clearly bothers her. "Okay. I take it you've talked to Jaina... we're on speaking terms again."

"That's great. Yeah, we've talked..." Her eyes wander off. "Are you hungry?"

Avizeh still sports a pit in her stomach from her last conversation with Mikasa, but she nods her head anyway. They have lunch at the mess together and each try their hardest to keep up a conversation but the whole time Avizeh can't stop re-living the night she lay beside her secret romance, told her, "I love you," and heard nothing in return. Meanwhile Clara is obviously upset about James, leaving Avizeh to wonder if something has happened. *Was he transferred to a different branch? Dismissed? Injured? Not... dead?*

Jaina takes a seat beside them and gives their conversation an air of normalcy.

"Can we go to Las Estrellas tomorrow? For my birthday?"

"I'm not sure I feel up to it," Clara responds.

"Please! You missed my last birthday and you probably won't be at my next one."

Clara looks at her and Avizeh sports her best sad face, something which she has perfected over the past week.

"Okay. We can go," Clara replies. Avizeh smiles at the small victory as she realizes she hasn't entirely lost her charm. Simultaneously, she contemplates tomorrow with dread.

*   *   *

Avizeh puts on her snowshoes and waits patiently for Jaina and Clara. When the other two finally drag themselves out of bed, they wish her a happy nineteenth birthday and grab three snowmobiles. Once they are halfway between the town and the base, Avizeh motions for them to stop.

"What's wrong, Avizeh?" Jaina turns and steps off her vehicle.

Avizeh takes a final moment to reflect on the words she practiced the night before. "I've given this a lot of thought and I've decided I can't do this anymore."

"Do what?" Jaina asks.

"This. I didn't choose this life and I can't do it any longer."

"Have you asked Colonel Mueller about a transfer?" The end of Jaina's sentence trails off as she realizes its inherent futility.

The wind steals the silence from them as Avizeh struggles to speak. "When I was in the United States I met up with the Vanguard."

Jaina shares a nervous look with Clara.

"They have a plan to release every single secret that our agencies have on file to public servers that anyone can access. Their thinking is that as long as everyone has a dirty secret that they're afraid will get out they can always be controlled and the surveillance state will always exist. As soon as there are no secrets, no one can be controlled and it'll finally end."

Jaina stares at her wide-eyed. "That..." She shakes her head. "That's treason. Never say this shit again, Avizeh. If I even think you'll go through with this I swear I will tell command."

"Would you? You wouldn't even walk away and let me try to escape? There's so little chance I'll succeed anyway. Besides, it could be fun to watch me try. I'd mostly be using the skills you taught me," Avizeh says with the faintest smile.

"You're serious? You're really going to do this? What's the end game for you?"

"When I see them next I'm going to alter the virus and have it delete any info on me so I can never be found."

"And then you're going to just let us pick up after the mess?"

"You don't have to," Avizeh replies. "You have a choice. You can leave."

Jaina huffs. "Look Avizeh, this sucks, I know it does, and I'm sorry for you. But I'm not going to let you get away with this. If you try something stupid I will stop you."

"Avizeh." Clara looks down at her. "What would you do, after you're freed?"

"I fell in love with someone."

Clara holds her gaze for a long time. "And you'll be free to do as you wish, as soon as all the info on you is deleted? With your skills..." She purses her lips. "You'd be free to help me look for James."

Jaina glances over at her in shock. "You'd... what happened to James?"

"I don't know. We lost him on a run in Afghanistan, in the mountains southwest of Kabul. We regrouped in the city and then we never even tried to find him." Clara's eyes water and a sudden intense pain burns through Avizeh. "I'll help you if you promise to find him. Alive or dead."

"How could you betray your country so easily?"

Clara turns to Jaina with a furious look. "Easily?" she nearly shouts. "Do you know how many years I've spent up here? Twelve years and the breaks I've been given to see my family and friends have barely amounted to one. We're not all capable of holding friends at arm's length like you. I won't leave him abandoned or dead. If you're so keen on stopping us you can turn us both in; you might even get a promotion out of it."

Avizeh looks back and forth between Jaina and Clara who eye each other intensely. Jaina tries to hold Clara's gaze. She turns and walks away from them, shaking her head and muttering to herself. Avizeh takes a breath and watches Jaina stop, back turned to them. After a few moments Jaina returns. "I'm not going to prison as a traitor."

Avizeh chuckles wearily. "Don't you think it's wrong that when someone asks you to do the right thing your first thought is, 'how screwed will I be?' I doubt this is what you thought serving would be like when you started. At some point you must have wondered if your actions did more harm than good. I know I have, and I refuse to continue this.

"In any case, you won't be in danger of being found, Jaina. Or you." She nods towards Clara. "I'll be the only one on the run. And if I manage it right there'll be no record of me. Beyond the few hundred people on the base who know what I look like, there won't be any pictures or any trace at all."

"So, what's the plan?" Clara asks.

"I think I can create a virus that Jaina can input into our systems that'll loop the cameras over the teleporters and it'll turn one of them into a ghost; even when it's recharging it won't show online. Clara, I need you to take a security shift and sneak out the one I tell you. That'll be all I need from you two. Aside from that, it's probably best you don't know anything else."

Avizeh locks eyes with Jaina. "I need to know you can do this. If not, then sell me out alone when we get back, but please, don't take Clara down with me and don't give me any false hope; I'm done with that."

"I'll help you." Jaina sighs and shakes her head while looking at the ground. She looks up to meet Avizeh's gaze and laughs. "Dammit, I actually liked you. I'm going to miss you. And God, the mess you're going to..."

After a moment of listening to the howling wind, Avizeh raises her arms. "We aren't going to get another chance to really talk again, no matter the outcome. I can't disappear without letting you know I care about you and I always will."

Jaina walks into Avizeh's arms and hugs her tightly. "Make it out alive so you can cause someone else trouble."

Chapter Eighteen
Southward Bound

Avizeh taps her feet nervously for an hour before being escorted into Colonel Mueller's office. As she enters, the Colonel looks up from his work with professional courtesy, but it is clear from his demeanor that he has grown tired of her.

"What is it, Jessica?"

Avizeh takes a deep breath. "I wanted to tell you... I've accepted your offer. I want to take the job in the United States."

Mueller suddenly grins.

Not a good look on you.

"I knew you couldn't turn it down. When can you be ready to ship out?"

"I'm ready now."

Mueller blinks; Avizeh realizes he isn't used to things going according to plan, particularly with her.

"Well, I'll have to contact someone who can watch you; you can't just roam free by yourself, not with a teleporter. We all know what happened last time."

Avizeh bites her lip.

"As soon as I find a guard we will ship you out."

"Thank you," Avizeh forces out through gritted teeth. As she leaves she thinks, *There's still time to change your mind...*

*   *   *

Avizeh averts her eyes from the rest of the women in the dormitory as she walks between the bunks. She remembers her first day at the base and smiles. *What an innocent, naïve kid I was back then. Lost and afraid.* She pauses and thinks perhaps she hasn't changed that much.

Clara rises from her seat and Avizeh notices her cheeks are puffy and her eyes have begun to water. She steps towards Avizeh, wraps her arms around her and slips a teleporter into her pants pocket.

"We heard you're heading out for good this time," Clara says loud enough for anyone nearby to hear, and perhaps explain the sudden show of emotion. "We're going to miss you."

Avizeh nods. "Thanks for teaching me English." She pauses, feeling a sudden weight in her chest. She suddenly realizes that she never said goodbye to her family, or to Clara before she had gone on her missions. People have always just disappeared from her life.

Clara notices Avizeh tear up and puts a finger under her chin. "Hey, cheer up; you've always landed on your feet before. Whatever you're doing, I'm sure you'll make it through just fine."

Avizeh is not so sure. She reminisces on the last conversation she had with her family, realizing that will probably be the last time she ever talks to them, regardless of what happens next. Avizeh forces herself to smile. "Thank you," is all she can think to say.

*   *   *

A hologram appears of a non-descript female soldier staring forward coldly. Avizeh steps up onto the teleport pad feeling nothing like the featureless warrior whose place she stands in. Colonel Mueller watches with silent approval as she stands in her ghost. With a deep breath, Avizeh looks down at the teleporter in her hands. She plugs in the coordinates and appears in a base surrounded by trees. As usual, two sergeants step up to greet her. Avizeh says, "Hello," while gingerly stuffing the teleporter in her backpack, careful to make sure it doesn't clink against the other one Clara secreted for her. The two officials lead her to an office where she spots the familiar face of Nathan Branch, a new detective novel in hand.

"Hello," Avizeh calls.

"Hello again," Nathan replies cheerily enough. "I didn't think I would see you again."

"Are you pleased?"

Nathan shrugs. Without another word, they walk out to his car and head towards Boston.

*   *   *

As soon as Nathan's snores can be heard from the next room, Avizeh sneaks out of the hotel and purchases a phone, careful to avoid CCTV cameras whenever possible. The next morning she tells Nathan that she has to stay at the hotel to fix some technical bugs with her gear and that she'd be stuck in all day. He doesn't bother to ask what problems she has and resigns himself to his room. Alone, Avizeh opens up her phone, finds 'Everything Cats' and gives a glowing five paws review to a salmon treat. Within minutes a follow-up review appears, with the words 'main' and 'school' capitalized. She picks up her backpack and walks out of the hotel, confident that her guard is busy chasing criminals and loose dames in his latest book. She chucks her portable phone in the nearest garbage can and heads to the corner of Main and School Street where she follows an older hipster with a beret down an alley and into a car. The man drives them to a warehouse on the outskirts of town. Inside the skeletal building are long tables where massive desktops are hooked up to even larger servers that line the walls. As she enters, the crowd of programmers gathers around her. One of them, a tall man with short gray hair and a scar across the middle of his nose introduces himself as Luke and says, "It's an honor to finally meet you, Jessica Brown. I've heard a lot about you. The crew in Asheville wouldn't have told you about this facility or how to access it unless they really believed in you, but I still need proof. How do we know you're the real deal?"

Avizeh reaches into her backpack, pulls out the two teleporters and puts them on a nearby table, where the Vanguard regard them as if they are the Holy Grail and the True Cross.

"I have an idea for how we can pull this off. But I have two conditions: one, you need to give me the virus for some editing before I leave. I'm okay with you releasing all the world's secrets except mine. If you release mine, then I die or spend eternity in a cell in a black ops prison and I'm not going to be your martyr."

"We're all in this boat together, Jessica."

"No, we're not. I'm not an American and my name isn't Jessica Brown, though you don't need to know what it really is. I'm from Afghanistan but I was forced to work for the CRD against my will. There's no constitutional protection for me so I'm not going to subject myself to any risk of being caught."

She waits until there is a general agreement from those in

the room.

"So, what's the plan?" Luke asks.

"We wait until it's 1 a.m., Fort Powell time. I have the exact coordinates for the women's dormitory bathroom. Every building outside the dormitories has cameras and sensors which could sound an alarm if they detect motion."

"Could?" a mousy woman asks from behind Avizeh.

Avizeh looks over her shoulder and shrugs. "Hopefully security is lax; I honestly don't know. Fort Powell is, after all, the most remote place on Earth. The best-case scenario is that there aren't security guards watching the cameras constantly. With any luck, they are there to make recruits at Fort Powell think that even they're being watched at all times and record their activities for rewatch if something goes wrong."

"And if they're not?"

"That's why we're going into the women's bathroom."

"That can't be where they keep their servers," a scrawny man asks, sounding a little unsure.

"No, but we should be able to access their computers with an Infiltrator, which I have."

"Where?" Luke demands.

"Somewhere safe. You don't think I'm stupid enough to give you everything you need, do you?"

Luke pauses, considering her words. He smiles. "Well, I'm glad we have someone clever leading us."

Avizeh gives a wry grin, poorly masking her worry at the thought of leading an operation to take down the world security system. "There's just one more thing: this teleporter has two charges. We can use it to arrive on the base. When we finish, you can take it and teleport to a country that's hostile to America, where they are less likely to follow and you can lay low. I'm going to take the other one and teleport to Afghanistan."

"Afghanistan? You really want to go back there?" a short man with a blond buzz cut interjects.

Avizeh grimaces as she thinks of her war-torn home. "The person who gave me this," she motions towards the extra teleporter, "is in love with someone who went missing there during a mission, and I promised her I would look for him. After we input the virus I'm going to teleport to Afghanistan. As soon as all the US secrets are out, a simple internet search will show where he was last seen. I'm going to find him."

"And then?" a stocky man, with two separated front teeth, muses aloud.

Avizeh shrugs. "I haven't thought that far. But I have to try. Which brings up my second condition: I need a passport so I can travel somewhere safe. And I'll need money to set up a new life."

Luke pauses. "Does twenty million dollars in a foreign bank account sound fair to you?"

Avizeh blanches, then quickly composes herself. "Really?"

"If you can help us take down the world security state, that'll be well worth it. What do you say?"

She pauses. "I want the passport and the bank account information before we go."

Luke puts his hands on his hips. "Okay. Can you wait a few minutes while we fix the printer?"

*   *   *

Avizeh watches the Vanguard with amazement. In a mere three hours they create a fake French identity for her, complete with ID card, healthcare card and passport, all of which sport the name 'Emma Martin,' which Luke explains is the most common girl's first name and last name in France, making a search more difficult.

"So, Emma Martin is the 'Jessica Brown' of France?" she

muses.

Luke prints out the information for her new bank account and hands her a USB with all her information as a backup. "Anything else?" he asks.

Avizeh's heart races as she realizes that this is the last possible moment she can back out of their agreement. She shakes her head.

"You sure?"

Avizeh's legs feel like jelly but she nods her head all the same.

"Good, let me introduce you to the team." Luke holds his hand outward as if presenting a new car. "Mike," he motions to a brawny man in a trench coat with thin blond hair and clear blue eyes. "Adrian," a thin hook-nosed man with high cheekbones and dark hair. "Daniel," a spry, younger fellow with a cheery smile.

Avizeh looks at each, wondering if these are their real names, and decides they must not be. She shakes each man's hand before turning to Luke. "Why can't the two of us just go? Or even just me?"

"Jessica, for decades all we've done is chip away at the global surveillance state. Then you came along and gave us a chance to smash the whole thing in one blow. We can't leave anything to chance. If there's some firewall or other security measure you don't know how to bypass, we might be able to help. Also, what if someone walks into the bathroom and tries to stop you?"

Avizeh frowns. "You won't kill anyone, will you?"

Luke meets her eyes. "Not if we don't have to."

"I have friends up there; friends who are on our side."

"Then we'll be careful, and we'll wait for your signal before doing anything rash," he addresses the last part to his three men.

Avizeh sighs; she doesn't like her original plan. This

sudden change makes her worry. She tries to press down the knots forming in her stomach. "Okay." She looks over at a clock on the wall.

"Is it time we go?" Luke asks.

"It's well past time," she replies. "It's past 3 a.m. at Fort Powell. Everyone will still be asleep but we can't wait any longer."

Luke nods. "All right, how do we do this?"

"Do you have international contacts? Preferably in a country not friendly to the US?"

"Does Cuba count?"

Avizeh thinks back on the countries she isn't allowed to visit. "That should work. Can you tell me where exactly they are?"

Luke shows Avizeh their Cuban supporters' address. She walks to the nearby table and grabs a teleporter. She inputs coordinates to a field a few miles from their safehouse. "Send these coordinates to them and make sure they are ready to pick you up as soon as you get back," she says while handing Luke the teleporter. He nods and walks towards a half-dozen people anxiously watching them. A few minutes later, Luke shoves the teleporter into the inside pocket of his coat.

"What next?"

Avizeh grabs her backpack, looking inside to see her laptop, a teleporter and the black burqa from her mission to Kabul nearly two years prior. She pulls out the teleporter and closes the bag. "Everyone put a hand on my shoulders and squeeze in tight." They do as she commands, their fingers painfully pressing the fabric of her shirt against her. She looks down and presses the 'jump' button.

Without the slightest transition on Avizeh and her literal hangers-on appear in the women's dormitory bathrooms at Fort Powell. She feels two hands dig deeper into her, while two more slacken; it seems each man struggles with vertigo in different ways. Without waiting for them to recover, Avizeh walks into a nearby bathroom stall and removes the lid. She pulls out a plastic bag containing her Infiltrator, walks back towards the men, sits down on the tiled floor and removes her laptop. She attaches the Infiltrator and anxiously waits for the system to start. The four men recover their balance and hover around her.

Avizeh prepares to send the virus and waits for the system to connect. She refreshes the Wi-Fi again and again before finally unhooking the Infiltrator. Her face slackens.

"There's too much interference," she says quietly. "I should have figured the walls are so thick that I couldn't get a signal through here."

Luke gives his men a nervous look. "I assume you don't know how to force open the doors to central command electronically?"

Avizeh meets his gaze. "I could try."

"Trying isn't going to work," Mike interrupts in a gruff voice that is too loud for Avizeh's liking. "If we go out there, in negative sixty degree weather in our clothes, we'll get hypothermia and severe frostbite in minutes. It's time for plan B." As he says this, Mike pulls out a football-sized mechanical device that Avizeh recognizes as an explosive.

"You'll wake up the whole base!" Avizeh snaps at him. "Hundreds of heavily-armed marines right on top of us."

"She's right," Adrian says, looking suddenly panicked. "We have to abort."

"We can't," Avizeh says, looking up at each man in turn. "Or at least, I can't. As soon as the base wakes up, whoever's monitoring the teleporters will see there was a jump from Boston to here. There's no turning back for me."

The members of the Vanguard each look to each other, silently debating whether to cut their losses and leave her stranded. "We've tried everything and nothing's worked,"

Adrian admits. "This has been our only real chance. We're never going to get someone as deep on the inside as her, and even if we did, they're going to beef up security here as soon as they catch her. Their complacency, thinking they were safe in a steel fortress at the bottom of the world, is the one thing we have going for us. It's this or nothing."

Luke considers Adrian's words before returning his gaze to Avizeh. "Plan B it is."

Avizeh bites her lip. *What a familiar feeling, having no choices but to stumble forward.*

"Once we're in, you're going to have to work fast." Luke stares into her eyes.

Avizeh nods solemnly. She puts her laptop in her backpack and rises to her feet. She walks to the door and slowly opens it. She leads the men between the bunks past women who sleep soundly, blissfully unaware that techies with explosives gently tiptoe past them. Avizeh looks over at Clara's bed and sees her lying down, eyes closed, and wonders if she is asleep or merely pretending. They pass Jaina's bed where she snores loudly, which almost makes Avizeh laugh.

She grabs the handle of the door and looks back to the four men. Luke nods for her to continue. As quietly as she can, she opens it and steps out. The chill hits her like a punch to her gut, freezing the air in her lungs. A wind howls across the plain. As soon as they are out, Avizeh closes the door behind her.

"Now," Avizeh forces out and marches towards the imposing central building. They reach the steel front door and she hugs herself for warmth. Mike places the explosive on the door with an adhesive and motions them to follow him behind another building.

"Cover your ears!" he yells.

Avizeh barely reaches up in time when a huge blast shakes her entire body and for a moment a warm gust breaks through the cold. Alarms sound and lights flash across the base.

"Come on!" Luke grabs her and pushes her forward. The group rushes past the debris and into the building, which is illuminated by flashing red emergency lights. Mike tarries to leave another explosive in the middle of the entryway. Avizeh runs down to her right and leads them into a conference room where she had been briefed on her missions. She sits down at one of the long tables and starts typing.

"I'm in!" she exclaims, only for Luke to shoot daggers with his eyes at her. She lowers her head and returns to her work, even as the men pile chairs at the entryway door. She works furiously, pulling through each line of defense. A few minutes in and she realizes she has to start all over.

Outside, a muffled cacophony of Antarctic wind and human shouts sound. Mike pulls out the detonator for the second explosive and triggers it. A blast shakes the room. Screams echo through the halls and Avizeh prays that Clara isn't among them. Avizeh has a sudden flashback to the mission at Kabul when she tried to work in a collapsing building.

"How much longer?" Adrian looks down at Avizeh. She doesn't bother answering, unsure herself. He gives a nervous look at Luke. "What do we do if they blow open the door?"

Luke doesn't look sure. Then he pulls out a handgun. "Hope some fire will keep them at bay."

"They'll have flashbangs and grenades; shooting won't stop them," Mike adds as he listens to the encroaching footsteps at the door.

A sudden burst blows a hole through the door and Avizeh screams. Chairs tumble aside. Dust and debris fill the room. Then Avizeh feels cold steel press against the side of her head.

"Don't shoot or Jessica Brown gets it!"

A tense silence follows. Dust settles, coating her keyboard and screen. The distant sound of Antarctic wind roars through the opening. Avizeh tries not to move her head as she looks up at the man holding the gun against her temple. "Keep working," he whispers, and she cannot tell if there is a genuine threat behind his command. She wipes off her keyboard and continues, shaking violently.

"Jessica," Colonel Mueller barks. "Jessica, are you all right?"

Avizeh looks up at Luke for confirmation. "They have a gun to my head. They're threatening to kill me unless you stay back."

"I'm coming in alone," Mueller calls.

"Anyone steps foot in here and I'll blow her brains out!"

Avizeh can't breathe. She tells herself that this is a ploy to keep the men just behind the walls at bay. She looks up at Luke. The panic in his face makes her wonder if he even knows what he is doing.

"Either I get to see her or we blow up the whole room."

Mike, Daniel and Adrian recover from the blast and congregate around Luke and Avizeh. "He's bluffing," Mike says.

"He isn't," Avizeh manages while typing madly with shaking hands.

"All right," Luke calls. "Just you."

Mueller gingerly steps over the ruins littering the entryway. Mike, Adrian and Daniel level their guns at him. He doesn't even look at them. Instead, his attention is firmly on Avizeh. "Jessica, what are you doing?"

Avizeh keeps typing.

"Jessica, look at me."

Avizeh stops. She stares blankly at the screen.

Luke turns down and follows her gaze. "She did it."

In a flash Mueller raises his sidearm and levels it at Avizeh. Luke presses against her back. A bullet grazes against the side of her head. The three other Vanguard members fire wildly at Mueller who goes down in their flurry of bullets. There's a sudden burst from the blasted entryway. Mike screams and falls to the ground.

Avizeh is on the ground, clutching at her head. The remaining three Vanguard members crouch behind the table with her. She hears footsteps across the entryway. The terrified former agent grabs her laptop, throws it into her backpack and pulls out the teleporter. A strong arm squeezes her shoulder.

"Everyone grab her," Luke orders. "Mike had the other teleporter. It's lost."

The other two grab onto her for their lives. Another burst of gunfire sends wooden splinters flying above them. Avizeh presses the jump button.

A calm silence broken only by the ringing in her ears pervades the world. The sky above them turns to night as the group finds themselves in a mostly empty parking lot in an abandoned mall with palm trees all around them. Avizeh takes a stabilizing breath. Then she retrieves the burqa and puts it on. She glances at the men and realizes that in their American clothes they will draw suspicion instantly. She wonders if it would be easier to abandon them, then remembers that a woman traveling alone would be just as dangerous. The three Americans look back and forth at each other, suddenly realizing they are in Kabul, a contingency that none of them have planned for.

"We have to go," Avizeh says, drawing the men from their stupor. "Our location will appear immediately in their system because we used the teleporter and I doubt it will take them long to regroup."

"We need to find a car and hotwire it," Luke offers.

"Too bad the one guy who could do that is bleeding to death at the South Pole." Adrian grimaces.

Avizeh looks back and forth between them. "You're serious? No one else knows?"

They all turn to her, saying nothing.

"Either way, we need to run, now," she says as she stands up.

Avizeh has no idea where they should go other than to get away from such a large, open area. She leads the men away from the mall and down the streets of Kabul. Avizeh notices that the city is ominously quiet. As they sprint down side streets and alleys she feels eyes peering down on them; three foreign men and a woman running through the streets? She can only imagine what people think as they peer through their windows at the odd group.

A sudden light shines down on them and the group freezes and looks up. On the second story of a nearby house, two American marines level submachine guns at them.

Avizeh throws her arms up and the men around her follow her lead. In Farsi, she yells, "Don't shoot, don't shoot!"

The soldiers pause for a moment before eyeing the three men beside her. "Don't move!" one of the men yells. The men from the Vanguard throw up their hands. Avizeh scans the alleyway and realizes there is no way she could run without being gunned down.

Fiery yellow light explodes from a roof on their right and the sound of gunfire screeches angrily across the city. Afghan men yell in Farsi, cursing the American intruders.

"Run like hell!" Avizeh screams and leads them away from the firefight.

Two more Americans appear out of thin air on the roof above them. They point their guns down at the group, then immediately duck as insurgents fire on them. Luke motions to his right and the four run down an alley, panting.

"What the hell's happening?" Luke roars.

"Local warlords," Avizeh explains. "One of the patrols must have engaged an American cohort and now Kabul's lighting up." With a smile, she adds, "Reminds me of my wedding night."

"There's no way we'll survive if we're on foot, dressed like this."

"Then we'll just have to blend in," Daniel barks. The group walks up to a house and Daniel fiddles with the garage handle. After a few frustrating instants, he lowers his gun to it. Luke grabs him and pulls him back.

"No, you idiot! That'll be too loud." He looks up and points to a light inside the house. Luke walks to the front door and kicks it open. The men storm in with all the professionalism of techies with guns as their shouting mixes with the yelling of the family inside. Avizeh follows them into a living room with a couch and outdated TV to find a woman with a crying baby in her arms and a small girl at her side standing in the hallway entrance while a wide-eyed man levels a pistol in shaking hands.

"Stop!" Avizeh orders in Farsi.

The shaking man eyes her.

"Don't shoot!" she calls. "We don't want to hurt you, we just need clothes and a vehicle to get out of here."

"Get out of my house! You're not welcome."

"Let us take three sets of men's clothes and a car and we'll be gone," Avizeh explains calmly. "You have a car, don't you?" She looks at the woman. Her expression tells Avizeh all she needs to know. "Lower your gun, sir."

The man looks from Avizeh to the three men who point shaking handguns at him. Slowly, he lowers his pistol.

"Where are the keys?"

"In my pocket."

"Don't shoot, he's going to get his keys," Avizeh says in

English. That causes the man to stop and give her a shocked and confused look. His eyes jump back and forth between the strange, armed men in his house and the woman who leads them. With no choice, he hands over his keys to Luke while Daniel picks up his pistol. The men each take turns going up and changing into the man's clothes. Luke and Adrian look ridiculous trying to stretch the man's clothes across their tall frames, while Daniel wears his stolen vestments as if they are his own. When they finish ransacking the man's wardrobe, the four intruders enter the garage to find an old blue Volkswagen bus at least three decades old. Avizeh offers a silent prayer that it still runs.

"Where are we going?" Daniel asks while climbing in the driver's seat.

Avizeh reaches into one of the backpacks and retrieves her laptop. She connects to the house's Wi-Fi, finds the Vanguard's server and does a search for James Dinapoli. She picks the last file, an official MIA report and reads:

Last known whereabouts, Kandahar.

"We need to get on the highway to Kandahar. Head southwest and drive fast."

Luke jumps out and raises the garage door, letting the sound of battle into the claustrophobic garage. He jumps into the back of the bus while Daniel pulls out slowly, moving clumsily in the narrow alley. Then they are off, tearing down the empty roads as gunfire bursts all around them and Avizeh has to shout directions from the back seat as RPGs roar to life. A pit grows in her stomach as she realizes they will never make it out alive in this chaos. Working as fast as she can, she connects to the American communications channel. She isolates all the communication lines, searching for one that might be friendly.

"Clara?"

After a moment the familiar voice replies. "Yes?"

"Oh, thank god you're alive! Listen, we're in a blue Volkswagen heading west but we're never going to make it. Are you here? Can you clear the way to the A-1?"

"I'll get on it."

The van rolls through the ongoing battle in Kabul. A bullet bursts through their back window and shoots through the front. Avizeh ducks and closes her eyes, expecting a fatal shot to come at any moment. She instinctively grabs the side of her head and feels dried blood where Mueller's bullet whizzed past her. After twenty minutes of weaving through the city, the sounds of combat recede until they resemble the low rumble of thunder in distant hills when Daniel suddenly slams on the brakes. Avizeh peers through her veil and sees four men with long beards in Afghan garb with submachine guns pointed at the bus.

Without looking back, Daniel asks, "What do we do, Emma?"

Luke looks down at the gun resting on his lap. Avizeh follows his gaze, knowing that they would be worthless.

One of the Afghans starts shouting.

"He's telling us to get out," Avizeh translates.

He shouts again.

"He says get out or he'll shoot."

He shouts a third time.

"It's a countdown. We're at two."

The man's head suddenly explodes in a spray of crimson mist. The three other men glance up but not before another falls to the ground. The last two start firing. Adrian jumps out and shoots at the first man, hitting him square in the chest. The last man turns to him and is taken down from behind. Adrian raises his gun just as a dark-haired woman in camouflage suit with an assault rifle steps down a set of stairs in a half-destroyed building.

"Adrian!" Avizeh calls as she steps out of the car. "Don't shoot."

Adrian lowers his shotgun while Clara scans the area around them. She turns to the Vanguard man and lowers her assault rifle. She presses a button on her earpiece, turning her comm off, then walks towards Avizeh.

"Avizeh, are you okay? Are these men your friends?"

"'Friend' is a strong word," she says as she remembers the feel of Luke's gun against her temple, "but they're about the only people who aren't trying to shoot me right now," the Afghan woman replies with as much humor as she can muster.

Clara looks at her seriously. "I can shadow you while you leave the city. Beyond that you're on your own."

Avizeh nods. "I found James. Sort of."

Clara's eyes fill with hope, then sudden dread. "Is he..."

"He's MIA, last seen in Kandahar. I'll find him, I promise."

"I'll go with you."

"No, you won't. The military will be turning over Kabul looking for us, giving us a head start. If you disappear, they will go looking for you. Either they'll think you're chasing after us or we captured you."

Clara grimaces. "To think you're telling me how to run an operation. You're right, you need to go. Only half the base has shown up so far. More will be appearing soon. They haven't told the new recruits your real name; I suppose they think four Americans can't hide in Kabul forever. But when they get desperate I'm sure it'll leak out. Be careful." She steps forward and hugs Avizeh, letting out a small sigh as she does. "I'm having flashbacks to when I first met you. You were freezing in a white burqa as you just flashed up to Antarctica. Now it looks like we've come full circle. I'm glad to have met you."

"You too," Avizeh replies, trying not to cry as she realizes this is the last time they will ever see each other, all while the world burns around them. "You're one of the only people I'm going to miss. And Jaina. Tell her goodbye for me. And be sentimental, she hates that."

Clara smiles. "I will, I promise."

"I'll find him, Clara."

Clara squeezes Avizeh and pulls back. "Go."

"Emma," Daniel says from beside her, "the fighting's getting closer."

The Afghan woman turns and jumps into the bullet-riddled bus. When she looks out the window, Clara is already gone.

*   *   *

Sunlight pours through their broken back window. Avizeh tries to sleep but she can't stop shaking and the bumpy road makes the bus jump every couple of miles. Luke reaches back, shakes her unnecessarily and points out the window.

"What's that sign say?"

Avizeh rubs her eyes. "Kandahar. Two miles."

The city appears like an oasis on their right side. Wearily, Avizeh pulls up her laptop. "Take a right," she instructs as they enter the city, directing them towards the coordinates where James Dinapoli was last seen. Daniel steers as best as he can while trying to remain calm. Avizeh worries that their bus might draw suspicion but as she looks out she realizes that a vehicle with obvious bullet holes through the windows isn't entirely uncommon.

"Stop!" Avizeh orders suddenly.

Daniel makes a rolling stop in a neighborhood filled with two and three-story mansions with palm trees and grass lawns. Avizeh hacks into each house's computers with her stolen Infiltrator, subtly activating their cameras and flipping through files.

"Drive down a block."

Daniel does as he is told and she continues her work. She takes over one computer and sees a large black banner with white writing underneath two scimitars. She finds a folder filled with video files, opens the first one and watches a man stand in front of the flag while reciting a manifesto. She fast forwards through it, then watches a similar one, before playing another video dated two weeks ago. A white American is on his knees flanked by men in ski masks and ammo vests while a third man yells threats at the camera. The American has been beaten, his face purpled, but Avizeh recognizes him, even if it has been a year since she has last seen him.

"That him?" Adrian asks.

Avizeh nods slowly. She turns off the grim scene and looks through the computer. "I'm guessing Zarrar Javed is our guy, given the amount of money in his accounts. I'm clarifying them with CIA and NSA files; seems like he runs Kandahar. Give me a moment, I'm trying to locate him through his cell phone... he's out at a café."

"So, what do we do? Rush in?"

Avizeh pauses. "No, I'm guessing there are armed guards inside with a lot more firepower than us. We have to find Javed. Go to the end and take a left."

Avizeh leads them through the busy streets in downtown Kandahar until she spots a café at the end of the road. She tells Daniel to park and looks out at the men drinking coffee on the outside tables, trying to guess which man he is by the pictures in his CIA file. She steps out of the car, laptop in hand.

"Emma, are you—" Luke whispers, as she ignores him and steps outside the bus.

The Afghan woman walks up to a huge man who is almost

as tall sitting down as Avizeh is standing. The giant laughs while slapping his knee beside three other men, all of whom have assault rifles at their sides. Avizeh takes a breath, walks up to them and sits at an empty chair at their table.

"Zarrar Javed?" Avizeh asks.

"Who said you could sit with us, bitch? Where is your husband? Why are you walking alone?"

"I apologize for my insolence. Let me make it up to you." She turns the laptop to face him. "This is your bank account, isn't it?" She presses a button, suddenly adding a massive sum to it. "Thirty million Afghanis, from my patron. I'm sure you've heard the Americans are taking Kabul in force. My patron believes in you and says you will need as much as he can spare when the Americans arrive and the war comes here." Avizeh closes her laptop and stands up. "Peace be upon you. Keep fighting the good fight."

The men regard her with a mix of anger, confusion and worry. Avizeh doesn't give them the chance to react as she practically runs to the bus. She leaps in and orders, "Drive. Fast."

"Why? What did you do?" Luke demands.

"The Americans should be here in a few minutes, in force."

Daniel takes off down the road, not needing an explanation to flee, unlike his superior.

"What did you do?" Luke repeats.

"The military gave me a bank account; I'm up to $200,000. Or, I was until just now. I just transferred it all to Javed. They'll be monitoring my account, they'll see the transfer and find him at the café. And just to make it more obvious, I hacked into his computer and used it to send the transfer order, which will lead them to his mansion."

They reach the highway and Avizeh tells Daniel to pull over.

"What now?" their driver yells.

"Pull over," Luke orders.

Daniel grumbles but does as he is told.

"Pull up a little farther so we can see the mansions." Avizeh removes her veil as she leans over Adrian to look out the window. The ever-familiar sound of gunfire breaks out though only for a second. An American appears on the roof out of nowhere. A dozen more pop into being around the complex. Luke glances worriedly back at Avizeh.

"Wait."

The doors to the mansion open and two navy SEALs carry a bleeding man out between them. His face is bruised, and he grimaces with pain, but he is clearly still alive. One of the SEALs pulls out a teleporter and they disappear.

Avizeh dons her veil, falls back against the seat and closes the door. "Okay, now we can go."

Chapter Nineteen
Choosing an Ending

As they drive through endless desert with no town or other cars in sight, Luke orders Daniel to pull over and the men toss their firearms into a ditch. Avizeh cringes as she thinks about what will happen when someone finds them, but realizes they have no other choice. She steps out of the van and throws the teleporter and Infiltrator alongside them. Then she picks up one of the handguns and points it at her discarded hardware. She takes a long time to level the weapon.

"Ever fired a gun before?" Adrian laughs beside her, knowing the answer.

"No, how hard can it be?"

"There's going to be some recoil. Hold it tight."

Avizeh aims. She pulls the trigger and feels a rumble through her arms. The Infiltrator bursts into pieces.

The men applaud her. Avizeh blushes, suddenly grateful for the burqa's cover. After the past few miserable months and recent near-death experiences, she appreciates the moment of levity. She takes aim at the teleporter when Daniel interjects.

"Whoa, whoa, whoa, can you just shoot that and not, I dunno, cause a rip in space-time?"

Avizeh gives him an incredulous look, then realizes he cannot see her. "It has no charge. It has a lot of toxic chemicals in it but they'll just drain into the ground. Not the best solution, but I don't think we should leave it here."

Luke nods his approval. She returns her gaze to the teleporter. She suddenly contemplates the object, remembering the first time she held one. Each time she did, she felt the tremendous power that comes with the ability to appear anywhere on Earth. She stops, wondering why she would ever destroy such a thing. Then she remembers Mueller appearing outside her hotel door in Virginia. She thinks of the American marines appearing out of thin air firing on her wedding party.

Avizeh pulls the trigger and watches the incredible machine burst to pieces.

"You know, when I was a kid, growing up in rural Kentucky, my uncle taught me how to shoot by firing his S&W .38 at a rusted old car that had been abandoned a mile past our property." Luke lets the wind eat his words. "I always thought that was a stupid waste. But you just shot the two most expensive pieces of hardware on planet Earth."

Avizeh, in a full burqa, shining silver-steel gun in hand, looks over at her three American counterparts as they survey their contraband gear in pieces in a ditch. Daniel shakes his head and laughs. The rest join in his mirth, completely overtaken by the absurdity of the last two days. Avizeh laughs, not believing where her life has taken her. She laughs far longer than anyone else. When she finishes, she tosses the gun into the ditch and the team covers the entire stash with loose dirt.

*   *   *

The reliable old Volkswagen follows the sun until the odd company reaches an Iranian-controlled checkpoint along the border between the two countries. Their vehicle rolls to a stop in front of a raisable gate. Inside a nearby booth a customs agent eyes the bullet hole in the window and gives a nervous glance at nearby armed guards who monitor the battered vehicle. Avizeh can feel each man looking at her in the rear-view mirror. She leans forward.

"As-salamu alaykum," she offers the universal Muslim greeting.

"As-salamu alaykum. Papers," he intones.

Avizeh pulls out her French passport and hands it to him. The Vanguard members follow and hand the agent their Swiss passports. The agent takes each passport and gives them a curious look, as if wondering what a bunch of Westerners are doing in Afghanistan. He opens Emma Martin's passport and his eyes narrow.

"Lift up your burqa, please."

Avizeh does as she is told, and he compares the photo to her. "My family is from Afghanistan," she explains. "But they moved to France where I was born. We are part of a news agency. I'm their translator."

"Now isn't a good time to be in Afghanistan," he replies.

"Is there ever a good time?"

He shrugs and runs the passport's bar codes through the computer. Avizeh's heart stops and she tries not to look at the men as she wonders how thorough their connections and expertise are. The agent stands up and looks down at the passports. He motions to the armed men who walk towards them.

"Step out of the vehicle."

"Why, what's wrong?"

There's a heavy thudding against the side of the van as one of the guards slams his palm down repeatedly on the hood.

Avizeh opens her side door and steps out. Her compatriots

copy her and exit the van. The two Iranian border guards rummage through the vehicle. One of them grabs her backpack and pulls out her laptop. She grimaces, hoping he will be careful, but keeps herself from saying anything. He tosses it on the seat then walks to the back and examines the back of the van. The man calls to the border agent and they return to their stations.

"Back into your vehicle," the agent calls, sounding disappointed. The four do as they are told. Avizeh gets in just in time to hear the agent ask, "How long will you be staying?"

"Until we can get a flight out," she replies. "Maybe three days."

"Where will you be staying?"

Avizeh blurts out her family's apartment address. "They're one of our contacts."

The guard nods and inputs the information into the computer. He stamps the passports and hands them back. "Welcome to Iran," he says while waving them forward past the rising gate.

The old Volkswagen rumbles back to life. Avizeh's mind races. For a moment she worries that this is just a trap; either an Iranian armored vehicle will cut them off or American marines will appear from thin air and shoot the tires. But nothing happens and the van rolls down the decrepit road. Avizeh pulls back her burqa, exposing her face. She leans back and puts a hand on her forehead. "I can't believe I ever agreed to this," she says.

Adrian laughs beside her. "Why did you?"

Avizeh remembers telling Mikasa, 'I love you,' and watching her turn away. She sees her family on a screen, thinking that is the closest she will ever be to them again. She thinks of all the times she's been called 'Jessica Brown,' now 'Emma Martin,' while no one but Clara and Jaina even speaks her real name. She thinks of the trip to Las Estrellas and

Jaina telling her that she has to keep friends at arm's length.

"Because I'm a human being, no matter how many times people told me I had to be otherwise."

Luke looks back at her through the rear-view mirror. "Any chance you're going to write a tell-all book?"

Avizeh meets his gaze. "Every secret in the world is out now except mine. You'll just have to make do." She winks and looks out the window.

*   *   *

Evening arrives as they reach Birjand. The exhausted group stops by a lively shopping mall for new sets of clothes. Long after the men have picked out their Western-style jeans and shirts, Avizeh joins them at the counter with a half-dozen outfits, light-colored hijabs which she can wear loosely in the Iranian fashion, and three new pairs of shoes. She places her new wardrobe on the counter alongside theirs and waits for the cashier to ring up the lot.

"Twenty million not enough for you to pay for your own clothes?"

"A gentleman always pays," she retorts with a smile. In truth, the ex-spy doesn't want to leave a money trail. She insists the Americans pay for everything and give her a substantial amount of cash from a nearby ATM before they leave. Luke bites his lip but decides against arguing with their translator.

The group check in to a hotel with the men sharing one room while she takes her own. After a much-needed shower Avizeh collapses on the bed and pulls up her laptop. She opens *CNN International* and watches a mid-forties anchor talk about the unprecedented worldwide privacy breach. In another window she simultaneously reads the headlines of major news articles. The NSA-CRD mass data collection and the leak of sextillions of private photos, video, emails and other information is the only story anyone is reporting on. Avizeh filters through page after page; every story is a different revelation from the leaks. One of the main stories lists all the scandals Congresspeople are involved in: their love affairs, insider trading and secret bank accounts. All but two of the five hundred and thirty-five representatives and senators have some scandal worthy of an ethics breach, impeachment, or even criminal sentencing, though she doubts there will be any repercussions for powerful people. Alongside these are revelations of worldwide fraud and price-rigging by international banks and outright conspiracy by oil companies hiring violent insurgents in the Third World to repress nationalistic politicians. Every world leader condemns the spying, which extends to them and their people, though there is substantial evidence that at least the UK prime minister and a few others knew about the program and openly aided their American counterparts. Mass protests choke major cities around the world. Even pop culture sites only discuss the leaks. Every few minutes a new article details another bombshell celebrity revelation.

On *CNN* a panel of Congress members furiously grill the head of the NSA who tries to shift all the blame on the now-deceased Colonel Mueller. Avizeh is torn over the dirty tactic; she is furious that the US government is trying to blame one rogue operative rather than the widespread culture that created and maintained the surveillance state apparatus. Yet, she smiles at the thought of her hostage-taker's name being confined to historical infamy.

For the first time in days Avizeh feels calm. As the world explodes around her she finally feels like she is safe, away from the chaos. Instead, everyone who held her and the world hostage are on trial. In this atmosphere Avizeh guesses that no one will be looking for her. There no longer exists any record of 'Avizeh Fatah.' Likewise, most of the new recruits only know her as 'Jessica Brown.' Those who know her real name are her friends. Either way, she suspects that everyone at Fort Powell will wipe their hands clean and transfer to a less controversial part of the military.

Avizeh closes her laptop, pulls her knees to her chest and sinks her head between them. She takes a deep breath. The mountain she has been carrying lifts off of her shoulders but there is still another weight holding her down. Two, actually. All that she has left in this life are her family and her love. She can tell her family she loves them unreservedly but cannot say anything of her life after the wedding night. She fears a loose word might endanger them or their position as refugees; no doubt the Iranian government would kill to recruit someone who destroyed the American surveillance state, regardless of whether she was willing to join them. Then there are her many sinful experiences, her failure to maintain a devout lifestyle, and her strictly haram relationship with a woman. Her love will have to be enough as she has nothing else to offer. *At least it's enough for Aamir, Laily and Mother. But Baba...* She pushes away the thought, refusing to worry until the time comes.

To Mikasa she can tell any secret, but she is afraid to say, "I love you." Those were words she thought she would never say again during her confinement in Fort Powell. When Omar kissed her and she felt nothing she feared she was incapable of love. Then she met Mikasa. At the end of their first trip together in Taiwan she wanted to say those three words but she was afraid; afraid she would never see her again, afraid that their love was a sin, afraid that she was too damaged to be in love. When she finally overcame all her doubts and declared her love it didn't matter and Mikasa turned away from her.

Avizeh unfolds, stretching out her legs and letting her head hit the pillow. She closes her eyes and hopes that sleep will sneak up on her. After a day of constant near-death experiences from Antarctica to Afghanistan, then a dangerous flight from Kabul to Kandahar and finally into Iran, she fears that her most painful trials are yet to come.

*   *   *

Avizeh's American counterparts knock on her door at eight in the morning. She angrily wonders why they are in such a hurry as she is more than content to finally do nothing for a change. After a quick breakfast the ad hoc team leaves and drives northward. Avizeh closes her eyes and tries to sleep even as the men talk excitedly about what they saw on the news the previous night.

"It worked! I can't believe it but it worked. Decades of trying and nothing and we did it in a night."

"The whole world's changed. Nothing will be like it was before. The big shots are finally getting what they deserve."

"Hey, none of you had anything embarrassing that got leaked, did you? No nudes or anything?" Luke ribs Daniel.

"I'm not ashamed of those. Besides, what's my petty drama to all the conspiracies in the world coming out at once?"

Avizeh wishes they would shut up. They have everything to look forward to; they'll be hailed as heroes by the rest of the Vanguard and they'll be 'forced' to go on vacation as they lie low, all while watching their political enemies squirm in front of Congressional committees. Once they reach Mashhad they can take a flight home and return to their lives. Avizeh has no such luxury. Her next step is making a life since she has nothing to return to. The Afghan-American-French woman from the Desert of Death warily contemplates her next move while trying to drown out their sense of self-flattery. On a sudden whim she leans forward and turns on the radio to a Persian pop station. The other three share annoyed looks but she doesn't care. Avizeh looks out the window at rolling hills and scant oases breaking up the arid mountainous landscape while her soul wanders around the chords and lyrics of songs she wishes she could relate to.

Time and space tumble through muddled consciousness as Avizeh drifts through daydreams. Signs appear announcing their arrival in the holy city of Mashhad, resting place of Imam Reza and Caliph Harun al-Rashid. Their bullet-strewn metal box circles around the airport until they find a hotel. Acting as translator, Avizeh reserves a room for one night for the three men, and another for five nights for herself. Again, Luke pays, this time looking more confused at the length of her stay than annoyance that he has to pay.

Avizeh steps into her room, lets her back hit the door and slides down until she is sitting down, knees raised in front of her. *I've wanted freedom for so long, now I don't know what to do with it.* She suddenly laughs at the word 'freedom.' Fort Powell had its own derivative language from standard English and 'freedom' had no connection with the word in the dictionary. 'Freedom' was a justification for every action her superiors took, proof of American righteousness and the sole possession of the US government, which it generously loaned out to its allies. For the first time in her life she is free to act but cannot decide what to do.

Which broken piece of my life should I try to pick up first? Should I call Mikasa? Tell her I'm coming to see her? Would anything I say matter if the most powerful words I can say mean nothing? She thinks of her family. *Will they accept me if I returned to them? I'm sure Mother, Aamir and Laily would cry and invite me back into their lives but Baba...* She wonders if she can live with them. Should she even try? *Maybe I can see each member of my family without confronting my father.* Ridiculous images come to her head. Like an American sitcom, she sees herself talking to her mother only to hide under the table when her father returns, while a laugh-track plays in the background. *What life is there for me anywhere?*

There's a knock at the door so hard it shakes her. Avizeh stands up, looks through the peephole and sees Luke standing in the hallway. She takes a deep breath, composing herself as best she can before opening the door.

"Emma," Luke says and she realizes he's sticking to their fake names even though no one is around. "I wanted to invite you over to our room for a celebration with the rest of the guys."

"Celebration? Of what?"

Luke laughs hard, watching dawning realization appear on her face. After catching his breath, he asks, "So, do you want to come over? It really wouldn't be the same without you."

Avizeh considers his words for a moment. She doesn't, but figures that she could benefit from escaping her thoughts, if only for a minute. She follows him back to the men's hotel room. Adrian and Daniel are seated on the couch. On the coffee table in front of them are two large containers of pomegranate juice and four cups.

"Alcohol is illegal, so we couldn't break out the bourbon," Luke explains. "I hear it's easy for locals to get booze but I figured we could behave ourselves for one night before we head out."

Avizeh sits down in a chair opposite the men and pours herself a glass of the sweet red juice.

"We have a lot to be grateful for," Luke begins an impromptu toast, "and a lot of people to be grateful to. First, to Mike. Our martyr for the cause." Luke raises his cup. The other two follow, calling "to Mike," before drinking. "Rest in peace. We won't forget his family. He'll always be our hero no matter what the news says about him in the coming days." Adrian and Daniel nod.

Luke lifts his glass again. "Of course, none of this would have happened without..." he trails off. Avizeh meets his glance, wondering if he honestly expects her to divulge her real name. "...our own, very mysterious angel, who delivered us from evil. To our angel." The men take a drink and Avizeh follows in.

"I've been called a lot of things; never an angel before," Avizeh says.

"So, Emma," Luke speaks her name with a terribly over-accentuated French accent. "Have you thought about what you're going to do after this?"

That question steals the mirth from her face. "I've been trying not to. Nothing ever seems to go to plan."

The men around her nod. After a moment of silence, Luke raises a questioning hand and says, "Well... if you ever need a job."

Avizeh glances over at him. "What else is there to do? Isn't the Vanguard done?"

Luke shrugs. "That's not all we are. We all have regular lives. Most of us work for tech companies or web design, but we've got people in everything."

Avizeh looks down, suddenly studying the carpet as she contemplates the offer to escape everything that she dreads. She shakes her head. "I have things I have to do. I can't."

Luke sighs. "Well, you know how to contact us."

"Five out of five paws?" she retorts to laughs.

The three Swiss journalists and their Afghan-French translator spend the afternoon sharing stories, jokes and talking about everything other than the chaos of the world around them. Avizeh feels so relaxed she even wonders if there is alcohol in the juice.

Their merriment trails off by evening. Each of the men looks like they want to keep talking but isn't sure of what else to say. The conversation continues unnaturally as the men talk just to talk. She can tell they are thinking of home. There will be chaos to deal with at their real jobs, amongst their families and in their communities. Every secret suddenly revealed will take their toll. This is the men's last night free of responsibility before they have to deal with the repercussions of their own actions.

Avizeh puts her cup down and stands up. "Thank you." She turns to the door but stops midway. "It was nice getting to know you all."

"This isn't goodbye, is it?" Daniel asks. "Aren't you going to see us off before our flight tomorrow?"

Avizeh shakes her head. "I have something I have to do, and I don't know what will happen afterward. Thank you though, for giving me a way out."

Luke stands up and offers her his hand. She shakes it. Adrian does the same, as does Daniel, who looks as if he is debating hugging her but refrains.

"Goodbye," she calls to them as she steps out, committing their faces to memory knowing she will never see them again.

*   *   *

Avizeh reenters her room and calls a taxi. She puts down the receiver and looks at herself in the mirror. A deep green hijab rests lazily on the back of her dark hair, contrasting with her bright orange abaya that clings tightly to her curves. She stares deep into her own eyes, wondering when she stopped being a scared girl and became the determined woman she sees looking back at her. She turns away from her reflection and leaves the comfort of her isolation. Avizeh meanders out of the hotel and hails the taxi. She gives the address to the balding driver who remains thankfully silent. The car passes through the middle-class tenements until they arrive at a run-down part of the city. The driver honks at children kicking a football in the street. Laundry hangs from windows. The streets crack until they are more gravel than pavement.

"Are you sure this is where you want to go?"

Avizeh repeats the address. The driver checks his phone's GPS and they continue. The taxi ascends a small knoll and stops in front of a run-down apartment complex. Avizeh eyes the fare, then hands him a wad of cash. "Keep the change," she says and grabs the door handle.

"Do you want me to wait for you?" the man offers.

"No, thank you," she replies. "It's fine."

"You're sure?"

Avizeh nods. "I've been to a lot worse neighborhoods. At least these aren't covered in bullet holes." She steps outside, just catching the stunned look on his face.

She walks up to the closest building and ascends the external stairs to the fifth floor. She stares at a worn metal door for a long time. Her hand rises, as if having a life of its own, and knocks.

Yellow light pours into the concrete hallway as Avizeh stares into her sister's face. Laily gasps and then launches herself on Avizeh, who wraps her arms around her. Avizeh feels her little sister sob even as she watches Aamir and her mother walk towards them. Her mother joins Laily in the hug, clutching Avizeh tightly as if afraid she might disappear. With no way to properly join in, Aamir lays a hand on Avizeh's shoulder and smiles at her. After a long moment Laily pulls back and Avizeh looks into her crying eyes, which are nearly the same height as her own.

"You keep growing. Soon you'll be taller than me!"

Laily laughs while wiping away tears. "And I'm not even wearing shoes like you! Wow, those are nice; new ones by the look of them," she says, looking down on Avizeh's bright multi-colored trainers. "Where did you get those?"

"Laily! Of all the things to ask, you want to know about her shoes?"

"Look at mine," Laily displays her worn pair of dirty sneakers, "how can I not notice?"

Avizeh smiles, even while cringing at her family's poverty. Laily sports torn blue jeans and a conservative white top with a long red shawl with loose threads. Her outfit is modest clothing for the West, though Avizeh imagines it scandalizes her Afghan parents. Her mother wears an old black burqa she kept from Afghanistan, though her veil is missing, showing her face. Aamir looks the least hard-pressed with his jeans and button-up shirt. Avizeh notices his face is clean-shaven and his hair meticulously cut. He poses as if he is more than just a poor refugee and Avizeh wonders if he is looking to impress a girl or if he already has.

"Has life been hard?" Avizeh asks. "Do you get enough food?"

"We manage," her mother reassures her. "We are safe here. That's—" She stops herself. Avizeh knows her mother well enough to know she was going to say, "That's better than we were in Farah," but she doesn't want Baba to hear. Avizeh looks over her shoulder and sees her father sitting at the dinner table, finishing what little rice is left. A cold silence seizes the group. Avizeh presses past her family and walks to the table to stand over her father. He looks forward, impassively.

"Baba."

He pauses and rigidly looks up into her face.

"I sacrificed everything to come back to this family in Farah. I nearly died to make it here. I won't risk anything to come back a third time if you can't tell me you're happy to see me." Avizeh holds her arms out at her sides. "Hug me or spend the rest of your life regretting it."

Her Baba holds her unflinching gaze. He looks years older than when they last spoke. She tries to read his eyes but cannot. All she can do is exert compassion for a man who lost his home and half his family.

The chair lets out a loud scraping sound as her Baba stands. Slowly and gently he wraps his arms around her and places a heavy palm on her back. Her tears flow freely, and she feels his repressed sobs rumble through her.

*   *   *

Few things bind people like shared loss. Each member of the Fatah family lost something unique to them when they abandoned Anar Dara. Simultaneously, they each gave up their pride. Mama put aside her traditional dress to better fit in with the less conservative country. Laily and Aamir went to school and worked knowing that they are looked down upon as poor refugees. Baba was the very last to surrender to the backbreaking grind of time. When he embraces Avizeh, he accepts that she is his daughter and that is enough. While he never says it, Avizeh knows he has given up on seeing his second wife and their children for a long while.

Avizeh doesn't mind sleeping on the floor in her siblings' room, though it briefly reminds her of the cold cell at Fort Powell. She accepts this mild suffering gladly to be with her family again. She listens to their every word and prods them to divulge every banality of their lives, even as she reveals nothing. Only Laily makes a fuss, demanding to know where her older sister has been. Then Avizeh pulls out a wad of cash and asks, "If I buy you a nice pair of shoes, will you shut up?"

One evening as the five sit at the dinner table, Avizeh says, "I want you to move somewhere nice."

"Where would we go?" her mother asks. "Paris? We can't travel until—"

"I mean here. At least somewhere cleaner. It can be somewhere cheap, just not this run-down ghetto." Eyes turn to Avizeh, waiting for confirmation of what everyone suspects. "I can pay for everything. I can wire money to you whenever you need it. Just tell me."

"Wire us? You aren't leaving again?" Laily gives her sister a look that is somewhere between pleading and angry.

"I have to," Avizeh replies without the slightest hesitation. *I have to. For love. And because if I don't, I will regret it for the rest of my life.*

"Will you ever come back?" her mother asks, afraid of the answer.

Avizeh looks around the table, suddenly realizing their melancholy. "Of course, I will! I could be back in a few months. I promise from now on I will always come back at least once a year. I want to watch you grow taller." Avizeh looks at her sister. "And I need to meet whichever girl Aamir is chasing after so I can warn her." She smiles at her brother, then turns to her mother. "It's not like before. I'm... free now. But I still have something I need to do."

*   *   *

The Afghan woman arrives in Sapporo dressed in a modest light pink Persian dress with a hijab worn low on the back of her hair. Avizeh takes a gently rocking bus to the eastern part of the city and watches snow fall softly on the quiet metropolis. As Avizeh steps out, she thinks she should be cold but Antarctica prepared her for northern Japan. She looks up to the night sky, wondering what the stars look like over Hokkaido, and lets a tiny snowflake fall on her cheek. She smiles a childish smile as it melts on her face. *I can adjust. If anything, maybe this is too warm.*

The lost Afghan woman walks down a few main streets

until she finds a small, two-story apartment complex. She walks up to the second floor and finds number '54.' Avizeh hears her heart pounding in her ears. She raises her hand to the door and finds herself standing in that position, fist trembling. She marvels that she has infiltrated the most secure base in the world, escaped a civil war in Kabul, yet stands terrified of knocking on a door. She takes a deep breath, closes her eyes, gathers up her courage and raps the door three times. The door swings open and Mikasa appears in its frame, hair pulled back in a ponytail, bags under her eyes and looking as if she is midway through a yawn. For a half-second she looks as if she cannot even comprehend what's before her. Sudden realization illuminates her face and she nearly jumps. For a long time, she just stares at Avizeh, dumbstruck.

Mikasa's lips press against Avizeh's. Her lover's hand touches the back of Avizeh's neck. Then she pulls back and looks into her eyes. "You blew up the world for me, that's so romantic. But now you've set the bar so high, what could you possibly get me for our anniversary?"

Avizeh laughs while holding back tears of joy. "I'll think of something. I shot a gun for the first time."

"At someone?"

"No, just some multi-million dollar quantum-leaping equipment that I buried in a desert before crossing the border with a group of cyber-terrorists."

"That is so 'you'." Mikasa shakes her finger. She looks over Avizeh's shoulder and asks, "Should I worry about someone coming to break my door down? Is our next vacation Guantanamo?"

Avizeh shakes her head. "I was always their dirty secret. I deleted what little files they had on me. They all know me as Jessica Brown, and I replaced my photo with a photo of a white girl with blonde hair. Some people know me, but they have no records, or images, meaning they can't trace me. Some of my friends are even prepared to lie to the sketch artists about what I look like so they can't find me. I'm finally free," she says with a shaking voice, half-laughing, half-crying. "Can I... can I come in?"

"No," Mikasa replies.

"Oh..."

"I have work. I started up the cinema I told you about. We're showing a '70s Italian film and serving spaghetti and meatballs. To be honest, I've always been shorthanded, alone and such, and I've had a hard time attracting anyone to work with me for a company that might be gone tomorrow. What do you say, care to join me?"

"Sounds like another adventure."

"With food! The best kind of adventure," Mikasa says as she locks the door behind her. She wraps her arm around Avizeh's, gives her a kiss and they walk together down the snow-covered sidewalk.

*   *   *

Mikasa discovers to her horror that Avizeh has no idea how to cook. Aside from her mother's lessons seven years ago, she hasn't cooked at all. Despite Avizeh's complete ineptitude Mikasa is able to scramble everything together for the guests. She runs up to the projector room panting after all the patrons are served while Avizeh sits on the couch behind it trying and failing not to blush a deep red at her own culinary failure. Mikasa turns on the digital projector and sits down beside Avizeh where the pair eat spaghetti with meatballs and garlic bread. The movie drags on and Mikasa looks clearly bored with the existential tangent the film takes. She turns to Avizeh with a sly smile. "I was going to wait until after the movie to ask what kept you away all that time but..."

Avizeh recounts all that has happened, even the part about Clara and James. Mikasa is hooked on every word and the movie fades into background noise.

"You're the most awesome person I've ever met. You risked your life for a friend, and then to see me. Even before I was willing to say, 'I love you.'"

Avizeh looks back at Mikasa tenderly. Exhaustion is clear in the way her shoulders sag and her every expression is sluggish but her eyes light up as she meets her love's gaze. Mikasa leans in, turns her head, kisses her, and pulls back just enough to whisper, "I love you." No words have ever sounded so sweet.

*   *   *

Mikasa waits by the door to let out the patrons as the film ends. The small audience of forty has nothing but good things to say about the cooking and the movie, both of which pleasantly surprise Mikasa, as she had been lackluster about both. As soon as the small group leaves, Mikasa gives Avizeh a conspiratorial grin and says, "Now the fun part."

After an hour of cleaning plates, floors and carpets, Mikasa locks the doors and they walk back towards her apartment. As they turn a corner, the sound of raucous men speaking English with American accents greet them as eight Americans in military garb walk towards the pair. Avizeh freezes as they approach.

"Hey cutie," one of them calls while his friends whistle at the two women.

"Come on," Mikasa grabs Avizeh's arm and leads her away. After they round the nearest corner, Mikasa lets go of her arm. "My god, you're shaking. Are you cold?"

"No, it's... what are they doing here?"

"Oh them? We get troops every now and then from the

Misawa base down south. They come up here for winter vacation to ski and visit the hot springs. They're harmless; well, as much as any horny drunk men are."

Avizeh takes a breath. They certainly didn't seem to be after any specific women and she tries to calm herself. When they get back to the apartment, Avizeh rushes to the window to shut the blinds. She thinks she hears someone outside and she peeks out only to see an elderly woman walking with a young girl.

"Come to bed, Avizeh."

The former spy looks over her shoulder and sees Mikasa smiling tiredly. Avizeh tears herself from the window and sidles over to join her love. She slips under the covers and feels Mikasa's warm hand reach across her belly as the soft touch of her lips caress her neck.

"We have so much to do together, Avizeh. We can go up to the mountains, celebrate the New Year soon... We can even hop over to China, or Korea. Promise me that whenever you aren't visiting your family, we'll travel."

Avizeh kisses her hand. "Until the money runs out."

"You said you have twenty million!"

"And you have expensive tastes," she retorts. Avizeh tightens her grip on Mikasa's hand. "I promised my family to visit every year, but I want to make my home with you, wherever you choose. After all that's happened, I want a life that lasts. I'll stay with you for as long as you'll have me."

Mikasa looks deep into her eyes, then suddenly bursts out laughing. Avizeh props herself up on her shoulder and watches with confusion and a little anger as Mikasa bawls beside her. After a moment, she collects herself and says, "'As long as you'll have me.' You're adorable. I love you." She leans over and kisses her.

Avizeh smiles, flips back over and grips Mikasa's hand, tightly.

Gary Girod was born in the woods of Oregon sometime during the last century. He fell in love with stories, true and fiction. In January 2019, he founded the French History Podcast, which covers the history of France from three million years ago to present. In 2020 Brain Lag published his first book, *The Maiden Voyage of New York City*. In 2021 he received his doctorate in European history from the University of Houston, writing about the origins of the mass domestic surveillance states in Britain and France.

He currently divides his time between writing fiction, world-traveling and wearing a suit while monologuing about the deeds of dead people.

www.ingramcontent.com/pod-product-compliance
Lightning Source LLC
Chambersburg PA
CBHW050804190726

48285CB00005B/1784

9781928011774